One Good Turn Deserves Nothing

An Eleanor Garrett Mystery
Book 3

K. McCrae

K. McCrae Books

First published 2024

ISBN: 978-1-8380322-5-8

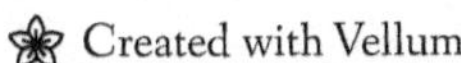 Created with Vellum

Chapter One

The grey clouds did nothing to lighten Eleanor Garrett's mood during the half hour journey to her new job. The single track lane led deeper and deeper into the vast expanse of large open fields, edged by endless lengths of hedges and dry stone walls that looked as though they wouldn't last another day and yet had been standing for hundreds of years. The only signs of life were the sheep, huddled together after a night of rain. An expanse of nothingness that echoed the void inside her. After months of living in a four-century-old cottage in the middle of nowhere, she wondered if she was making a mistake. Exchanging one place of isolation for another.

Darryl Westwood swung the Land Rover into the car park of the Minstrel-Wood archaeological site and, avoiding the potholes, parked under a large ancient oak tree. Its branches blocking the dim morning sun-light and bringing a chill to the air. Eleanor made no effort to move from her seat.

'There's no need to be nervous,' Darryl whispered with amusement in his voice.

She suddenly realised she had been playing with her necklace. Twisting the chain round her finger. She dropped it with a nervous laugh. First-day nerves, that's all it is.

'Will you take that stupid grin off your face?' she teased.

Darryl hadn't stopped smiling since she had got the job in the gift shop. 'Why should I? It's going to be great.'

He had been giddy with excitement since he had first mentioned the job, and Eleanor, in desperate need of some civilised conversation, had agreed to attend an interview.

'We'll be working together, we can have lunch together—' he continued.

'Not exactly,' Eleanor cut him off. 'You'll be knee deep in mud in your trench and I'll be in the gift shop. And, let's face it, it's not exactly the kind of job that dreams are made of.'

'Maybe not for you, but at least it's a job.'

He's right, Eleanor thought. Teaching had been her dream. Even though there were teaching jobs available, she had already proved to herself she couldn't go back to that life after losing both her husband and son nineteen months ago. The memories it evoked were too painful. She had resigned herself to the fact that she was almost forty now; too old for a career change. But she had always prided herself on doing a good job, no matter what it was, and this job was going to be no different.

She climbed out of the Land Rover and shivered from the early autumn breeze as Darryl walked round the car and joined her. The wind was blowing his grey speckled, dark hair around his tanned face, as his wide grin remained firmly in place. She couldn't help but smile at his excitement.

'Where's your badge?' he asked, his smile turning into a comical frown.

Eleanor begrudgingly pulled a plastic name badge from her coat pocket. 'You don't have to wear one of these.'

'I guess I'm not as special as you,' he said as she attached it to her dark green polo shirt emblazoned with the Minstrel-Wood logo, the only item provided for her uniform. The black trousers and flat, comfy shoes were her own, of which she was grateful.

Eleanor gave a mock laugh at his attempt at humour and they set off on the long walk towards the main building that housed the museum, the tea-room and the gift shop. Darryl almost skipped like a child as they passed the shed-like building that served as the main reception. His delight was unbearable and, for a man in his forties, could have been considered by some as highly inappropriate.

They continued up the gently sloping path, past the main entrance for the museum, and on till they reached the gift shop, entering through a pair of double glass doors that would normally be the exit for visitors after making their way through the museum. The gift shop itself was more of a wide corridor than a room. Shelves were mounted on any vacant high wall space with cabinets beneath them. In the centre of the room were more display cabinets with open compartments, reminding Eleanor of an over-sized cutlery drawer. But instead of knives and forks, each area contained smaller items clearly meant for the younger visitors. Such as pens, key-rings and small plastic toys.

On their arrival, Darryl introduced her to Sahara. The teenage shop assistant bounced on the balls of her feet like a child on the morning of their birthday, impatiently waiting to open their presents. She held her arms stiffly by her side, holding herself back in her excitement. Though Eleanor soon noticed that this was probably an attempt to hide the hole in the seam of her trousers that had once been black, but had faded to grey with time. Her well-worn shoes would have been more appropriate for the hot summer months. The girl was extremely excitable, friendly and helpful, though the word manic often popped into Eleanor's mind.

'I'm so glad it's you that's come to work here,' she said after Darryl had left for his trench, where a large Roman mosaic waited for him. 'When Darryl told me you'd got the job, I just knew we would get on. Darryl's great, so it only makes sense that his partner would be too.'

Eleanor raised her eyebrows and pitied the young girl's naivety.

'You're much nicer than the last woman,' Sahara went on. 'Horrid woman, she was. Bossy cow. Everything had to be just so. She used to even straighten the carrier bags, so they were all level. Barmy! Thankfully, she handed in her notice after one of the archaeologists accused her of stealing.' Sahara put on a high-pitched, haughty voice in imitation. '"I'm not putting up with your accusations." She did go on.' Her loud burst of laughter made Eleanor jump. 'She had a right go at him,' Sahara continued, 'although I think I'd be pretty annoyed too if somebody accused me of stealing. It wasn't nice to see neither, especially with visitors around. He left that day, the archaeologist, I mean—'

'Not gossiping, I hope,' said a man's voice from behind them.

They turned together to see a man of around sixty in a smart suit and tie enter the room. He was little shorter than Eleanor, his hair was smoothed flat and his face immaculately shaved, though beads of sweat were gathered along his brow. Mr Nelson, the site manager, had clearly had a stressful morning already. He was marching into the gift shop to prepare for opening.

'Oh no, Mr Nelson,' Sahara said, her hands held behind her back as though standing to attention.

'Good. I can't abide gossip,' he said, looking down his nose at her. 'Now, firstly, I would like to formally welcome you here, Eleanor. I'm sure we'll all get on like one big happy family. We are a friendly bunch here, all in all.' He gave a hint of a smile before glancing at the black, leather-bound clipboard he held close to his chest and hurrying on. 'And now, down to business. I have a couple of notices for you this morning, before we open. We are due some heavy rain this afternoon and it's only going to be getting worse as the week goes on, so you'll need to be prepared with the mop.'

'Yes, Mr Nelson,' Sahara nodded efficiently.

'Unfortunately,' Mr Nelson said, turning his attention to Eleanor, 'the place tends to get very muddy when there's rain. With health and safety being paramount, we must keep the floors as clean and dry as possible. Though we should count ourselves lucky after the heatwave we have been experiencing this past summer.' Pulling himself up straight, he turned his attention back to both of them. 'Secondly, we have two school parties in this morning.'

Mr Nelson's voice faded into a haze. Only vaguely aware of the conversation continuing on around her, Eleanor fought the wave of emotions that rose within her. A sickness that had plagued her ever since her beloved son's death entered her stomach, together with the familiar lump in her throat.

'Of course, it's quite quiet during term time,' Sahara was saying. 'It's during the school holidays things get really busy. A couple of school parties should give you a little taste of things to come.'

Eleanor stood, unable to speak as Sahara continued gabbling.

'There's usually more staff on during the holidays, though. But, you just wait and see. They grab everything they can reach; pull everything off the rails. There's just something in them that tells them they have to touch everything and then just drop it wherever they want.'

Clutching at the ring that hung from her necklace, Eleanor forced herself back into the room. For Sahara's sake, more than her own.

'Yes, thank you, Sahara.' Mr Nelson frowned.

'Sorry, Mr Nelson, but you know it's true.'

'It should be a nice quiet morning for you to get the hang of things,' Mr Nelson said encouragingly to Eleanor, 'and here in the gift shop, you don't need to worry yourself about needing any archaeological terminology. The most difficult question you'll receive here is for directions to the toilets.'

Both he and Sahara laughed loudly.

'Even though they've just walked straight past them,' Sahara added.

'Ahem,' Mr Nelson reined himself in, his hand jingling what sounded like coins or keys in his pocket. 'Although, living with an archaeologist yourself,' he went on, 'I wouldn't be at all surprised if you had picked up a few terms here and there. Maybe we should all come to you for help in that department if ever it is needed.'

Eleanor made an effort to laugh at his light-hearted humour. *Be professional, Eleanor. Of course, there would be school parties. It was inevitable.* She clenched her fists and breathed deeply while the conversation continued. *You can do this.*

'Right, it's almost time to open up.' Mr Nelson glanced at his watch. 'There's just one more thing. Now I'm sure it's nothing to worry about at this stage. I just need to make you aware of the fact. Head office has been onto me with reports of stealing.'

'Stealing?' Sahara exclaimed, making Eleanor jump at the high-pitched squeal.

'Now, as I said, I'm sure it's nothing to worry about,' he endeavoured to calm Sahara. 'They haven't been very specific, which, between you and me, isn't very helpful, so I don't know if we're talking about a substantial amount or the odd pencil sharpener. I'm having a meeting with them later today to find out the details—'

'Sorry, Mr Nelson,' Sahara interrupted, 'but it'll be those kids. I swear they sneak stuff into their pockets. When there's only two of us here, we can't watch all of 'em all the time. This is where they take stuff from,' Sahara moved across to the low cabinet situated in the centre of the shop. 'It's all small stuff. I mean, look at this: rubbers, pencil sharpeners, little toys. It's crazy, and far too inviting for kids that know no better.'

'Don't worry yourself,' Mr Nelson told her. 'I'm sure it'll all sort itself out. You just need to be aware that there is an issue. I will try to make myself available to be an extra set of eyes during the busiest times.'

'Yes, Mr Nelson. Thank you.'

Eleanor frowned at Sahara's assumptions. During her years as a teacher, the children were, on the most part, well-behaved, and teachers tended to know which children they needed to watch carefully, but she held her tongue.

'Well, come on ladies, it's time I got down to the ticket office and opened up. Hopefully, the computers have decided to work properly now. Life is always a little more difficult without the use of the booking system.' He gave an enormous sigh before continuing. 'Good luck, Eleanor. If you have any questions ask Sahara, here. There's not much she doesn't know that's worth knowing. I'd be lost without her.'

Mr Nelson's adulation was greatly appreciated as Sahara failed to hide a smile.

'Anything she can't deal with, I'm around and about all day. I'm sure Sahara has mentioned the priorities already, such as tea and coffee is available from the kitchen in the tea-room next door—'

'Darryl has already told me I need to sample the café's scones,' Eleanor said in approval.

'Tea-room,' he replied.

'Pardon?'

'It's a tea-room, not a café.'

Chapter Two

Darryl glanced up at the darkening sky. The morning, though cloudy, had mostly been bright. But over the last couple of hours, a coldness around his shoulders made them stiff, necessitating the need for the extra jumper he often carried in his bag. It had been a slow morning, visitor-wise, other than a group of school children who had ambled past the trench with hardly a second glance. He pulled on his jumper and returned to scraping and brushing at the earth, revealing more of the Roman mosaic that lay beneath him.

'Darryl,' Larry called from further along the trench.

There was only one thing that would cause that tone in his voice. A curious but excited tone. In a moment, Darryl had moved closer. The large pads strapped to his knees for comfort's sake gave a comical appearance as he walked across the boards that were placed in the trench to protect the mosaic beneath. He lowered himself to his knees while Larry gently prodded and scraped with his trowel around a small object hidden in the ground.

'Another pin?' Darryl asked.

He struggled to see, but at first glance, a thin length of what looked like metal or bone was sticking up out of the earth. Only two centimetres showed before it disappeared into the earth, but that was enough to make Darryl's heart race. He was relieved when Larry put down his small trowel and retrieved his Leatherman from his back pocket. He opened the blade and continued. Larry had always favoured his Leatherman to the comparatively bulky trowel, claiming it was easier to control for delicate times like this. 'Perfect for all eventualities' he had said. But, for Darryl, it also removed the possibility of hiding his view. Though the trowel itself was small and slender, specially designed for delicate archaeological finds, he didn't like to risk missing a moment when a new artefact that had been hidden for hundreds, perhaps thousands of years beneath the earth, first came to light.

'May be a brooch,' Larry whispered in concentration.

He removed the earth, piece by piece, each segment no larger than the tip of the knife. Uncovering something that had the two men holding their breath with anticipation.

'Pass me my brush,' Larry asked, not removing his eyes from the delicate operation.

Darryl quickly looked around, picked up Larry's brush from beside his bag, and handed it to him. For the next few moments, they were silent. Larry switched between knife and brush in expert movements during the surgical process. Picking away at the earth with the knife, then sweeping it gently away. Little by little, he unearthed the mystery object. Suddenly, Larry let out a huge, resigned sigh.

'It's a pin.' He had reached the end of the object, and he lifted it away from the ground.

Darryl sat back on his heels. 'How many is that now?'

'Don't know. I lost count when we hit triple figures.'

'From this trench?'

'From the site.' Larry laid the pin on the palm of his hand and held it up for them both to see.

'Looks like it's bone,' Darryl said, peering at it closely.

Larry turned it gently in his hand, brushing off specks of dirt for a clearer examination while they both scrutinised the find.

'And more elaborately carved than a lot of the others,' Larry said. 'I'd better get on and record it,' he continued eventually, though sounding reluctant.

'I'll leave you to that.' Darryl understood the hesitancy in his voice. The recording aspect of the job wasn't as much fun as the actual excavation work. Unfortunately, the end of their excavating time for this year was drawing to an end, and they would soon spend their time inside recording and conserving. Interesting work, but incomparable to being in the field, searching and uncovering artefacts. Never knowing what he may find next.

He stood to return to his own area of the mosaic that he had been working on all morning and looked down towards the main site, more specifically, the gift shop. The trench where he stood was at least a five-minute walk from the main site; set out in a field on its own and only relatively recently discovered.

'Go down and see her,' Larry said. 'You're not going to be able to concentrate on anything else until you do.'

Darryl laughed apologetically. His conversation that morning had been a little one-sided and had ended abruptly when Larry finally yelled, *'I get it, you're happy she's working here'*. They had been friends for many years, and worked on a few digs together before this one. And though they had laughed at his outburst, Darryl had tried to keep Eleanor out of his conversations after that.

Taking advantage of the respite from being on his knees, he stretched his back and shoulders. A visitor to the site was walking towards them. The wide-brimmed hat and long trench coat were immediately recognisable. The man had been several times over the last couple of months or so. Each time, he looked markedly older and more frail. Darryl watched as he coughed, almost doubling over with the effort, but the wind had taken the sound long before it reached the trench. The man had a keen interest in their work and was always friendly towards them. Darryl suspected he had more than just a hobbyist's knowledge of archaeology. But there was something else that intrigued Darryl, and this time he decided to put his theory to the test.

He returned to his knees and continued scraping and brushing at his area of the mosaic, while Larry rummaged through his kit bag at the other end of the trench. They were both out of sight from any oncoming visitor by the high bank that surrounded them, created when the trench had originally been dug. He waited for the old man to arrive above them, behind the barrier that separated the visitor's path and the trench. With their heads down, working, they often didn't see visitors arriving until they were already there. And this was what Darryl was counting on.

When the man reached the barrier, Darryl pretended not to notice him, absorbing himself in his work. Only risking surreptitious glances in his direction as the man continued past. As Darryl suspected, he didn't stop until he reached Larry. He looked down into the trench, his shoulders hunched and his sagging face making him appear much older than the reality. Darryl had supposed him to be in his sixties, but today, he looked closer to eighty.

'Good morning.' His frail voice croaked.

Larry looked up with a jolt, surprised by the sound. Darryl hesitated to see if Larry would answer him, but he turned away and pointedly ignored him. Darryl stared at the dirt covered mosaic in front of him without seeing it. He could hear the man's wheezing breaths as he stood there waiting for some kind of reaction from Larry that never came.

Not able to stand it any longer, Darryl called over to him, 'Good morning,' he said, trying to ease the awkward silence. 'As you can see, we haven't progressed very far since the last time you were here. It's been less than a week this time, hasn't it?'

'I know, but time's running out.' Even though the man answered Darryl's question, he spoke directly towards Larry.

Larry continued to hide his face while he rummaged through his large leather bag. His jerky movements were uncharacteristic for someone usually so laid back.

'That sounds a bit ominous.' Darryl gave a light-hearted laugh, immediately regretting both his remark and his decision to test his theory.

'Not to worry,' the man said, bursting into heavy coughing for a moment. Once he had caught his breath, he turned his gaze on Darryl. 'It's amazing this mosaic has escaped modern-day ploughing,' he said. 'You're lucky to have this opportunity.'

He paused. The man's sad eyes bored through Darryl, pleading with him, appealing for something Darryl was unable to give. The man spluttered a moment as if he was about to cough again, instead he said,

'Thank you.'

The sincerity in his voice was heart-breaking.

'I'm sorry, but thank you for what?' Darryl asked.

'Taking the time to talk to me. It's very much appreciated.' He coughed a little more and then seemed to rally his spirits. 'Any news on the funding yet?' he asked.

Darryl rolled his eyes ostentatiously. 'Nothing yet, but we keep asking,' Darryl said, obliging the man's wish to change the subject. 'We simply *need* to put more trenches in this field. With this mosaic here, there must be more to find.'

'I agree,' the old man said enthusiastically. 'You don't put a mosaic like this just any old where. Keep fighting, won't you?'

He turned back to face Larry, who was still rummaging through his bag. 'I'm getting tired now. I think I'll go and sit down for a while. I'll be in the tea-room for an hour or so. Maybe longer if I need to.'

There was a pause. Clearly, he hoped Larry would make some kind of acknowledgement, but his gaze fell to the ground at the silence that followed, and he pulled himself away.

Darryl sat on his heels, watching the old man hobbling his way along the path. He felt an inexplicable rage as Larry finished with his bag and returned to work as though nothing had happened. During the last four or five visits, Larry had always ignored this man. Before, there had been nothing definite. A sense, a feeling as Darryl had always been the first to acknowledge the man's presence. But this time there was no denying it, and this time Darryl couldn't ignore it.

'Larry.'

Larry ignored him.

'Larry,' Darryl called again, louder.

'I don't want to talk about it.'

Darryl was partly relieved that at least he had acknowledged there was an issue. He put down his trowel and stood. Hesitantly, he walked over to Larry and, putting his hand gently on Larry's shoulder, he said, 'Please?'

'I don't want to talk about it.' Larry's firmness made Darryl hesitate further.

'I can see there's a problem,' Darryl said gently. 'I just want to help.'

His plea was met with silence, with only the sound of Larry's trowel scraping at the earth a little more forcefully than normal.

'He seems like a nice guy,' Darryl continued.

'Don't be fooled. It's all an act,' Larry mumbled.

Finally, Larry had spoken. Darryl persisted, hopeful that he would continue.

'How can I help,' Darryl continued, 'if I don't know—'

'He's my dad,' Larry snapped and stopped his work, though continued to stare at the ground.

Darryl staggered slightly. Not knowing what to say, he stammered, 'Your - your—'

'Yes, my dad. We haven't spoken for a long time and I don't intend to start now.' Larry's tone was sharp and pragmatic, but his breathing was heavy with anger.

'But why?'

Larry ignored the question. His head down, he began working again, his knuckles white as he gripped his trowel hard.

'He looks ill,' Darryl continued. 'I'm worried about him. I don't like the sound of all this "not much time left."'

'He's dying,' Larry said bluntly. 'He has cancer.'

'Then why won't you speak to him?'

Again, there was silence.

'Maybe he'd like a reconciliation,' Darryl put forward, trying to keep his voice calm, still shocked by Larry's announcement.

'I *know* what he wants, and it's not a reconciliation.'

After a silent moment, Larry stood and looked around. There were no visitors close by; the midday lull as visitors had their lunch.

'Dad was an archaeologist, too. Until he decided to steal the artefacts he was digging up.' Larry spat out the words from pent up anger. 'At least that's how it started.' Larry began pacing up and down the boards. 'He'd take unreported items from the trench he was working in. But then he moved on to bigger artefacts, stealing from archives and museums. That's when he got caught.'

Darryl was speechless. Unable to find the right words to say, he remained silent and watched Larry pace, his hands clenching and unclenching at his sides. A far cry from Larry's usual carefree demeanour. Though Larry had been reluctant to speak of the situation, now he had started, he wasn't going to stop until he had finished.

'He went to prison a few years ago, always professing his innocence, but then who doesn't?' Larry went on. 'He was released about a year ago and has been trying to convince me ever since that he was set up. It was all a mistake. But we both know the truth. He did it, but refuses to face the consequences.'

Eventually, Larry stopped pacing and blew out an enormous breath. Darryl's initial anger at Larry's disrespect towards the old man was replaced with guilt.

'That must have been awful to go through,' he said gently. 'You know you can talk to me about this stuff if you ever need to.'

Larry smiled back at him with more of a smirk than a smile. 'Since when have I ever been one for wallowing in self-pity? You know me, I'd rather ignore the whole situation.'

'I know, but – well, you know I'm here.' Darryl placed a comforting hand on his shoulder and Larry seemed to calm a little. 'I can't help but think, though,' Darryl began hesitantly, 'he is still your father. Once he's gone, there are no second chances.'

Larry simply shook his head.

'If he's innocent—'

'Oh, he's not innocent,' Larry interrupted.

'But, you said—'

'I said he has always professed his innocence, *claiming* to have been set up. But he's not innocent.'

'How can you be so sure if he's still saying he's innocent even now?' Darryl paused as Larry turned away and moved back towards his work place. In desperation, Darryl continued.

'It's obvious that it's you he comes to see. Maybe you could give him the benefit of the doubt?'

'He's not here for me. All he wants is...' Larry broke off, swallowing hard.

'Hey, come on. What is it?'

Larry cast a sweeping glance at their surroundings. Nobody was around, but still he whispered, 'I *know* he's guilty.' Larry stared directly at Darryl for a moment, chewing on his lip. 'He gave me something,' he continued awkwardly, 'Before he was put away - I didn't know what it was to start with, it was just a box – he asked me to keep it safe for him. I didn't know what he'd been up to,' he implored. 'It was only later I found out and realised he must have known that the police were on to him. He just needed a place to hide his latest hoard.' Bitterness shot through his voice. He continued in a more rushed, almost panicked tone. 'With the police buzzing around, I shoved it under one of the floorboards in the attic room. That's what he's come back for now. Not for me, but for his stolen stash.'

Larry turned determinedly back to his work, leaving Darryl struggling to take it all in. He found it difficult to believe that the man that had stood in front of them a short time ago was someone looking to take a stolen artefact back into his short life. He was a man looking for love. The love of his son.

A few moments of silence passed before Darryl spoke again. 'I can't believe he's here for an artefact. What good would it do him if he's dying? Just give him one more chance to explain.'

'No, Darryl. Just give it a rest.'

Darryl held his tongue. Silenced by Larry's harsh tone.

Chapter Three

Eleanor blew the few strands of hair that insisted on hanging down in front of her face out of the way, only for them to return to their original position. She had spent the last half an hour replacing all the items that the children from the first school party had left lying around. Searching for the homes of Roman helmet key-rings, mini mosaics, replica Roman coins, and note-books with the Minstrel-wood logo emblazoned on the front. More curiously, there were also various soft and furry, or small and plastic animals that seemed to have no relevance to either the site or the Romans.

'They're not exactly archaeological, are they?' she said, while her stomach rumbled with hunger.

'They're *not* archaeological, but there's some great wildlife round this area, too.' Sahara had just returned with a box from the stockroom full of books, toys, and paper bags. 'There are some red kites nesting near here, which I believe are quite endangered. Or they were. Something like that.' She took the paper bags from the top of the box and put them behind the counter, and Eleanor began to unpack the other items. 'There's also a large badger sett in one of the fields. I've never seen it as it's really well hidden, and to be honest, I've never gone looking for it, but I've been told it's on the other side of the river, I think. Some of the others here know where it is. One of the biggest in the country, it is, so they say.'

Once happy the till area was tidy, Sahara joined Eleanor to replenish the rest of the items. 'There's even talk of reintroducing otters in the river. I really hope that happens.' Sahara's shoulders melted like a nine-year-old's, and with the tilt of her head and a look of serene bliss on her face she continued, 'I love otters, they're so cute.'

Eleanor was searching for the home of a small plastic badger she had found on the floor as an elderly couple ambled through the shop, heading directly for the exit. They gave friendly smiles, but weren't interested in stopping.

'They're regulars,' Sahara whispered as the couple left. 'They only come for tea and cake.'

Eleanor's stomach rumbled again at the thought of being so close to the tea-room; only a corridor between them. Delicious smells had been drifting through all morning.

Eleanor's shoulders suddenly stiffened at the sound of children's voices drifting down the corridor. Though unable to find the right compartment for the plastic badger, she quickly pushed it into her pocket; she could deal with that later. Right now, she had other priorities.

She watched as the thirty or so children descended on the gift shop. Running out from the museum corridor where they arrived three abreast, before they scattered across the room like locusts. This time, Mr Nelson arrived with the group. He stood with his head held high, his shoulders back, and his hands held behind his back. Surveying his domain, covertly watching for any wandering hands.

Eleanor, though grateful for the extra set of eyes, braced herself for the added pressure of being under observation herself while the children whirled around her, seemingly with no self-restraint or control. *Keep on top of the chaos before it gets too bad,* she told herself, distracting her mind from searching for her dead son's face in the crowd.

The children had chased each other into the gift shop, eager to spend their money on items that would mostly be lost or broken before they made it home. A small child with a plastic sword made a swipe at an imaginary monster and hit Eleanor instead. The girl, of around six or seven years of age, didn't stop to apologise. She continued with her imaginary battle, leaving Eleanor breathless and speechless. This wasn't how she remembered school trips. She saw a child drop a pack of coloured pencils on the floor, while another dropped a plastic sheep into the plastic bird compartment, which was closer. Mindful of keeping the floor clear with so many children running around, she firstly picked the up pencils. Removing the sheep from the bird compartment, she searched the sections for the others. It didn't take long till she understood why the child had left it with the birds, as frustration set in. She swiped at a fly buzzing round her head. *That's all I need,* she thought, noticing at least three or four flies had entered the shop. Eventually, she found the sheep and turned to replace the pencils. A disproportionate amount of pride filled her as she knew where they were displayed. Suddenly, a child ran past and almost knocked her over. She gave the smallest of yelps as he did so. Looking around the room, she saw Mr Nelson's eyes were on her.

Come on, Eleanor. It's not hard. She returned a feeble smile while absentmindedly taking a step backwards. She froze at the sound of a crack. Something hard was under her heel. She slowly looked down with dread. Below her foot was a crushed wooden Roman soldier. Her weight had squashed the shield against him, causing a crack to run its length and detaching both his head and sword-bearing arm from his body. Eleanor scooped up the pieces, and as she stood, Mr Nelson was standing by her side. He held out a black plastic bin that usually lived behind the till. She gave a light-hearted and pathetic laugh in apology while dropping the pieces into the bin.

'You don't need to do it all at once,' he said gently. 'You'll drive yourself mad that way.' He replaced the bin behind the cash desk and returned to his spot on the opposite side of the shop.

Eleanor took a deep breath. Her desire to prove her competency was more than a frivolous wish. It was a crutch. A greatly needed distraction. *I need to do a good job,* she insisted.

The blonde-haired girl, who was still waving her sword around, suddenly dropped it with a squeal of delight when she saw a complete Roman soldier's outfit. Eleanor made a beeline for the sword. She didn't see the plastic cow that had been dropped at her feet. Stepping on it, it slid across the floor, taking her foot with it. The room stopped at the sound of her howl as she flung out her arms, hoping to hold on to something to stop herself from falling. She felt the edge of a shelf with her fingertips and reached out, but instead of being a help, the shelf came down with her. All the baseball caps and neatly folded t-shirts tumbled down with it.

Mr Nelson was once again by her side. 'Are you alright? What on earth happened?'

'I'm sorry,' Eleanor sat, stunned. 'Nobody else got hit, did they?'

'No, no, not at all.' Mr Nelson helped her to her feet. 'It's not as easy as it looks, is it?'

'I'm so sorry. I'm honestly not usually this clumsy.' Eleanor brushed herself down, trying to ignore the adult's judgemental eyes and the children's sniggers.

'Don't worry about it,' Mr Nelson said. 'It's just first day nerves, I'm sure. Take it one thing at a time. It'll take a while before you learn where everything is, for one thing. I still keep finding things in here I never knew we had.'

Eleanor appreciated his friendly encouragement and sympathy.

'Thank you,' she said, taking another swipe at one of the flies that was buzzing near her ear.

Mr Nelson laughed at her. 'I'm afraid you'll need to get used to those, too.'

Together, they put the shelf back on the wall, and lifted the t-shirts in armfuls, returning them to the shelf. 'There's a job for you,' he said with a teasing smile. 'They'll all need refolding. But later. Right now, just watch. You'll learn a lot quicker that way.'

'But—'

Mr Nelson put up a hand to stop her.

'Forget the chaos. As long as nobody's going to get hurt, it's fine. Everything will be just fine.'

Eleanor's cheeks burned with humiliation, but she took Mr Nelson's advice and, fighting every instinct in her body, stood and watched.

Sahara worked hard on the till, but her face was alive with the activity. She served each child with the utmost attention. Helping them with their change and making sure they were holding on tightly to their packed paper bag, before she moved on to the next. A couple of times, a child approached Eleanor, pushing their money into her hand.

One child in particular was so excited with his toy he had to tell Eleanor all about it before he would join the queue that she was directing him towards.

'It's a castle,' he exclaimed. 'Just a teeny, weeny castle, but if you look on the bottom,' he said conspiratorially, 'it's a pencil sharpener.'

Eleanor couldn't help but smile at the boy's wide eyes and

excitement. 'That's lovely,' she said, exaggerating the delight in her voice. She tried to return what she thought was an extravagant amount of ten pounds to the boy. 'But I'm afraid I can't—'

'But it doesn't look like a pencil sharpener,' the boy interrupted in wonder. 'Just like magic. It's not what you think it is.'

'Isn't that incredible?' She held up his money between them, stretching out the written on old note like a barrier. 'Now, go and join the queue so you can buy it before your class leaves you behind. You're going to be the last one.'

The boy turned, and seeing his classmates queuing up, ready to go, looked terrified that he might have to leave without taking his castle-shaped pencil sharpener with him. He ran to the till where Sahara was finishing with her last customer; a girl who was wearing her new plastic roman helmet and gripping it tightly with both hands. Pulling it down onto her head as though she was expecting a hurricane.

Eleanor took a deep breath in the relative calm, and noted Mr Nelson was leaving, moving towards his office. It was now safe to begin the job of reorganising the shop.

'Watch where you're going.' A gruff voice bellowed a moment later.

Eleanor saw an elderly man grab the arm of the boy she had just been talking with. He had bought his pencil sharpener and was running to join the rest of his class. The teachers were already by the door and ready to leave, and from the expression on his face, the boy truly believed he risked being left behind. The boy started to cry and Eleanor immediately stepped forward.

'Excuse me, sir. Please let go of him,' she said forcefully. Her arm moved protectively around the boy's shoulders as her motherly instincts took over.

'He nearly knocked me over, running about the place.' The man started coughing and let go of the boy.

'Are you alright?' Eleanor asked the child, crouching down to his level and wiping his tears away.

One of the teachers arrived at Eleanor's side and quickly whisked the boy away, hardly giving an acknowledgement of the heated situation.

'You shouldn't let them run about in here,' the man spluttered.

'In a perfect world, I would agree, but they are children,' she said, taking a swipe at the fly that was still insistently buzzing around her head, only adding to her annoyance. 'It's what children do. And it's no excuse to go shouting at him like that.'

'I'll shout at who I want to shout at—' A full burst of coughing coincided with the reappearance of Mr Nelson.

'Thank you, Eleanor. I'll take it from here.'

Eleanor stopped with a jolt. Grasping the situation, she stepped back in panic. Shouting at one of the visitors was surely not the best course of action.

'I'm sorry, Mr Nelson, I—'

'Why don't you take a break? We'll discuss this later.'

She slowly backed away, her insides burning, while Mr Nelson spoke quietly and calmly to the man. Apologies were given on Eleanor's behalf, and the old man was invited to step into Mr Nelson's office.

'I don't want to sit in your office,' the man growled. 'There's nothing I want to hear from you and all you'll hear from me is the truth. Is that what you want?' He stared wide-eyed at Mr Nelson for a moment before heading in the direction of the toilets a little further down the corridor. Leaving Mr Nelson standing waiting in the quiet.

Mr Nelson's words, *we'll discuss this later,* repeated in Eleanor's mind. What did he mean by that?

'Don't worry about him,' Sahara whispered from behind.

She was surreptitiously watching the scene from the till. 'He has a go at somebody every time he comes here.'

Eleanor moved closer to continue the whispered conversation.

'But has anybody else ever argued back?' Eleanor subconsciously swiped at another fly.

Sahara thought for a moment, then shook her head. 'I just try and ignore him. He looks really sick now, though. He's been getting worse and worse with each visit, and now – I've never seen him looking so bad.'

Mr Nelson continued to wait in the gift shop doorway where the entrance of the toilets was visible. Rocking from the balls of his feet to his heels, and back again. Holding in his impatience while he waited. As soon as the old man exited, Mr Nelson approached him again. They spoke quietly together for a moment and this time the man accompanied Mr Nelson to his office. Eleanor hadn't taken in the man's pale complexion, his hunched stature, or his dark eyes at the time. Sahara was right; he didn't look well at all.

'Go get some lunch,' Sahara said. 'You'll need it by now, I bet. It's quite sad and lonely in the staff room. Most of us tend to go to the tea-room instead. Especially like now, when it'll probably be empty. You can treat yourself to some of that baking Darryl's been telling you about. It is really good.'

Eleanor looked at her watch at the same time as her stomach rumbled loudly. It was nearly half-past two. No wonder she had been quick to answer back with hunger getting the better of her. So much for efficiency and competency. Her heart sank with the thought that she had never lost a job on her first day before.

Chapter Four

Darryl traipsed across the field, returning from his lunch. His head down with concern, he fought against the growing wind. He knew he had to do something to help Larry, but was at a loss. He had intended to visit the gift shop, hoping to discuss his dilemma with Eleanor, but, before he had reached the doorway, he could hear the noise from a school party. Probably the same one that had wandered disinterestedly past his trench about an hour earlier. It was immediately apparent that it would not be possible.

He took a moment to watch her from the entrance. The excitement he had felt about her working there soon dissipated. He cringed at the sight of the children running round the shop with a deafening din. Her smile was stiff and forced, something he had seen too many times before. He knew the sweat that trickled down her face would have more to do with anxiety than hard work. She had enough to deal with. He couldn't burden her with his problems, too.

Back at the mosaic, he hopped impatiently from one foot to another while he watched a family group with a pushchair slowly make their way past. Once they were at a safe distance away, Darryl took a deep breath.

'Larry, I'm sorry, mate, but—'

'That sounds worrying,' Larry cut him off.

Darryl hesitated at Larry's defensive tone.

'Any sentence that starts "I'm sorry, but" can't be good.' Larry was still on his knees, working; hiding his face. The gentle scraping sound from his trowel suddenly became more forceful.

'You're right, but I have to say it. Please, just listen.'

Larry continued working and didn't say a word, so Darryl continued.

'You know that I lost my father several years ago. Even though I was there for him at the end, with his dementia, he never knew it. Every time he asked for me, he expected to see a little boy. He didn't know who I was. It tore me apart to think that he believed his son didn't care about him and didn't want to see him. I know it's stupid, but in a way I regret not being there for my dad, even though I was. Does that make any sense?'

Larry continued working, giving no indication of whether he was listening, let alone any reply to the question.

'You have this opportunity to speak to him,' Darryl went on. 'You don't have to like him, but family ties and all that, he's still your dad and I'm telling you, you will regret it if you don't.'

Larry gave an enormous sigh, his frustration evident. He stood and faced Darryl. Darryl had never seen such a look of anger from him before.

'Please, hear me out,' Darryl blurted, aware that he wouldn't have another chance. 'You may not regret it immediately, or even for quite a while, but eventually you'll look back and think, what if? Isn't a ten-minute conversation worth trying if it avoids all that misery in later life?'

'You don't understand,' Larry growled. 'You don't under-stand what he put us through.'

'No, I don't. You're right. But I do understand how much it hurts when your own family thinks you don't care enough about them to have a quick conversation, and how much *you* will regret it.'

'I make it a policy never to regret anything. A completely pointless emotion,' Larry said derisively.

'He's your father.'

'He's a man who left his son and wife to deal with the consequences of his actions. What kind of man does that?' Larry's voice had risen with his anger.

'I don't know. Maybe you should ask *him*.'

Larry quietly seethed at Darryl's impudence, but Darryl had to try every way he could to change Larry's mind. Although, it seemed whatever he said only made matters worse. His last option was humour, which he knew would go one of two ways. Ease the tension, or make him take a swipe.

'I could always come and hold your hand if that helps,' he said tentatively, trying his best to add a comical touch to his voice. He held his breath and waited for Larry's reaction.

They stared at each other in the silence that followed.

'I have never known you to be so -,' Larry began through clenched teeth, 'so – soft.'

Darryl let out a burst of laughter with his own relief.

'What's that saying?' Larry continued. 'You can't teach an old dog new tricks? Well, he is an old dog.' The tension may have eased, but Larry was still defensive.

'He's also dying,' Darryl implored. 'That changes a person's perspective. One of the last times my dad did remember me, he was in tears. He knew what was coming and that he would forget me. It not only broke my heart, but it broke his, too. Once he's gone, he's gone forever and there's something about knowing when the end is near that changes everything.'

Darryl could almost see the torment going on inside Larry's

head as he looked off into the distance, his eyes darting from place to place, but at least it meant that he was thinking about it.

'I had one hell of a time trying to convince the police that I had nothing to do with it.' Larry rubbed his eyes, trying to hold back tears. 'All the time knowing that I had what they were looking for. But I couldn't rat on my own dad. Even now I can't —' He broke off and squeezed his eyes shut tight. Shaking his head forcefully, he said, 'I can never forgive him.'

'I'm not asking you to forgive, just to talk to him,' Darryl said gently.

'One of these days,' Larry whispered, 'you're just going to have to accept that there's no hope for some people. They are just plain bad. And *you're* just a soft touch,' he added with the slightest of smiles.

'I'll try if you will.'

'OK,' Larry nodded in exasperation. 'I'll try, but don't go getting your hopes up.'

The delicious smells of home cooked soup and freshly baked bread had been wafting across the corridor from the tea-room all morning. After Sahara's suggestion to have her lunch there, Eleanor didn't need any further persuasion, especially at the thought of the sandwich she had made that morning still sat in her bag, squashed and limp. After the morning she'd had, she needed something with a little more substance. Her hands were still trembling from her argument.

A couple were examining a poster-sized aerial photograph of the site as she entered the tea-room. One of the many posters around the walls, each one depicting a different viewpoint, or of particular artefacts that had been discovered there over the years. The couple left a moment later, leaving the tea-room empty of visitors, and remnants of a busy lunchtime scattered across the tables.

Light from the glass double doors that led to a patio flooded the room, reflecting off the lace-patterned plastic tablecloths.

Being Darryl's place of work, she had visited before, but as Darryl had never been with her, she had never introduced herself to any of the other staff members.

'Hi,' she said brightly to the waitress, who was busy piling crockery onto a tray from one of the tables. Like Eleanor, her hair was tied back in a ponytail, and she even had the same escaped strands hanging down around her face. In her twenties, she was fit and strong. 'I'm—'

'Eleanor, yeah I know. I'm Kate,' she said. 'Or Katy, I'll answer to both.'

With a loud clatter, she added more plates to her already towering pile, and dropped the cutlery to one side.

'Darryl's told us all about you,' Kate continued abruptly. 'I don't have time to show you around. Got to get cleared and ready for the afternoon and I haven't had my lunch yet.'

Eleanor was about to apologise for her intrusion when Kate carried on quickly.

'That's Rochelle,' she nodded towards a teenage girl with black hair in plaited pigtails sat at a table in the corner eating chips, dressed in the same black and white, old-fashioned waitress uniform as Kate. Her large eyes were framed by a bold, thick line of black eyeliner. Rochelle looked up from her magazine and lifted a hand in acknowledgement, still holding on to the chip that she had just dipped in ketchup. Her mouth too full to speak.

'And you've probably heard about Mo, but don't worry, her bark's much worse than her bite,' Kate went on to more clattering cutlery.

'Mo?' Eleanor squeaked, hoping she wasn't about to have another argument.

'The cook. Darryl might have called her Maureen, I suppose. Of course, she works in the kitchen, which is just as well.' Kate piled the last cup and saucer from the table onto her tray and looked up at Eleanor for the first time. 'And best it stays that way, too.'

Eleanor paused for a moment, trying to remember Darryl ever mentioning anything about a Mo, a Maureen, her bark or bite. Although Darryl had only been there a few months himself, she also knew he had a tendency to focus on the positive, omitting the negative entirely. Especially if it would have any influence on a decision. Like the decision as to whether or not to take this job.

Kate must have realised from her blank face as she continued, 'Put it this way, the Romans would have loved her. She could have taken on an entire legion by herself with that mouth. Come on, I'm going to the kitchen. I'll show you where everything is, if you can bear with me.' She hauled the crockery laden tray up off the table and into her arms. Then, marched off to the kitchen before finally dumping it next to a large dishwasher. A man who looked in his seventies began helping her unload the tray while she stretched out the tired muscles in her arms. The clattering continued as the man loaded the crockery and cutlery into large trays, spraying food debris off with an overhead spray that splashed over more than just the crockery.

'This is Oli,' Kate went on.

'Hi,' Eleanor said enthusiastically.

The man hardly turned to look at her. It seemed an effort for the short stocky man to glance towards her from under his heavy eyebrows. His thinning grey hair doing its best to hide the bald patch.

'Mo is over there,' Kate continued quickly, gesturing

towards the other side of the kitchen with a flick of her hand.

Eleanor could just make out the back of a woman in a blue dress with a white apron tied at her back. The view was obscured by a large open shelving unit in the centre of the room, filled with pots and pans that almost touched the ceiling.

'All hands to the deck, I see.' Eleanor's attempt to lighten the mood in the busy kitchen was greeted only by tired and unhappy faces.

'Lunchtime and straight after is always the busiest time of the day,' Kate quickly went on. 'Here's where you make your tea or coffee. You'll need to use the kettle because the hot water tank isn't working, as usual,' she drawled, pointing to the area immediately opposite the door. 'I'm afraid staff teas and coffees are made in the kitchen. Only paying customers get the proper stuff. If there's any food you want, just ask. The discount's not great, but it's something.'

'Can I have a scone?' Eleanor said quickly. The sight of the large plump scones on the counter in the tea-room had made her salivate as she'd walked past.

'Sure,' Kate said and pointed behind Eleanor to a counter next to the door, where there were piles of white ceramic ramekins. Though there were two sizes, they were both relatively small.

'The smaller ramekins are for the butter, the larger ones for the jam. You do those yourself,' she said as she exited the kitchen with an empty tray under her arm, 'then help yourself to a scone back in the tea-room. We only have the ones left on display at the moment, but they're still fresh from this morning.' The door swung shut behind her.

Eleanor stepped to the counter as more crashing and clattering continued. She stared at the ramekins, her shoulders tight and raised almost to her ears. Her stomach rumbled again and with a deep breath, she turned her attention back to her lunch.

Two enormous tubs sat on the counter to her right. One of jam and one of butter. As she scraped a small portion of butter out of the large square tub and into its respective ramekin, Larry walked into the kitchen immediately to her right.

'Hi, Larry,' she breathed with relief. A friendly face after her disastrous morning.

But he walked straight past. He took a few more steps before turning back towards the door as though he had forgotten something; distracted and staring at the floor.

'Hi, Larry,' she tried again.

This time, he jolted at her voice.

'Eleanor! Hi. How's your first day going?' he gabbled.

Eleanor hesitated. 'OK, I think,' was the version she opted for, pushing everything else from her mind. 'Have you come for a coffee?'

'I – yes. Coffee. I came to get a coffee,' he said, turning again and heading back towards the kettle. 'Do you want one?'

'Please, thank you,' Eleanor replied.

He turned his back on her and busied himself with making the coffees. His distracted behaviour was uncharacteristic, to say the least.

'I thought I'd treat myself to a scone,' Eleanor continued over her shoulder as she pulled the lid off the large pot of jam. 'Darryl's told me how good they are.'

With a spoon, she scooped it from the pot and watched the deep red, thick jam plop unappetisingly into its respective ramekin just as Kate came back through the door, carrying another tray piled full of plates, soup bowls and mugs. A man's gruff voice called after her.

'Scone and coffee,' he bellowed, followed by a fit of deep coughing.

Eleanor froze. It was the same low, gruff voice as earlier, and her shoulders stiffened once again.

Chapter Five

Everything in the kitchen suddenly stopped, and the room went quiet. The only sounds were the old man's coughs and the gradually intensifying pitch of the boiling kettle. Kate hesitated in the doorway while everyone in the kitchen turned towards her.

'I'll be with you in just a moment,' Kate called back. The kindness in her voice didn't match her expression.

'That man,' Maureen growled, appearing at Eleanor's side. 'Every time that man comes in here, he orders a scone, and yet every time he complains about them.'

'Don't worry, Mo. I'll deal with him.' Kate looked harassed as she dumped her heavy tray down by the dishwasher.

'Why don't you get Rochelle to do it? She's just sitting there doing nothing,' Maureen said, wielding a plastic spatula covered in brown goo in the air.

'She's not doing nothing,' Kate snapped back. 'She's having her lunch. It doesn't matter, anyway. He's already had plenty of pops at me. I'm getting used to it.'

'Well, I'm telling you now,' Maureen shouted over her. 'if he complains about my scones today, I'll go out there and tell him exactly what I think of him. Mark my words.' Her wrinkled face sagged, accentuated by her deep frown. Wisps of white hair attempted to escape the many pins and hairnet. 'Why doesn't he just hurry up and die?'

Eleanor tried to hold back a gasp.

Kate rolled her eyes. 'Speak your mind, why don't you?' she said with sarcasm.

'What?' Maureen asked. 'Nelson told me last time he was here that he's dying and we should all humour him. Personally, I don't see why we should put up with him making our lives miserable. Even if it is just for a few more months.'

'Maybe he has a point.' Kate stretched her aching arms again.

'And what would that be? I'm sure the miserable old—'

'Mo!' Kate warned.

'I was only going to say codger. I'm sure he eats so fast he's not able to taste them anyway,' Maureen continued. 'They should be savoured. Award-winning scones, these are,' she said directed at Eleanor. Her deep frown suddenly returned. 'Who are you?' she asked abruptly.

'E - Eleanor,' she stuttered at the sudden assault. 'Darr—'

'Oh yes, Darryl's partner.' She looked Eleanor up and down as though deciding whether she was worthy, before returning to the counter where she had been working, mumbling under her breath.

Kate grabbed a glass from the counter next to Eleanor and filled it with water from the nearby tap.

'While I'm here,' Eleanor said, keen to be helpful, and trying to appease her guilt at shouting at a dying man, 'I'll do the butter and jam for you, if you like.'

'Thanks, that would be great,' she said, and then drank nearly the full glass in one go. She stopped and breathed deeply before she continued. 'Lots of jam. He likes lots of jam.'

She finished the last mouthful in the glass while Eleanor took two more ramekins from their respective piles.

'I think he's had a go at me every time he's been here,' Kate continued, 'and, unfortunately, Mo's right. I think we all wish he would hurry up and die.'

A smash behind them made both Eleanor and Kate jump. Unfortunately, Kate's glass ended up smashed on the floor, along with the coffee mug Larry had just dropped.

'It just slipped in my fingers,' he whispered.

'Larry!' Mo exclaimed, her fists pushed into her hips and staring at him wildly. 'We'll have no cups left at this rate.'

'I'm so sorry, Mo. You know how clumsy I can be.' A flicker of Larry's usual cheekiness came through in his reply.

'It's a good job it's you,' Mo said as her frown changed into a teenage love-sick smile. 'But maybe you should try to be just a little less clumsy around my kitchen.'

His nonchalant shrug conveyed the unspoken understanding that it would never happen. With one coffee still in his hand, he turned to Eleanor.

'Here, you take this one.'

'Don't worry,' Eleanor said with concern. 'I'm sure I can make my own coffee. I think you may need it more than I do.'

'No, I insist. You have this one, and to make up for my clumsiness,' he continued a little louder with a glance towards Maureen, 'I'll clear up the glass as well. It was my fault anyway.'

'Too right, you will,' Kate added.

While Larry headed towards a large cupboard to one side of the kitchen, Eleanor returned to serving up another helping of butter and jam for the old man.

Kate filled up another glass of water, and with her back towards Maureen, she whispered, 'Cook's a bit touchy when it comes to breaking stuff. You have been warned. Unless you're Larry.'

Eleanor felt a smile tugging at the corners of her mouth as she began to understand Kate's sense of humour.

'I can't find the dustpan and brush,' came Larry's voice from the cupboard.

Kate rolled her eyes again. 'Men,' she growled under her breath before replying to him. 'Just because you can't find anything there doesn't mean there's nothing there to find. You're going to need the mop, too,' she said, tip-toeing around the puddle of coffee stretched across the floor as she made her way towards him.

Eleanor was relieved that Kate had shown a little sign of friendliness after her abrupt welcome. She wondered where she had heard that phrase before as the busy sounds of crockery clattering and saucepans banging continued behind her. It was only a moment before she remembered it was something she had heard Darryl say several times, especially during their long walks past open fields where he clearly longed to search through the mud for who-knows-what.

'Thanks, Kate,' came Larry's voice from the direction of the cupboard and, a moment later, Kate was by Eleanor's side again, downing the last mouthful of her drink.

'I'll be back in a minute for the jam and butter. You can just leave it here,' she said.

'Are you an archaeologist, too?' Eleanor asked.

'No,' Kate answered. 'Why would you think that?'

'Just something you said. It's exactly the kind of thing Darryl says.'

'I've just picked it up since working here, I guess.' She shrugged and moved towards the door, almost bumping into Mr Nelson as he entered the kitchen.

'It's always just as busy in here after lunch as it is during lunch,' he joked, after jostling at the near miss with Kate and finding both Eleanor and Larry inside. He gave a quizzical look towards Larry, who was now crouched, picking up the pieces of china and glass. Stepping next to Eleanor, Mr Nelson quietly said, 'I hope you weren't too traumatised by our friend earlier.' He flicked his eyes with a shift of his head towards the sound of coughing that was coming from the tea-room. 'We all know what he's like and you don't need to worry. I'll handle everything.'

'Thank you,' Eleanor said, relieved. She hadn't been looking forward to explaining to Darryl that she had lost her job on her first day. 'And I'm just about to get out of everyone's way. This is obviously not a good time of day to be coming in here,' she said with an apologetic smile.

Feeling a little easier from Mr Nelson's reassurance, she put her coffee and her own two ramekins on a tray and left the kitchen. Kate was already serving a scone onto a small side plate when Eleanor arrived for her own. They said nothing, but Kate gave a cynical smile before placing the scone laden plate on a tray and turning to the large coffee machine on the back counter. While Eleanor focused on choosing her scone; her mouth watering at the anticipation, the sound of hissing grew louder behind her as Kate heated milk for the old man's coffee.

Because of the limited space of the tea-room, Eleanor couldn't keep a sizeable distance from the man, but at least she could be out of his eye line and she headed for a table behind him. Rochelle had lifted her magazine, hiding her face completely, presumably for the same reason. Thankfully, he was more preoccupied with watching the comings and goings of the tea-room as he watched Kate return to the kitchen, arriving at the same time as Mr Nelson hurrying out. *A second close collision,* Eleanor thought. His scurried march across the tea-room gave the impression that he was as eager to get out of the kitchen as Eleanor had been.

She placed her tray on the table, the plastic table cloth still sticky from lunch, and made herself as comfortable as she could. She cut her scone in half as Kate returned from the kitchen, breaking the ominous silence. There was no thanks when she placed the man's order on his table. Not even a grunt of acknowledgement. Instead, his head followed Larry as he passed by after he had exited the kitchen immediately behind Kate. He had caught Eleanor's attention, too. With his head hung low and his hands deep in his pockets, he seemed to have given up on his coffee. She made a mental note to ask Darryl later if there was a problem.

The room returned to silence while she quietly spread the jam on her scone, except for the odd cough from the man in front of her and the shufflings of his heavy movements. She suddenly jumped as he dropped a piece of his cutlery on to his plate. The quietness of the room had intensified the loud clatter, and she turned her attention back to her scone until the old man's coughing pulled her focus once again. It started as a heave of his shoulders. That juddering that you have when trying to stifle a cough when your mouth is full. But it seemed to get worse. Trying to stand, he struggled to get out of his chair. His hands now clutched at his throat. Eleanor's instincts kicked in. Her first aid training had never been needed as a teacher, but it was still there, lurking somewhere in her mind. She scrambled out of her seat and came round to look at him. His face, though bluish earlier, was now bright red.

'Cough,' she told him. 'Can you cough?'

The man continued to splutter, spitting crumbs of scone and dollops of jam all over Eleanor as he tried to breathe. Ignoring the splats that had landed on her face, she moved round behind him. Desperately trying to remember the correct position of her fist, she attempted the Heimlich manoeuvre. Learning in the school hall with friends and colleagues was a stark contrast to the real-life situation. Once. Twice. She was about to try a third time when the man suddenly dropped through her arms.

Eleanor stood bewildered. Everyone stared at her. Mr Nelson had returned during the chaos. His phone against his ear. The room fell silent as the man hit the floor.

Chapter Six

Darryl anxiously raised his head and looked past the earth mound that surrounded the trench. There was still no sign of Larry. Although it had been no time at all, it seemed like hours before Larry appeared and Darryl's stomach sank at the sight of him. He cursed himself as imaginary heated words between father and son immediately began playing out in his head. Watching Larry striding across the field with his head down and his hands shoved deep into his pockets, he failed to convince himself it was due to the cold that accompanied the continually greying sky. With the imaginary argument still running in his head, Darryl braced himself for the actual argument that was to come.

'I couldn't do it,' Larry snapped as he approached the trench.

Stunned for a moment, Darryl's apprehension turned to frustration. 'What happened?' he asked. 'Did you see him at all?'

Larry hesitated. His eyes flicked from one side to the other. 'He wasn't there when I arrived, so I hung about in the kitchen and then-'

The pause only added to Darryl's already frayed nerves.

'Then it happened,' Larry spat. 'He saunters into the tea-room and just bellows his order across the room like nobody else on this planet matters. "Scone and coffee,"' Larry mimicked his father's gruff tone. 'As long as he gets what he wants, the rest of the world can go to hell.'

Larry's anger gave Darryl reason to pause. 'That's a bit harsh, don't you think?' he said tentatively. 'It was just a coffee order.'

'But that's how he is with everything,' Larry snapped back. 'I'm sorry, Darryl. I tried. But he hasn't changed. You should have heard what they were saying about him in the kitchen. Everybody hates him, it's not just me.'

As Larry spoke, Darryl felt a wave of sadness wash over him at the spite contained in the word *hate*, and he struggled to continue. 'I really think you'd be—'

'I tried, and that's that,' Larry interrupted. 'He's still the same belligerent, arrogant – sod he always was.'

'Maybe—'

'No, Darryl. I don't want to hear any more excuses for him. In fact, I don't want to talk about him at all.'

Larry stormed across the planks and returned to his position on the mosaic, resuming his work in a rage. Darryl was left with the awful feeling he had just made things worse. The thought of going down to the tea-room himself crossed his mind. A civilised conversation between the two men. After all, he had always been polite to Darryl. But he ultimately decided to honour Larry's wishes and let it be. At least for now.

Larry had never spoken to him like that before. The cold and silence of the afternoon only intensified the tension between them. Darryl often lifted his head, trying to catch a glimpse of any indication that Larry was willing to talk. But

Larry kept his head down and showed no signs of approach-ability.

~

'Yes. Yes, I'm still here,' Mr Nelson continued into the phone, breaking the silence that had filled the room. 'I think – I think you'd better get here as quickly as you can. I think he may be dead.' His words echoed in the room and the silence thickened. Even his own efficiency faltered. He held his hand over the tele-phone speaker and told everyone that the ambulance was on its way before his attention was pulled back by the person on the other end of the phone. 'Yes, yes. I'm still here.'

'There's blood,' Rochelle whispered, staring at Eleanor.

Eleanor wiped her face with her hand. Her arm was heavy as she lifted it. Looking at her hand, she saw the remnants of the man's scone and jam.

'It's just jam.' Her voice quivered as she spoke. She desper-ately wanted to wipe the gunk from her face further, but found her limbs were too heavy to move.

'No, there's blood,' Rochelle repeated as the shock subsided and hysterics moved in.

Kate quickly moved across to her and placed an arm around her shoulder. She spoke soothingly in an unsuccessful effort to console the young girl. Eleanor's knees threatened to buckle as she realised what had just happened. A man had died in her arms. She had failed to save him. Her gaze wandered around the room at the stunned faces. She hadn't noticed Sahara, who now stood in the tea-room entrance. Nor Mo and Oli, standing at the kitchen door. Suddenly, Mr Nelson's voice boomed, causing Eleanor to jump in surprise as visitors appeared over Sahara's shoulder.

'Sorry, the tea-room is closed. Sahara, could you please...'

Sahara quickly hustled the visitors away and towards the gift shop. Mr Nelson one-handedly closed the doors to the tea-room while still holding on to his mobile.

'Have you killed him?' Mo asked loudly.

Eleanor stared at her in disbelief. She didn't kill him. She tried to save him.

'Thank God for that,' Mo went on. 'I've got work to do.' She turned abruptly and disappeared into the kitchen.

'But...' Eleanor was too exhausted to argue.

Instead, Mr Nelson spoke gently to her. 'Why don't you go to the ladies and clean yourself up? On second thoughts, use the facilities for the disabled. No chance of you being interrupted there. A bit more privacy that way.'

Eleanor couldn't move. Her entire body was numb.

'Katy,' Mr Nelson called across the room gently. 'If I sit with Rochelle, could you...?'

Kate seemed to understand immediately and withdrew from Rochelle, much to Rochelle's annoyance. Eleanor found her hand being taken and pulled gently. Bit by bit, Kate coaxed her away from the body that lay at her feet.

The cool, refreshing water on Eleanor's face helped revive her. Though Kate had been hesitant to leave, Eleanor assured her she would be OK. Once left in the small, clinically tiled, white room that provided a toilet and basin, she lifted her head and looked in the mirror in front of her. A couple of tiny dots of red jam were still stubbornly stuck to her left cheek. She wiped them away with her damp hands, her cheek scratched as she wiped her fingers across it. Though not painful, she cursed at the shock. Taking a closer look, she saw a tiny fragment of glass on her finger. She peered back into the mirror. The small specks of what she had thought were jam on her face, spread and a fine line of red had appeared where the glass had scratched her cheek. She watched, stunned, as the tiny dots gradually increased in size. Adrenaline now fuelling her body, she raced back to the tea-room.

As soon as Eleanor entered, she saw Kate had returned to the corner with Rochelle, comforting the silently sobbing teenager. Someone had draped one of the plastic tablecloths over the dead man's body on the floor. And his table, where his order of scone and coffee should have been, was empty.

'Stop,' Eleanor cried as she saw Mr Nelson disappear through the door to the kitchen, carrying a tray. She raced across the room. 'Stop!' she cried again as she burst through the door.

He had already laid the tray by the dishwasher and was picking up the plate ready to scrape the scone into the waste disposal unit. About to throw away what Eleanor believed was vital evidence.

'Is this from his table?' she demanded, peering at the scone, looking for any telltale sparkles from broken glass.

'Yes, yes, it is. Eleanor, you need to clean yourself up.'

'It's blood,' she announced. 'Rochelle was right. It's blood.'

'What are you talking about?' said Mr Nelson.

She glanced up at the looks of bewilderment and continued. 'When he was choking, he spat scone at me. He must also have spat blood and pieces of glass. I found a piece still on me.'

'Glass!' Mr Nelson exclaimed. 'Don't be ridiculous. Are you saying Maureen put glass in the scones?'

'Who's insulting my scones?' Mo's voice came from the other side of the kitchen. 'These are award-winning scones, I'll have you know.'

'No, that's not what I'm saying. Mine was fine.'

'Fine!' Mo exclaimed. 'Is that all? Just fine?'

Eleanor ignored her. 'I'm saying somebody put glass in *his* scone.' Although, she saw nothing in the scone. 'Or his jam,' she went on and changed her focus to the jam. Using a teaspoon to stir it slowly in the small, shallow ramekin, she saw tiny fragments of glass. The thick jam disguised them well. It wasn't surprising the old man hadn't noticed them. That is, not until he chewed and swallowed them. The glass ripping at his throat.

Mr Nelson exited the kitchen with his phone back by his ear.

'Police, please.'

Eleanor heard before the door swung shut behind him.

'It appears there may have been a murder.'

Chapter Seven

At the mention of murder, Rochelle immediately burst into tears again, before the sound was muffled by the kitchen door as it swung closed. Distracted for only a moment, Eleanor turned her attention away from the victim's ramekin of jam and towards the large pot-full, stirring it with a spoon, searching for more evidence of glass. All the while, Maureen persisted with her tirade at the slightest hint of an insult about her cooking, real or imaginary. Despite her thorough search, Eleanor couldn't find any trace of glass in the large pot of jam, but before she could continue, Mr Nelson burst back into the room.

'I have been instructed,' he announced, 'to clear the area and make sure that nobody touches anything.'

'So what are we going to do?' Maureen said. 'Just sit around waiting?'

'That is exactly what we're going to do. If we all stay in one corner of the tea-room, that should be clear enough for the authorities.' He stood holding the door open with an expectant look on his face.

Maureen begrudgingly agreed and marched out of the kitchen. Although Eleanor wanted to keep searching, she followed with Oli behind her. He had lingered in the kitchen, taking his time before finally making his way out. His fingers grasped so tightly around a walking stick his knuckles were white. He remained quiet as he moved through the tea-room, keeping his eyes firmly focused away from the victim laid out on the floor only to join Maureen, where she had found herself a table with a good view of the tablecloth covered body.

Taking into account Oli's reaction, let alone Rochelle's, Eleanor hesitantly approached Mr Nelson. 'Maybe we shouldn't be in here. Considering...' she said with a sideways glance towards Rochelle.

The girl was still sobbing into Kate's shoulder with no sign of easing. And, as he had only just asked Maureen not to lift the tablecloth that hid the dead man's body, he eagerly agreed.

'On second thoughts,' he announced to the room. 'I think maybe some fresh air will do us some good. We don't want to go too far, as I'm sure the police will need to talk to all of us, but I don't see any harm in moving out onto the patio. Yes. Fresh air. That's what we need,' he said with over-the-top enthusiasm in an attempt to drown out Maureen's and Oli's groans.

'Moving again! Why do we need to move?' Maureen moaned. 'My old bones won't put up with all this to-ing and fro-ing. And besides, I've got a good view from here.'

'Your old bones don't stop you dancing round the kitchen during the quieter times,' Mr Nelson teased her.

Mo only answered with a non-committal sound that only confirmed the possibility that he may be right, and she followed everyone else out to the patio. She certainly couldn't argue with everybody else's eagerness to remove themselves from the room.

'Now, come on, everybody outside,' Mr Nelson continued, even though most were already on their way. 'We'll all feel so much better out in the fresh air.'

It wasn't until Eleanor glimpsed herself in the glass door's reflection that she realised remnants of scone and jam still covered her shirt. And whatever else may be there.

'Mr Nelson, do you have a clean shirt I could borrow?' she asked. 'Besides, I think the police may want to take this one with them.'

'Yes, of course. That's good thinking on your part, Eleanor.' Once the small group was on the patio, he said again, 'Now, everything will be just fine. There's no need for anybody to worry. This will all just be a bad memory soon.' He checked to make sure that everybody had sat themselves at the tables on the patio, and then he and Eleanor left together for his office.

'I don't know why I didn't think of it before,' he said as they entered his office.

'Maybe because we were all a little preoccupied with other things,' Eleanor mumbled, suddenly feeling tired.

He opened a large cupboard full of orderly placed stationery items. Pens, pencils, envelopes, and other such paraphernalia. The top shelf seemed to be reserved for staff shirts. While he searched for the correct size, Eleanor's eyes wandered over the pictures that were displayed on the wall directly opposite. There were so many of them it was difficult not to.

'Here we are,' he said, passing the shirt to Eleanor. 'I see you're admiring my photographs.'

Eleanor wouldn't have used the word admiring, but she held her tongue. She remembered him showing them off when she had come for her interview and how bored she was then. People standing around grinning in their shorts and wide-brimmed hats. None of it meant anything to her. A forced smile was suffice for her reply.

'I'd better get outside to wait for the ambulance or police. Whoever decides to arrive first,' he joked. 'I suppose I ought to close the site, too,' he said thoughtfully. He held the door open for Eleanor, ready to leave, and placed a hand on her arm as she passed him. 'Now, remember, you've had a great shock, so take care of yourself. Everything is going to be just fine.'

Not so fine for the dead man, Eleanor thought.

They left his office together and Mr Nelson strode importantly towards the exit doors while Eleanor headed back to the toilets to change. Breathing deeply in the quiet, she took a moment to settle herself. She tried to steady her hands, but they continued to tremble. The sight of the residue on her shirt brought a sickness to her throat as the memory of the dying man's face forced itself into her mind.

After she changed her shirt, she made her way back to the patio area, faltering at the sight of Mr Nelson through a window, as he was only now walking down to the main entrance. *The job of a manager,* she thought, *looking after the well-being of everybody else.* But she didn't want to listen to any more of his constant bolstering and unhelpful consoling and was glad she had missed his most recent pep talk on the patio.

Reaching the end of the corridor with the tea-room on the left, she glanced to the right. Directly through the entrance-way to the gift shop, she saw Sahara standing at the till with her back towards her. Her hand slipped down into her pocket as the till drawer closed. The memory of Mr Nelson's announcement that morning of a thief came into her head. No more than a second and it was over. But the glance over her shoulder, as she must have realised Eleanor was there, was a very guilty one. Eleanor turned quickly away and continued into the tea-room. She left her old shirt on one of the tables and continued out onto the patio. Though her heart sank with disappointment, she pushed the event out of her mind. There were bigger problems to deal with.

Chapter Eight

Everyone glanced up at her when Eleanor arrived on the patio. They had found their own spots without her and, feeling like an outsider, she stayed on her feet and on her own. Nervous energy still tingling, she paced back and forth. Maureen and Oli remained together, sat on the edge of the patio. Both hunched over and mumbling to each other. Like a mother, Kate gently consoled Rochelle, whose sobs had quietened to sniffles.

'I know. It must have been awful for you.' Kate spoke gently and calmly.

Rochelle nodded, staring vacantly at the lace-patterned, plastic tablecloth that laid over the table in front of her; struggling to free itself from the clips around the table's edge in the growing wind.

'You had the best seat in the house,' Kate joked. 'I'll bet you'll be the one who'll be able to help the police the most.'

Rochelle shook her head vigorously. Her eyes were wide with terror.

'It's OK. I'll stay with you if you want,' Kate went on.

Rochelle seemed to calm a little at this.

'Do you remember seeing anything that might help them? Maybe somebody stirring the jam or adding anything?'

Rochelle's eyes began darting around wildly, shaking her head again.

Leave it to the police, Eleanor thought. *She's clearly distraught. You'll do more harm than good.*

'It's OK,' Kate continued gently, squeezing Rochelle's shoulders tighter. 'It's OK.'

Movement inside the tea-room pulled Eleanor's focus. The inside doors had opened and Mr Nelson entered with police officers and a group of people covered head to toe in white overalls. Eleanor surreptitiously watched through the windows while the others remained in their seats. Mr Nelson, in his ever efficient manner, was pointing to a black bulbous blob that was attached to the ceiling at the entrance to the gift shop doorway. *CCTV. That must surely be of some help.* The room had suddenly become busy with one person bending down next to the body, while someone else made their way towards the kitchen, and others busied themselves with various pieces of equipment. Eleanor suddenly found herself face to face with an officer through the window as he walked across the room towards the patio doors. With an incomprehensible feeling of guilt, she turned quickly and walked away, waiting for a reprimand behind her. The door opened to the patio, and the officer stood at the door, guard-like. There was no reprimand, but the feeling of being confined and watched over set Eleanor's nerves on edge. Further enhanced by the fact that every so often, Maureen tutted loudly at the officer, as though the old man's death were nothing more than an inconvenience. Soon, another officer joined them on the patio and took statements from each. Their names, what they saw, what they did. The same story over and over. As soon as the officer reached Maureen, the inevitable eruption came. Eleanor turned away. The constant outbursts were already starting to wear on her. She gazed out over the miles of open fields around them. Surrounded by a vast, isolated landscape.

Once statements were taken, the second officer disappeared back inside. Eventually, the door opened again and a small, middle-aged woman in an old, well-worn black trouser suit joined them on the patio. She introduced herself as DI Hutchins and the man that stood next to her as DS Johnson. She hunched her shoulders from the chilly wind and looked up towards the grey clouds. Subconsciously imitating her, Eleanor felt a drop of rain land on her face. The DI popped her head back through the door. After a brief discussion, or it could have been considered a minor argument, DI Hutchins told everyone to make their way round the outside of the building to the gift shop. Even Maureen was grateful at the idea of getting back inside and out of the cold and rain.

'And who are you?' DI Hutchins asked on finding Sahara perched on the edge of the counter as they all entered the gift shop.

She immediately jumped off like a naughty child. 'Sahara. I work here in the shop.'

'Has one of my officers taken your statement?' She spoke to Sahara but glanced over towards the officer by the door, who nodded his confirmation.

'Yes.' Sahara nodded eagerly. 'But I didn't see nothing. What happened?' Her eyes flicked towards Eleanor.

Standing separately from the huddle of other staff members, Eleanor avoided eye contact.

'Then you can go,' the DI spoke over her, ignoring her question. 'If we need you, we know how to contact you.' She turned her back on Sahara and spoke to the room. 'Are there no chairs? Well, just perch where best you can.'

She waved her hands around in what Eleanor thought was a very dismissive manner as the group shuffled towards the side cabinets. They pushed the neatly displayed items aside to make room for themselves to sit. Eleanor perched on the edge of one of the low display tables full of plastic animals in the middle of the room.

'Now, Mrs Eleanor Garrett,' the DI said, casting a roaming eye over the group.

'Yes, that's me,' Eleanor said, raising her hand automatically like a schoolchild.

'You were with the man when he died, I believe.'

Eleanor nodded. She pulled her arms across her as she remembered the feeling of his body slide through them and down to the floor. 'He was choking. I tried to help.' Her eyes involuntarily flicked towards the door of the tea-room just across the corridor and a wave of nausea came over her.

'Do we have a name for the victim yet?' the DI asked DS Johnson.

In her mind, Eleanor saw everybody's faces staring at her. 'Have you killed him yet?' Maureen's voice rang in her head.

'No, not yet,' the DS replied. 'They're still running his prints.'

'Did you know the man?' the DI turned back to Eleanor.

'No, I was sitting at the table behind him.' Eleanor pushed the image of his angry face shouting at her that morning out of her mind. She didn't know him and was glad about it. 'Once I realised he was choking, I tried to help.'

'So, you were...' The DI looked around her with that aimless look again. 'You were...' She wandered over to the tea-room door and peered through the glass insert. Turning back to the shop, she gave a large humph sound. 'Come on, come with me.' She gave a minimal flick towards Eleanor and wandered off down the corridor.

Eleanor struggled to her feet and by the time she had caught up, DI Hutchins was talking with an officer outside Mr Nelson's office, with Mr Nelson himself standing in the doorway. As she got closer, she heard Larry's name and realised they must have been discussing the CCTV footage. She had almost forgotten that he had been in the kitchen just before the incident and was selfishly relieved to hear that he would be joining them. For her sake, even if not for his.

'Good, good. That should help,' DI Hutchins said. 'You're finished in here now, are you?'

'Yes,' the officer said. 'I have the most recent footage here,' he said, indicating the laptop he was carrying under his arm. 'I can—'

'Good,' the DI interrupted. 'I'll have this room, then.'

'That is my office,' Mr Nelson said, importantly.

'And we thank you for your cooperation,' she replied quickly before walking straight past him into the room.

She glanced behind her and waved for Eleanor to follow. Inside the room, she looked around her with a heavy sigh.

'There's not much here, is there? Never mind. As we can't get in the cafe, we'll have to do the best we can in here.' She looked up at Eleanor. 'Now, if the victim was sat in the chair there,' she pointed to Mr Nelson's office chair on the far side of the office, opposite the door, 'how far away from him would you say you were?'

Eleanor stared at the empty chair facing her. 'He was facing the other way. I was behind him,' she said vacantly.

'OK.' DI Hutchins moved round the table and swivelled the chair until it faced the wall behind it.

Eleanor felt this was a completely unnecessary act. She was just explaining that she was sitting behind the man, but she continued. She judged the distance as best she could and explained the positioning of her own table and the surrounding chairs that would have been between them.

'Hmm,' the DI hummed thoughtfully, staring at the space in front of her as though staring at the physical table and chairs Eleanor had just described. 'And this is where you were when he began coughing?' she asked.

'Choking,' Eleanor corrected.

'What were you doing yourself?' the DI continued.

'I was having my lunch,' Eleanor said.

'This was about half two, quarter to three, wasn't it? That's a late lunch.'

'It had been a busy morning.' Eleanor shrugged.

'What happened next?' DI Hutchins asked.

Eleanor took a deep breath. Reliving the moment was the last thing she wanted to do. 'I got up to help him. I learnt the Heimlich manoeuvre when I was a teacher and I guess the impulse just kicked in.'

'Hmm, and where would you say the others were at this point?'

'Rochelle was the only other person in the tea-room at the time. Everyone else was in the kitchen, I think.'

'Where would that be?' DI Hutchins waved her arms in the air as if to indicate in relation to where they were standing now.

'Rochelle was sat in the corner over that way.' Eleanor pointed past the corner of Mr Nelson's office and through the wall into the distance. 'And the kitchen is that way,' pointing to her right, past the stationary cupboard.

DI Hutchins stared in the directions Eleanor had pointed. 'So that makes the doorway over here?' She waved an arm behind her and off to the left.

Eleanor nodded.

'What about,' the DI said thoughtfully, 'immediately before the incident? Were you already seated when he arrived?'

'No, I was in the kitchen. I came through soon after, though. He hadn't even received his order when I sat down.'

'Who brought him his order?'

'Kate,' Eleanor replied.

'Kate,' the DI mumbled to herself. 'That would be Katherine Reeves.' Turning her focus back to Eleanor, she said, 'And that was the order of the scone...'

'and coffee.' Eleanor finished.

'Hmm. That will be all...'

'I can go home?' Eleanor asked hopefully.

'You can go back to the shop and join your colleagues. Don't worry, I'm sure this won't take long.'

Eleanor returned to the gift shop, where murmurs and whispers abruptly stopped as soon as she entered. She quietly crossed the room and resumed her perched position on the central display case.

DI Hutchins, who had been following behind, spoke with the officer who had taken their statements earlier before turning her attention to the room.

'Miss Maureen Bradbury?' she asked the room.

'Don't you go blaming my scones,' Maureen blurted, standing in protest. 'Award winning scones, they are. Every time he came in here, he complained about my scones, but it didn't stop him ordering them again the next time.'

The DI gave a knowing look towards the officer she had just spoken with, who had clearly informed her about the earlier event when Maureen had given a similar outburst. 'So, he was a regular visitor. Could you come with me—'

'I'm not going anywhere,' Maureen said firmly, crossing her arms in defiance and sat back down on the cabinet.

DI Hutchins had no choice other than to leave her to rant.

'My old bones can't cope with all this to-ing and fro-ing. I didn't even know the man. I never even talked to him. He would just complain and then leave. I would have liked to have given him a piece of my mind—'

'Would you?' the DI interrupted, her eyebrows raising.

Maureen suddenly went quiet. A momentary pause before continuing.

'Of course I would.' She held her head high, defying anybody to complain about her scones. 'I would have told him that they are award-winning scones, and if he had a problem with them, then he would need to take that up with the judges of the 2018 Baking Championship of Cragbourne County. And, if you're inferring,' she continued defiantly, 'that I would have killed him over it, then you are sadly mistaken. After seventy-two years of life experience, I wouldn't need to resort to such a crude method of justice. I have my first place certificate to prove I'm in the right.'

'The glass was in the jam,' Eleanor said, tired of Maureen's ranting. 'Not the scone.'

'How do you know that?' the DI said, bringing her focus back to Eleanor.

Eleanor looked at her. She could see the real question in her eyes. 'Because I saw it,' Eleanor replied.

'Don't you start having a go at her.' Maureen stood again and, to Eleanor's surprise, defended her. 'She's a hero. Tried to save his life – even if he didn't deserve it,' she added wistfully. 'And what does she get in return? A face full of glass and snide insinuations from you. She's probably going to be disfigured for life now, thanks to that no good—'

'Miss Bradbury, will you please sit down?' DI Hutchins said firmly. 'I am not making any insinuations, snide or otherwise. I am simply doing my job. We are investigating a potential murder and from early CCTV results, at this point, the number of people who could have committed it is limited.'

Eleanor should have felt relief at the silence that followed.

Maureen was, at last, quiet. But, instead, suspicions filled the room. The fact had now been implied, if not directly said. One of the people present in that room was a murderer. Everybody looked at each other. All with the same thought in their head. Suspicions flowed and most of them were heading towards Eleanor.

Chapter Nine

Darryl spent the next half an hour or so torturing himself with thoughts of what he could do. He watched Larry cautiously, hoping for some sign that he would be open to conversation. But it didn't come. Instead, Larry kept his head down, focused on his work. Though his actions seemed a little more forceful than usual. Darryl had felt a few drops of rain and he knew this could be his last chance to talk to him on his own. Depending on how heavy the rain became, they may need to leave the trench soon. He finally summoned the courage to speak.

He sat back on his haunches and said, 'Larry, please, just listen to me—'

'No.' Larry interrupted. 'Just let nature run its course and have done with it.'

Not ready to give up, Darryl continued. 'I can't just let him die—'

'Let who die?' came a young but stern voice from outside the trench.

Both Darryl and Larry looked up with a jolt to see a police officer arriving at the trench. They had both been so engrossed in their own thoughts, they hadn't seen him walking along the visitor path towards them.

'We're not letting anybody die,' Darryl said with an attempt at light-hearted humour. 'We were – we were talking about his father,' Darryl said hesitantly. He continued, more for Larry's benefit than the officer's. 'He is dying of cancer and I believe there are other issues that need to be addressed before that day arrives.'

'Leave it,' Larry snapped back at him under his breath.

'Your name, please?' the officer asked, frowning with uncertainty.

At first, Darryl was taken aback by the question. The officer was quite young, maybe early twenties, and seemed out of his depth.

'Darryl, Darryl Westwood,' he said, losing his patience over the ridiculousness of the situation. 'Honestly, we're not *seriously* letting him die—'

'It sounded pretty serious.' The officer stared sternly at him.

'When you arrived, I was about to say, I can't just let him die... without trying to help,' Darryl tried to clarify.

'I really think you need to come with me.' The officer's stern stare flickered.

His shallow breathing gave away his agitation and Darryl could see he was not yet ready for this level of responsibility. He finally turned to Larry. 'And your name?'

'Larry Chambers.'

The officer's blunt demeanour changed to curiosity as there seemed to be a sign of recognition of Larry's name.

'Could you both come with me, please? We need to ask you some questions.'

'Because of what I said?' Darryl asked.

'This must be some kind of joke.' Larry laughed derisively.

'It's no joke, sir. But if you could, please follow me.'

'What is all this about?' Darryl asked again, clenching his fists nervously.

'I need you to come with me to make a statement.'

'A statement for what?' Darryl persisted, taking advantage of the fact that the young officer was becoming flustered with his questions.

'Could you both please follow me and all will become clear.'

Darryl and Larry looked at each other. Larry shrugged and climbed out of the trench. Darryl began putting his tools into his bag, but the officer told him to stop.

'I need you to come now, sir. There will be time for that later.'

'We can't just leave all our tools lying around.'

'The site is closed. You have nothing to worry about,' the officer said.

'What are you talking about? The site is closed? And it feels like rain. We can't just leave our tools out in the rain.' He looked towards Larry for support but only received another shrug in return.

Only when he was climbing out of the trench did he see the ambulance and several police cars and vans. All the tension between Darryl and Larry suddenly disappeared.

Chapter Ten

Larry entered the gift shop, his brow furrowed at the scene in front of him. 'What's going on?'

Eleanor couldn't help but feel a wave of relief at seeing a friendly face. Although Darryl hadn't been anywhere near the tea-room at the time of the death, his absence was a disappointment as she had hoped he would arrive with Larry. Initially Darryl's friend after working on previous sites together, over the last few months, she had become accustomed to his quirks and habits. His brightly coloured waistcoats and beloved old red Ferrari, in contrast to Darryl's jeans and t-shirts, and second-hand Land Rover. Always cleanly shaven against Darryl's rough stubble. He was always the gentleman with Eleanor, although, sometimes she considered his attitude a little too bachelor-like for her liking.

'You are Larry Chambers?' asked DI Hutchins, shifting her attention from the young officer that had arrived with Larry before he disappeared again back down the corridor.

'Yes,' he replied, giving the DI a passing glance as he tried to take in the sight of everyone crammed into the small gift shop.

'Are you aware of what's happened, Mr Chambers?'

'No, not really. Other than I saw the ambulance outside and I'm guessing from the fact that you lot are here, it's not good news.'

A semblance of his usual cheeky-self tried to break through, though he still looked pale from earlier.

'Mr Chambers,' the DI drawled. 'A man may have been murdered here this afternoon, and according to CCTV you were here at or around the time of the incident.'

Larry hesitated. Shock written across his face. 'Murdered?' he whispered. 'No. I don't believe it. I – I'm sorry,' he said sincerely. 'Who was it?' When his question was met with silence, he continued. 'I didn't see anything. I certainly didn't see anyone being murdered.'

'Could you please tell me why you were here this afternoon, around two thirty?' the DI asked.

'That must have been around the time I came in for a coffee.'

'Yet you left empty-handed,' the DS said.

Larry turned to him curiously.

'On the CCTV you weren't carrying anything when you left,' the DS clarified.

'I downed it in the kitchen and then left again. Please, who was it?'

'Did you see anything out of the ordinary while you were in the kitchen?' DI Hutchins persisted.

'No.' He stared at the floor in front of him, his brow furrowed with concentration. 'Mo was cooking, Kate was coming and going with tray-fulls of stuff, Eleanor was dishing up jam—'

'Sorry? Eleanor...?' DI Hutchins' interest was piqued.

As her gaze landed on Eleanor, she immediately saw what DI Hutchins was thinking and panic took hold.

'Eleanor,' he nodded towards her, 'she was spooning jam

into those stupid little dishes. You can never get enough jam in those things. They really should be bigger.' He laughed at his liking for jam. 'Although, maybe not,' he continued, running a hand over his slightly rounded stomach with a frown.

'I was helping myself to jam for my scone,' Eleanor quickly clarified. 'For my lunch. I told you earlier that I was having a scone for my lunch and Kate told me to do my own jam and butter. That's what the staff do. When – the man,' Eleanor said, gesturing towards the tea-room, 'came in and ordered a scone, I offered to do his jam and butter too. I was just trying to be nice.'

The DI continued to glare at her questioningly.

'I've done nothing wrong,' Eleanor exclaimed. 'All I've done is try to help and yet I'm feeling like a criminal. And no,' Eleanor continued at the expression on the DI's face, 'it's not because of a guilty conscience.'

DI Hutchins sighed and put her hands in her pockets. Her facial expression now seemed to say, *Are you finished?*

Going for the easy option? Eleanor thought, her temper rising.

'Where did this dishing up of the jam take place?' DI Hutchins said after a moment's silence.

'In the kitchen,' Eleanor whispered, her voice hoarse from tension. She clenched her fists, trying to keep calm.

'In the kitchen,' DI Hutchins repeated. She wandered over to the tea-room and peered through the glass insert in the door again. Turning back to Eleanor and with a wave of her hand, she wordlessly invited Eleanor to join her in Mr Nelson's office again.

Eleanor rose from her make-shift seat. Passing Larry on her exit, she gave his arm a quick squeeze. Guilt and regret were evident on his face. But she understood he wasn't to blame.

Back in the office, DI Hutchins was looking around. 'Now, you're going to have to help me. I've had one quick look in the kitchen so far, but that's not really enough for what we need. So, if we pretend this door is the kitchen door, where were you dishing up the jam?'

'The counter is right next to the door,' Eleanor said. 'Behind us.'

The DI turned to the area behind them and outlined a counter with her hands. 'Here? Like this?'

Eleanor nodded.

'OK. Walk me through what happened,' DI Hutchins said.

Eleanor stared at her blankly. 'I served out some butter and—'

'No, no,' DI Hutchins said, holding back her impatience. 'Pretend you're getting yourself your jam and whatsits now, and show me what you did. What happened, who came and went, and when?'

'I was here,' Eleanor said. 'obviously,' she added with a nervous laugh. 'Kate was going backwards and forwards between the tea-room and the dishwasher, clearing tables.'

'The dishwasher. That's opposite the door, isn't it?' At Eleanor's nod, she moved to the desk. 'So, the desk is now the dishwasher.' She moved back next to Eleanor as if standing at the jam counter. 'Carry on.'

'While I was helping myself to the jam, the … man,' Eleanor said awkwardly, not knowing what else to call him, 'came into the tea-room.'

'How do you know that? Can you see into the tea-room from here? The door's to one side.'

'No, but the door was open. Kate was coming through it at the time. I heard him shout his order. *Everyone* heard him shout his order,' she drawled. 'It was clear from Kate's reaction that he wasn't well liked, so I—'

'What reaction was that?' DI Hutchins interrupted.

'Well, nothing really.'

'Hold on. You said "from her reaction"...' the DI persevered.

'It was just – she – I don't know.' Eleanor tried to remember the small subconscious motion that would have led her to this belief. But then putting it into words was another thing. 'A roll of the eyes maybe, calling back her reply through gritted teeth? I don't know. Nothing specific. But later she said he had already had a go at her before, so—'

'He had already had a go at her?' DI Hutchins was intrigued.

'Yes, but not today. Another time when he was here.'

'So, there was history between them.'

'No, not really,' Eleanor flustered. 'Not in that way—'

'Please continue, Mrs Garrett,' DI Hutchins interrupted again.

'But—'

The DI raised her eyebrows.

'All she meant,' Eleanor said, determined to explain, 'was that because she had already gone through it before, it wouldn't be anything new if he had a go at her again. So, with that in mind, she was happy to take his order out to him. She didn't care what he said to her.' Eleanor gave an enormous sigh; grateful that the DI had given her the chance to explain.

'Are you telling me,' DI Hutchins said thoughtfully, 'Miss Reeves *wanted* to take the order out?'

Eleanor could not answer. Shock had taken her voice. No matter what she said, things were looking worse for Kate.

In the silence, DI Hutchins continued. 'So, while you were dishing up the jam, Miss Reeves was making his coffee? Where would that have been? I seem to remember a kettle next to the dishwasher, here?' DI Hutchins indicated one side of the desk that had now become both dishwasher and coffee area.

'Yes,' Eleanor managed, not thinking properly. 'No,' she suddenly blurted. 'Larry was making coffee there.'

'Larry Chambers? The archaeologist was making the dead man's coffee?'

'No, of course not.' Eleanor laughed nervously. 'Just one for himself, and one for me. He offered to make mine at the same time,' she said as an aside. 'Kate was still busy with Oli at the dishwasher at this point, clearing her tray. But customers have their coffee made from the proper machine outside in the tea-room.'

'When did Mr Chambers enter the kitchen?' the DI asked.

'A few moments before Kate entered with her tray, I think.'

'So, Mr Chambers was already in the kitchen when the victim arrived?'

Eleanor nodded, not wanting to say anymore than was necessary in case the DI twisted her words again.

'And then?'

Eleanor thought carefully about what happened next. Mundane tasks are rarely worth remembering.

'Larry dropped one of the coffees behind us,' she suddenly remembered.

'Why?' DI Hutchins asked.

'Sorry?'

'Why did he drop his coffee?' she clarified.

'I don't know, I didn't see. He was behind me. Just a silly accident, I suppose. He said it slipped.'

DI Hutchins nodded thoughtfully.

'And then Kate dropped her glass next to me, here.' Eleanor pointed at the floor beside her.

'Here, but you said she was over there?'

'She was,' Eleanor flustered, 'but once she'd finished unloading her tray, she came and got a glass of water.'

'A glass of water? Why here?'

'The glasses are kept on the same counter with the jam and butter. There's a drinking water tap next to the counter.'

'That's convenient,' DI Hutchins mused.

Eleanor floundered, wondering whether she meant the tap was convenient for the glasses or the glasses were convenient for Eleanor to break, crush and put pieces in the jam. Worried it was the latter, her mind whirled.

'Just another silly accident?' the DI asked.

'Sorry?'

'Miss Reeves dropping her glass, another silly accident I suppose?'

'She jumped,' Eleanor said. 'We both jumped at the sudden smash from Larry's mug.'

'So, *she* smashed the glass?' the DI mused.

'Yes.' Eleanor's voice squeaked from the guilt that ran through her. 'Like I said, we jumped,' she tried to clarify.

'What happened then?' DI Hutchins said, ignoring her.

Eleanor held back her urge to scream in exasperation. The DI wasn't listening, only to the parts that suited her.

'Larry gave me my mug of coffee and said he was going to make another one for himself,' she gabbled, infuriated.

'And where was Miss Reeves?' The DI looked around the room as though expecting to see the real Kate there.

'She went to help Larry find the dustpan and brush from the cupboard.'

'Which was where?'

'The filing cabinet,' Eleanor said with contempt, nodding towards a filing cabinet that was conveniently placed around the same area as the door to the cupboard would have been.

'So, you were left alone with the jam?'

'Only for a moment. She got the dustpan and brush and was straight back. Had some more water and then left. I went back into the tea-room to get my scone and then sat down at the table behind the—' She waved her hand in the air madly while staring at an imaginary body lying on the floor.

'And where was Miss Reeves at this point?'

Eleanor paused for thought. 'She was already in the tea-room getting his scone when I arrived to get mine,' Eleanor said victoriously.

'So, you weren't there when she returned to the kitchen for his jam.'

Deflated, Eleanor whispered, 'No.'

'Now, let me see if I've got this straight. Firstly, you were left with the jam and broken glass on the floor.'

'Yes, but—'

'And then,' DI Hutchins interrupted, 'Miss Reeves, Mr Chambers, Miss Bradbury—'

'I'm sorry,' Eleanor interrupted. 'I don't know all their surnames.'

DI Hutchins looked at her curiously and began again. 'So, Katherine, Larry, Maureen and Oliver were all in the kitchen after you left?'

'Yes – oh, and Mr Nelson came into the kitchen, too, just as I was about to leave.'

'Mr Nelson,' she stressed the words and the fact that Eleanor seemed to know that surname. 'Quite the little hive of activity. Where would the pieces of broken glass and cup have been put?'

'I don't know,' Eleanor's voice squeaked. 'It's my first day here.'

'Well, that's rather unfortunate.'

Eleanor looked at her quizzically.

'For all this to happen on your first day.'

That morning Eleanor had pulled down a shelf, got into an argument with a visitor, insulted the cook and failed to save a dying man. She felt numb from exhaustion and didn't have the energy to make any reply.

'OK,' the DI went on, 'I may need you to go through some of it again once we have access to the café.'

'Tea-room,' Eleanor replied without thinking.

'Pardon?'

'It's a tea-room, not a café.'

DI Hutchins stared at her, eyebrows raised.

Chapter Eleven

Darryl jittered impatiently from one foot to the other while the young uniformed officer finished writing in his small notebook.

'I believe the Senior Investigating Officer will want to speak to you,' he told Darryl importantly. 'If you could please wait here.' He hardly gave Darryl a second glance before turning on his heel and marching down the museum corridor that led towards the gift shop and tea-room.

Darryl had reiterated that the officer had misinterpreted his comment while writing what he referred to as Darryl's statement. The whole situation was ludicrous, and Darryl still had the heavy feeling of not being believed in his stomach.

Instead, he waited as patiently as he could, trying to distract himself with the items on display at the museum entrance. Excavated items from the site over the years; a display cabinet with Roman shoes, a plinth holding a replica of an ornate ceramic jug, among others. He hadn't been working there long, only six months, and hadn't had the chance to see everything they housed. But he stared vacantly at the exhibits. A moment later the main doors behind him opened and Sahara came rushing in to escape a sudden heavy downpour.

'Hiya, Darryl,' she said cheerfully, shaking the rain from her hair. 'What you doing here?'

'I could ask you the same. Why are you not with the others in the gift shop?'

'They didn't want me. Sent me home.' She shrugged and gave a disapproving look.

'Do you know what's going on?' Darryl asked. 'They won't tell me a thing.'

'All I know is, somebody died in the tea-room this afternoon,' she whispered, though there was nobody else around to hear her.

'Died? Who? How?'

'I've no idea. It's nothing to do with me. I've told them what I saw, which was nothing, and now I'm waiting to go home. But Kate is still in there and she usually gives me a lift.' She turned to look back out the glass doors. 'Look at that rain. I don't want to be walking home in this. I don't suppose you could give me a lift into town, could you?'

'Of course,' Darryl said, still flustered at the news. 'Once I know what's going on with Eleanor. And it would seem they want to talk to me some more, too. Come to think of it, I might be here for quite a while,' he said as panic sank in at the possible thought that his overheard comment could link him to the death. 'Do you know why they're all being kept in there?'

Sahara shook her head. 'Probably 'cause there's nowhere else big enough for all of 'em.'

'No,' Darryl gave a slight smile at Sahara's misunderstanding, 'I mean, why are they still here? Surely it doesn't take this long to take statements and whatever they do.'

Sahara shrugged, still running her fingers through her long hair, gently shaking it in an attempt to dry it. 'I don't really know what's going on. All I keep hearing is Mo going on about her scones. I think she may have poisoned someone. But then again,' she said thoughtfully, 'that probably wouldn't explain why Eleanor left there earlier covered in blood.'

'What?' Darryl exclaimed.

'Yeah, all over her face, it was. I saw Kate taking her off to the loos to get cleaned up.'

Darryl turned and ran down the corridor, heading for the gift shop. He turned a corner and was stopped a couple of metres away from the entrance.

'I'm sorry, sir, you can't come in here,' said an officer in uniform.

'But my partner is in there and I need to know if she's alright,' he gabbled.

'I'm sorry, but nobody can enter right now.' He stepped forward, holding up an arm to block Darryl's way.

'Eleanor,' he called. 'Are you OK?'

'Sir, please—'

'Eleanor!' he yelled over the officer.

'Sir,' the officer shouted him down. 'Please step away. Nobody can enter.'

Darryl took a step backwards. With no reply from Eleanor, he found himself unable to argue, or even speak.

Eleanor had returned to the gift shop and was immediately conscious of the many pairs of eyes that followed her across the room. She was just as much a suspect as any of them. In fact, in their eyes, probably more so as she was the outsider. She perched back down on the edge of the display cabinet next to Larry, relieved to have one friend in the room. On their return, the DI addressed the room and asked for a quick run-down of where each person was just before the man's death.

'In the kitchen, of course,' Mo spoke up first in her usual sarcastic tone. 'Where else would you find the cook?'

DI Hutchins took no notice of Maureen's sarcasm and turned to the person sat next to her, Oli.

'Dishwashin'. Didn't move from me spot.'

'I was here, there and everywhere,' Mr Nelson interjected from the other side of the room. His managerial status somehow keeping him separate from the rest of the staff. 'I go wherever I'm needed, but that's not very helpful for you, I'm sure. I spent most of my time before the incident in the gift shop, I believe. I popped in to the kitchen for a brief moment to speak with Maureen, but then I was out again, quick as a flash. There's always so much to do.'

Eleanor was sure the DI's gaze glazed over half-way through Mr Nelson's monologue as the sound of coins and keys jingled in his pocket while he subconsciously played with them. Once he had finished speaking, she turned to Kate, the next in line after Oli.

'I was back and forth with trays, clearing the tables.'

Red faced and trembling in the corner was the last, Rochelle. Tears and streaks of make-up stained her cheeks. DI Hutchins stared at her, waiting.

'I was having my lunch at the table in the corner,' Rochelle said finally. She pointed determinedly towards the tea-room as though pointing at her specific table. 'I didn't get up. I didn't move. Not till I was told to by...' She nodded towards Mr Nelson. She seemed unable to say anymore.

'Hmm,' came DI Hutchins's reply.

Eleanor carefully listened to everyone's account. It took her by surprise when she realised she was subconsciously checking they matched her own memory. Guilt swept in. These were

Darryl's colleagues. How could she even think of accusing any of them of murder? But, then again, she couldn't deny that it had to be one of them.

After a silent moment of thought, followed by an enormous sigh, DI Hutchins asked Kate to follow her to the office. The room was silent as they left.

'I think we're going to be here for quite a while,' Larry whispered from Eleanor's left.

'Surely not,' Eleanor said. 'Once they've finished this preamble bit, I'm sure we'll all get home soon. Won't be long.'

'I don't know.' He shook his head sadly. 'Let's face it, it's a closed room scenario. One of us here killed this man, and we don't even know who he is. Was,' he corrected.

'An old cantankerous man who had clearly never heard of the word *consideration*,' Eleanor grumbled under her breath.

'An old man?' Larry asked.

'Mo said he was already dying apparently,' she said, distracted by an officer who appeared at the doorway searching for the DI. She glanced at Larry and was reminded of how pale he had looked earlier. He certainly wasn't looking any better now. She smiled and tried to sound encouraging. 'It'll be fine. You'll see.'

He didn't return her smile, instead he quietly asked, 'Could you do me a favour? They might let you speak to Darryl, him being your partner. Could you pass him my keys? Just in case we are here for hours. Someone needs to feed my cat.'

'I didn't know you had a cat,' Eleanor jolted with surprise. She would never have considered Larry an animal lover.

'Didn't Darryl tell you? Yeah, a kitten, really. I've only had her a couple of weeks. Still at that cute stage.'

Eleanor noticed his smile at the thought of his kitten didn't reach his eyes. She longed to ask what was worrying him.

'He's probably getting sick of hearing about her, actually.'

Larry continued with a slight laugh. 'I've been talking about her all morning.' Larry reached in his pocket and passed Eleanor his keys. 'As you say, hopefully we'll all be able to go soon, and I'm sure it won't be necessary, but if need be—'

'Of course,' Eleanor agreed and took his keys from his hand and placed them in her pocket. Pleased to help in any way she could.

Raised voices from the corridor pulled their attention. Darryl's voice came loud and clear, arguing with presumably one of the many officers that seemed to be on guard. He called out her name. Though she was relieved to hear his voice, the look on the officer's face at the doorway made her think twice about replying.

Chapter Twelve

Darryl, angry with himself as much as the officer, decided he wasn't ready to give in yet.

'I just need to know if she's alright,' he implored.

'It's OK.' A woman who looked in her fifties and dressed in a black trouser suit that looked uncomfortably tight around the waist appeared from Mr Nelson's office. Her grey streaked hair fell limply around her face.

She turned to the young officer that had taken Darryl's statement who was by her side and asked, 'Is this him?'

He nodded far too enthusiastically for the situation.

'You can let him through,' she went on, waving her hand dismissively.

Begrudgingly, the officer who had been standing in Darryl's way stood aside. Darryl rushed ahead towards the shop.

'One moment,' the woman called, stopping him just at the entrance. 'Darryl Westwood, is that right?'

'Yes. What's going on here? Is Eleanor hurt?' he asked. His impatience getting the better of him. His glance flicked back and forth between the suited woman and Eleanor. From where he now stood, he could at least see her, and she looked OK, if maybe a little pale.

'I'm DI Hutchins and I'd like to ask you a few questions first.'

Darryl couldn't help but let out a sigh of impatience.

'I understand you were discussing leaving a man to die,' she said abruptly.

Darryl laughed with frustration. 'I thought I had explained that,' he said with a sideways glance towards the young officer. 'We were discussing -' Darryl hesitated and turned towards Larry, who was sitting by Eleanor's side and avoiding his eyes. It wasn't something Larry would want everybody to know about, but the police were involved now. What choice did he have? '— discussing Larry's father, who is dying of cancer.'

Sighs of sympathy filled the room. He saw Eleanor place a hand gently on Larry's arm.

'I wanted to do something for him before he dies. But, I was interrupted by -' he thought better of insulting the young officer before continuing '- by the officer here, before I could finish what I was saying. I didn't want to leave him to die without doing something to help. But what has that got to do with all this? Look, I'm asked to give a statement and then told to wait like a dog, and nobody will tell me what's going on.'

DI Hutchins waved her hand towards the group, perched in various places around the shop, ordering Darryl silently to join them.

Trying telepathy now, are we? he thought angrily as he finally got his wish and raced across the room to be with Eleanor. He had already reached the small toy display unit and was perching next to Eleanor on the other side from Larry when the DI continued.

'There has been a suspected murder here this afternoon, and I would appreciate your full cooperation.'

'Murder? Who? How?' Darryl exclaimed, putting an arm around Eleanor, though he was disappointed to see Larry stand and move away at the same time.

DI Hutchins ignored his questions, turned and came face to face with Kate. She had appeared quietly behind her, and the startled DI was clearly not expecting to see her there. While they spoke quietly together, Darryl whispered to Eleanor.

'What's going on? Sahara said she saw you covered in blood. Are you alright?'

Eleanor's eyes flicked towards the DI. She was clearly uncomfortable with her presence and he waited. A moment later, DI Hutchins and Kate left the shop, presumably returning to Mr Nelson's office. Once she was out of sight, Eleanor went into a tirade. Her voice was barely audible amidst the sound of Mr Nelson fiddling with the keys and coins in his pocket.

'There was a man choking, or so I thought,' she whispered breathlessly. 'I tried to help him, but then I found out he was murdered, so there was no way I could have helped him.'

'Murdered? How can you be sure?' Darryl said, speaking over her.

'There was glass in his jam.'

'In his jam?'

'He had jam with his scone,' she explained. Her hands flexing animatedly in her lap.

'But Sahara said you were covered in blood.'

'It was the jam,' she interrupted impatiently. 'He coughed his scone and jam all over me when I was trying to help him. It wasn't until I was cleaning myself up that I found glass and realised that there was blood, too.' Her voice became higher and more panicked with each sentence. 'Somebody put glass in his jam.'

'Are you sure it was just in *his* jam?'

'Yes, I'm sure. There wasn't any in mine. I spread my jam so thinly I would have noticed, but apparently he likes – liked,' she corrected, 'his jam and would have had it dolloped on his scone really thick. Somebody murdered him and ever since, we've all been sitting here waiting for each to be interrogated. According to the CCTV, we were the only ones who had the opportunity to – do it. It was one of us. And I think she believes it was me because I was the one who served up his jam,' she finished frenetically.

'OK, calm down.' Darryl said gently, trying his best not to sound patronising.

After a moment's breath, her voice returned to the gentle whisper.

'Larry's convinced that they're not going to let us go until they've solved the case. Here,' she said, pulling Larry's keys from her pocket. 'He asked if you can feed his cat.' She dropped the keys into Darryl's hand. 'By the looks of it, you're more likely to be getting out of here than I am.'

He looked curiously across to Larry, who had moved across to the glass-panelled door after he left his seat. He stood staring outside at the rain, gazing into the distance.

'Larry doesn't have a cat,' he said.

'Well, he said he's been going on about her all morning,' Eleanor went on incredulously, her voice rising again. 'And, to top it all off, I saw Sahara stealing.'

'What?' Darryl was certain she couldn't have said what he thought she'd said.

'She stole from the till,' she said frantically. 'Mr Nelson told us this morning that head office had said things were going missing and we needed to keep an eye out. And there she was, stealing. It's no wonder she was so quick to blame the school parties.'

Confused by her last remark, Darryl chose to ignore it. Instead, he took hold of her hands, which were clenching and unclenching in her lap.

'Are you sure? What did you actually see?' he asked gently, but she didn't seem to be listening.

'She's obviously done it before, too. She knew what she was doing.' Eleanor stared towards the counter with the till as she explained, as though watching the events in her mind's eye. Her voice calm as she spoke. 'She was angled in such a way that her back would have been to the CCTV, blocking the view of the till opening and of her taking the money out. Though she gave a very guilty look behind her when she realised I was there. I should tell Mr Nelson.'

'Are we talking great wads or just a note or two?' Darryl asked, trying to keep his voice low.

'It doesn't matter how much. It's wrong.' Eleanor returned to her high pitch exasperated tone.

'Don't worry about it,' Darryl said, trying to calm her again.

'I didn't at the time. We had bigger problems, but I'm now beginning to wonder what you've got me into here.'

'She probably needs it. She's not exactly dressed affluently, is she?' He tried to appeal to Eleanor's sympathetic side. 'I believe she lives in that rough estate, too, poor girl.'

'More like she's stealing for drugs, then,' Eleanor snapped.

'Are you kidding me?' Darryl knew she was stressed, but maybe she had taken a step too far with this accusation. 'Does she look like she takes drugs?'

The jingle of Mr Nelson's coins and keys continued, the noise exacerbating Eleanor's infuriation. She hesitated at Darryl's firm tone.

'No,' she said guiltily. 'Not to me, but I'm no expert,' she added.

'Eleanor, don't be such a snob.' Darryl laughed with that half-hearted laugh that suggested there was nothing funny about this.

An uneasy pause followed. Eleanor glared at him. Unable to believe what he had just said. Had he actually called her a snob?

'Mr Nelson. May I speak with you?' she said defiantly, staring directly at Darryl. Immediately, the sound of Mr Nelson's keys stopped.

Darryl's face dropped. 'You're not—'

Eleanor's expression cut him short as she raised her eyebrows.

'Yes, I am,' she whispered in reply. 'Stealing is wrong, under any circumstances.'

Mr Nelson stood by the opposite wall. His authority was now lacking as the police had taken over and he was no longer of any help to them. He had turned to look at Eleanor expectantly, but she got up forcefully and moved towards him. DI Hutchins returned to the gift shop as she did so.

'Going somewhere, Mrs Garrett?' she asked.

'No,' Eleanor said, suddenly realising that all eyes were now upon her. Nervously, she continued. 'I have something I wish to discuss with Mr Nelson. Just while we're waiting,' she added with a nervous laugh.

'And what's that then?' the DI asked.

'Well, it doesn't have anything to do with this,' Eleanor said awkwardly.

'I'll be the judge of that.'

Eleanor remained silent at DI Hutchins' persistence until she raised her eyebrows in defiance. Under different circumstances, it would have been a comical match to the expression she herself had just given Darryl.

'Well – I – it really doesn't matter,' she floundered.

'Now I really want to hear it.' DI Hutchins folded her arms, her stance indicating that she had no intention of moving until Eleanor had said her piece.

'Mr Nelson,' Eleanor turned and spoke directly to him, trying her best to shut out the fact that everybody was watching her. 'I'm really sorry to say that – that, earlier, after I changed my shirt, and – and, I'm very sorry to have to tell you that – in light of the news you gave us this morning – from Head Office—'

'Get on with it,' drawled DI Hutchins.

Eleanor took a deep breath. 'I saw Sahara taking money out of the till,' she blurted.

'Of course you did. She works the till,' he said with a quizzical smile.

'No, I mean, she then put the money in her pocket.'

'Are you certain?' Mr Nelson said amongst the audible gasps from the other staff, and the groan from Darryl.

Eleanor nodded, not wanting to say any more. She had already said too much.

'Sahara is the girl who works in the gift shop, I take it,' DI Hutchins said.

'Yes,' Mr Nelson stammered. 'I will deal with this most severely if this is true.'

'She left, didn't she?' DI Hutchins asked the DS, standing by the door. 'Wasn't she sent home?'

The DS nodded.

'Not in this rain,' Darryl mumbled.

'I'm sorry, what was that?' DI Hutchins turned back to the room. She had heard Darryl's grumbling but couldn't make out who it had come from.

'I said not in this rain,' Darryl said after a brief pause. 'It's a long walk back to town, and she's waiting for a lift.'

'Is there not a bus?'

'Not right out here. She'd need to walk at least fifteen minutes to the nearest bus stop, and a lift's better anyway, as she's always short...' Darryl's words trailed off.

'As she's always short of cash? Is that what you were going to say?' DI Hutchins asked. 'So where is she now?'

'Sheltering in the museum entrance,' Darryl said begrudgingly.

Wordlessly, the DS communicated he would fetch her, and he disappeared down the corridor.

'Well, this will be interesting,' the DI said.

'Is this really necessary?' Eleanor asked, regretting her outburst at Darryl's childish remark.

'I don't know,' the DI replied. 'But unless we ask, we don't find out. Anything could be relevant in circumstances like these.'

The police officer returned with Sahara. She looked timid and clearly confused as to why she had been summoned.

'Sahara, isn't it?' the DI stepped forward to talk to her.

The girl nodded hesitantly.

Eleanor, now perched on the cabinet by the wall next to Mr Nelson, tried to disappear into her surroundings. She dropped her head and hid her face as she peered surreptitiously at the scene in front of her, and hoped she wouldn't be involved anymore.

'Would you mind emptying your trouser pockets for me, please?' The DI took a step closer to the girl.

'What? Why?' Sahara furrowed her brow and automatically took a step back. 'I've nothing in my pockets. What's this about?'

'Please, indulge me,' DI Hutchins said in a gentle tone.

Sahara slowly put her hands in her pocket and just as slowly pulled out a ten-pound note.

'Where did this money come from?' DI Hutchins asked calmly, taking hold of the note.

'It's mine. I – I brought it with me,' she stammered.

Everyone turned to look at Eleanor, including DI Hutchins.

'I'm sorry, Sahara,' Eleanor said gently. 'But that's not yours. I recognise it from earlier.'

She had seen a glimpse of green ink as Sahara had taken the note out of her pocket. Somebody who had been counting a pile of notes had written the amount on the top note in green ink. Eleanor had noticed it when the child with the castle pencil sharpener had handed it to her to pay. It had brought back memories of when she had watched the same thing being done in a local pub she had worked in during her younger days. An evening job to help her through university.

'It had gone in the till when one of the school children paid for their pencil sharpener earlier,' she went on, 'He had come to me, thinking I would be able to take it.'

'You recognise it?' asked DI Hutchins.

'The writing. Someone's written five hundred pounds on it.'

DI Hutchins checked the note and nodded, mainly to herself, but the implication was clear.

'Did the victim see you take this money?' she asked Sahara.

'What?' Sahara gazed around the room frantically, surrounded by staring eyes.

'Please answer my question. Did he catch you removing the money from the till?'

'I – I –' Sahara burst into tears.

'No, he didn't,' Eleanor said on her behalf. 'It happened after he'd... It was when I was on my way back from changing my shirt that I saw her, so it was definitely after.'

Sahara continued to sob. Mr Nelson, who had been sitting upright and perched on the edge of the cabinet, had been held back by the presence of the police. He finally stood authoritatively.

'Is this true, Sahara?' he boomed.

'I – I –'

'I'll take that as a yes.' His voice full of regret.

'But—'

'You have disappointed me. Leave now and no more will be said.' He stood looking down at her. An intimidating authority figure for the young girl. 'If you don't need her anymore,' he added as an aside to DI Hutchins.

The DI shook her head while Sahara stood quietly, tears running down her cheeks. Unable to speak as her glances flicked between Eleanor and Mr Nelson.

'Sahara, please leave,' Mr Nelson said, quietly but firmly.

Darryl stood suddenly. 'You can't,' he exclaimed. 'Eleanor, tell them.'

'Tell them what? I saw her take the money,' she said quietly, acutely aware of eyes glaring at her.

'But Mr Nelson,' Sahara's voice trembled. 'I – I don't understand. You—' She stopped suddenly, before starting again. 'I'm a good worker, Mr Nelson. Why—'

'When Head Office told me there was a thief, I never would have believed it was you. Please leave,' he repeated with a more forceful tone.

'You know that—'

'Please leave, now,' Mr Nelson snapped.

Sahara stared at him for a moment. Tears streamed down her face, but there was nothing more she could say. She turned and ran from the room.

'Do you wish to press charges, Mr Nelson?' DI Hutchins said, sounding bored.

Eleanor assumed now she had discovered that it couldn't

have had any bearing on the murder, it would only cause extra paperwork.

'No, I'll deal with it.' Mr Nelson sat heavily on the cabinet, causing it to jolt as he landed. Clearly dazed by what had happened.

Weary and frustrated, Eleanor's head drooped forward once more. All she had done since she had arrived that morning was to try to be helpful, prove herself competent, and everything had gone wrong.

'You're quite the vindictive so-and-so, aren't you?'

Mo's voice was harsh, and Eleanor was astounded when she looked up and realised that the remark had been directed at her.

'Vindictive!' she exclaimed. That was the final straw. 'She was stealing. I'm just trying to help—'

'Help? Is that what you call it?' Mo growled with contempt. 'Were you *helping* when trying to save that miserable old git's life, too?'

'OK, I think that's enough,' DI Hutchins stopped Eleanor from replying. 'You are a very duty bound woman, aren't you?'

Eleanor looked at her suspiciously.

'I try to be. Surely that's a good thing.'

'Of course,' DI Hutchins replied gently. 'You speak up when you see someone stealing. You helped try to save the life of a man that's choking, you help dish out the man's jam. Did you help clean up the broken glass too?' she asked.

'What are you insinuating?' Darryl asked angrily as audible gasps came from around the room.

Eleanor felt everyone's eyes on her once again.

'It was just a question. I'm not insinuating anything,' the DI said.

'Well, maybe you should.' Mo stood. Her face was full of anger. 'Let's face it, she had the means and opportunity. I've seen enough of these TV programmes to know how this works.'

'But no motive, Mrs Bradbury.'

'Maybe she was just trying to be helpful, as she seems so keen on doing. Did you bump the old guy off because we were all moaning about him? With his constant complaining and belligerent attitude.' Maureen turned back to the DI. 'There you go. There's your motive. A true modern-day vigilante.'

Chapter Thirteen

Darryl watched Eleanor sheepishly make her way back to the empty space next to him and sit. With everybody turning on her, he had to admit, it wasn't looking good for her, but at least there couldn't have been any motive for her to have killed this man. Though DI Hutchins hadn't contradicted Mo's theory when she had broken up the argument that had followed, surely she couldn't possibly have believed it. He took hold of Eleanor's hand and squeezed gently; he shouldn't have called her a snob.

A plain-clothes officer walked determinedly into the gift shop, breaking the ominous stillness of the room. He spoke quietly to the DI.

'Chambers... Chambers... I've heard that name before,' the DI said quietly. Only just in earshot.

Old man... always coughing... Darryl heard the words in his head. And now the name, Chambers. He looked around wildly, stopping at Larry, who was still staring out the window at the rain. Everything connected rapidly, and just as they did so, Larry turned back to the room. His face was no longer angry, but full of sadness.

'Mr *Larry* Chambers,' DI Hutchins said, turning towards Larry.

'He's my father,' Larry said.

His voice was so pragmatic he was clearly resigned to the situation. It made Darryl wonder how long he had known, or at least suspected. The room went silent. Even Mo.

'From what everyone has said, I had hoped it wasn't him, but I can't deny it to myself anymore, can I?' Larry went on.

'Mate, I'm so sorry,' Darryl moved to console him, but Larry raised a hand to stop him.

After their conversation that morning, Darryl knew his head would be in turmoil. Accepting the death of his father from cancer was one thing. But to come to terms with murder was quite another.

'Why would anybody want to murder your father?' Eleanor asked in a gentle whisper.

'That's a good question, Mrs Garrett.' DI Hutchins had walked over and was now standing directly in front of Larry. 'I'm sorry for your loss, Mr Chambers. I hope you understand that I do need to ask you some questions.'

Larry quietly stared back, his nostrils flaring.

'Could you follow me, please,' the DI turned and walked away expecting him to follow, but he stood fixed to his spot.

Maybe it was the silence that made her turn back, but something made her realise he wasn't following.

'I'd rather stay here,' he stammered.

'OK.'

She wasn't happy about it, but whether that was for his sake or hers, Darryl couldn't tell.

'You came to the tea-room to meet him?' she asked.

'No. I came to speak with him. There's a difference.' Larry dropped his head and stared at the floor. 'But when I got here, I couldn't go through with it and I left again.'

'From what everybody has said here, you must have realised it was your father,' she said. 'Why didn't you say anything?' Silence followed her question, and so she continued. 'Why did you say you came to get coffee?'

'Like I said, I hoped it wasn't him.'

'That doesn't explain why you lied to us.'

Again, there was silence.

'Once more, Mr Chambers, why didn't you say anything?' the DI persevered, gently but firmly. After more silence she continued, 'Are you sure you wouldn't like to come—'

'No,' he answered more firmly than was necessary. 'I don't know why I didn't say anything. I guess I didn't want to get in to the whole thing about me and my dad not speaking for years if I didn't have to.'

'Estranged, were you?' she asked.

'Being a thief will do that.'

'My sergeant has told me he was in prison for theft. Only released a few months ago.'

Larry nodded. 'To be perfectly blunt, I didn't want anything to do with him. Not then, and not now.'

'Is that why he was here, to see you?' she asked.

Larry nodded, his movements heavy.

'He was a regular, wasn't he? Came several times over the last few months, so I understand. Did you speak during any of his visits?'

'No.' Larry shifted uncomfortably from one foot to another.

'I can vouch for that,' Darryl said tentatively. 'Every time his dad came in, Larry would always ignore him. Believe me, he really didn't want anything to do with him.' He gave an apologetic laugh, not wanting to interrupt, but the guilt at the thought that he was the one who had convinced Larry to see his father overruled his good sense. So he continued. 'He only came down to the tea-room today because I persuaded him. It was me that thought he should try for a reconciliation.'

'But the reconciliation didn't happen,' she said. 'Only his murder.'

'What are you saying?' Darryl asked. 'Are you suggesting Larry would kill his own father, especially when he was already dying? If it wasn't for me, he wouldn't have been anywhere near the place.' Darryl wished he had respected Larry's wishes and let him seethe in silence.

'Darryl, please,' Larry pleaded.

'If you really didn't like him that much, I'm afraid it doesn't look good,' DI Hutchins said.

Darryl felt the blood drain from his face as he realised what he had done. The opposite of what he had hoped.

A pause followed. So quiet everybody in the room could have been holding their breath. Larry returned to staring at the floor while the plain-clothes officer stepped forward and showed DI Hutchins a tablet. He pointed to one specific part of the screen.

'It says on your father's records,' she said, focusing back on Larry, 'that one of the items he stole was never found. Would you know anything about that?'

'No,' Larry said defiantly. 'Like I said, I was ashamed of him and wanted nothing to do with him.'

'And yet here he was, pestering you at work.' DI Hutchins folded her arms and tapped her index finger on her biceps thoughtfully. 'Now, let me think. *You* cleared up the broken glass along with your coffee cup, I believe. The dish of jam was just sitting there. Could have been tempting.'

'When he was already dying?' Larry blurted angrily. 'Why would I bother putting myself at risk when his cancer was going to do the job for me?'

'Look at it from my perspective. It all just seems a bit too convenient, don't you think?'

With a derisive laugh, Larry leaned back against the door frame. 'Come on then,' he said. 'Bring on all your questions. I've heard them all before.'

Darryl winced at his sarcasm. That would not be the way to win the police over to his side, as was proved by DI Hutchins as she raised an eyebrow. Eleanor's hand squeezed his as emotions in the room grew stronger.

'Yes, he was a thief,' Larry said, getting angrier by the second. 'Yes, there was an artefact that was never found. And no,' Larry said, pushing himself forcefully away from the door frame. His momentum causing him to take a seemingly aggressive step forward. 'I don't know where it is. But, according to you guys, because I'm his son, I must have known what he was up to. Well, I didn't and just in case you missed it, let me clarify again for you – where did he hide the missing artefact? I. Don't. Know. I didn't know then and I don't know now.'

Darryl found his own muscles tensing at Larry's reaction. Their own argument from this morning was nothing compared to now.

DI Hutchins stood, staring. Silent for what seemed like an age. Darryl couldn't decide whether she was trying to process everything that he had said, or if it was an attempt to prove to Larry, he couldn't intimidate her.

Finally, she spoke. 'And this is the reason you were estranged?' Her firm tone was quiet but made it plain she was the one in charge.

'You soon learn that having a thief for a father isn't really an endearing quality.'

'I think it may be beneficial to have a chat down the station,' she continued in her calm but firm manner.

Larry put his head in his hands. 'I was hounded by you guys

before. Please, think about it,' he implored. 'Why would he hide something like that with his son? I'm going to be the first place you look. And you did, back when he was first arrested. And I was cleared.' He spat his words with disdain.

'Still, I'd like you to come to the station with me, Mr Chambers. We need to talk about this further, and I'm sure we can get everything cleared up in no time. This really isn't the place for this sort of conversation.'

Larry let out a heavy, tired sigh and trudged towards the door.

'What?' Darryl exclaimed as Larry left the room with one of the officers, while DI Hutchins stood talking with her sergeant. He looked fiercely at everyone sitting around the room, doing nothing to help. 'This is wrong,' he yelled in frustration.

'Of course it's wrong,' said Mr Nelson quietly. 'We know that, but what can we do if the police want to talk to him?'

'He's the only one who had any kind of motive,' Mo said. 'I know he's your friend, Darryl, and I'll be really sorry not to see that cheeky face around here anymore, but sometimes you have to face facts.'

'It wasn't him,' Darryl said defiantly.

'Oh really? So, who was it?' Mo continued. 'Eleanor? She's the only other person under suspicion. It's between the two of them.'

Eleanor stood and stared at Maureen. Darryl took hold of her arm, but she shook him off. The room was closing in around her.

'Sorry, but I don't know you,' Maureen went on pragmatically, 'and I don't know what you're capable of.'

'Murder? You think I'm capable of murder?'

'I'm saying, I don't know. Are you?' Maureen's pragmatic tone was as if she had been asking if she wanted a coffee.

Eleanor could only stare at her. Her voice lost in outrage.

Maureen shrugged her shoulders. 'I guess someone here is, and as I spend quite a lot of my waking hours working with everyone else, I think I'd prefer it if it was you.'

'I think that's enough,' Mr Nelson announced loudly. 'Let's leave the arguing and finger pointing to the police. For now, let's all go home and take things easy for the rest of the day. The site's closed, anyway.'

DI Hutchins had finished her conversation with the DS and Eleanor couldn't help but notice her standing quietly with her hands in her pockets and a slight tilt of her head. Infuriated by the woman's amusement of their arguments. From her apparent age, Eleanor guessed she must have been close to retirement, and she looked like she didn't care anymore. Happy to take the easy way out. Happy to watch the chaos left behind by her questions.

For the first time in a long time, Rochelle's quiet, frightened voice spoke. 'Maybe we'll wake up in the morning and find that it's all just been a bad dream.' Still shaking, she sat hunched as though in the arctic circle rather than the warm gift shop.

Eleanor looked around her at the resigned attitudes of Larry's so-called friends. Part of Eleanor had at first been relieved when the DI's attention had moved elsewhere. She'd had visions of being taken off to prison, there and then. But then, Larry didn't do it, either, and the thought of him spending a lifetime in prison for something he didn't do made her blood boil.

'Let's not,' Eleanor suddenly blurted to the room. 'Let's not all go home and pretend our friend hasn't just been taken off to prison.' She turned to the DI, who was about to speak, but Eleanor had heard enough. 'You've got the wrong man,' she implored. 'It could have been anyone here; Mr Nelson, Mo, Oli or Kate. '

'Only my friends get to call me Mo, and you're not one of them,' Maureen shouted over her, but Eleanor went on.

'All of them were in the kitchen with the jam at some point.' Eleanor ignored the angry looks and continued. After all, Maureen had just accused her. 'Everybody here has a story. They all have a past. You've found out Larry's, so you're going to stop there?'

'Like what?' DI Hutchins asked, but Eleanor didn't hear and continued.

'Everybody heard the glass smash. That was certainly no secret. By the sounds of it, he antagonised everybody in the place—'

'You mean like *you're* doing right now?' interrupted Maureen again.

'You've heard about how he had already had a go at Kate several times,' Eleanor went on, ignoring Maureen's snide remark and Darryl's shifting around on his perch. 'And heaven forbid if anybody should insult Maureen's scones.' She purposefully stressed her full name.

Everyone gasped at her audacity.

'Don't you start on my scones,' Maureen said angrily.

'Why?' Eleanor demanded. 'You go screaming and shouting at everyone as though nobody else's opinion matters but yours. I'm sorry to tell you, but other people's opinions do count and not everybody cares about scones as if they are a life or death matter.'

'So, not happy with getting Sahara sacked, you're determined to get one of us put away, too.'

'I just want the right person to be put away, not the first one that seems convenient.'

'Like what?' DI Hutchins shouted over the arguing couple.

Eleanor turned to her, startled.

'Pardon?' Eleanor was taken aback.

'Like what? You said everybody has their story. So tell me. And,' the DI continued nonchalantly, 'to make it clear, Mr Chambers has not been arrested. He is assisting with our enquiries. We are far from *putting anyone away*.' She stressed the repetition of Eleanor's words.

Eleanor's anger seemed to fizzle out inside her. Instead, she was left floundering.

'Would you prefer...?' DI Hutchins made the sweeping motion with her hand, inviting Eleanor to return to the privacy of Mr Nelson's office.

She was about to agree when Maureen's voice mumbled from the side of the room.

'Yeah, you'd like that. Go on, disappear. As if we're not going to know that anything that's said will not have come from you.'

Eleanor put out her hand to stop Darryl from making a comeback.

'I'd rather stay here, if I may,' she told the DI.

Maureen had proved herself to be one of those people who like to complain, whatever the situation. She hadn't stuck up for Eleanor earlier. It was simply something else she could argue about. DI Hutchins smiled at her knowingly, but unhappy with the suggestion.

'I think it would be better, Mrs Garrett, if we—'

'It's OK,' Maureen said. 'You have my permission to go and hide.'

Even though Eleanor knew she was being manipulated by Maureen, she couldn't stop herself from refusing the DI's offer. After all, she mused, I'm not doing anything wrong and others may join me once they realise that.

'I think it would be better,' Eleanor imitated, 'if we stay here. After all, it's in everyone's best interest to find the actual murderer, and surely, if anyone is arguing against that, we need to ask ourselves why?'

The room was silent other than a *harrumph* from Maureen. DI Hutchins hesitantly agreed. With everybody staring at her, Eleanor began to doubt herself. If she was going to make anybody understand her motives, she needed to choose carefully. Of course, there was no point discussing Darryl, as he wasn't anywhere near the tea-room at the time. From what she had seen, Kate seemed the most reasonable and hoped she would understand.

'Well, I don't believe Kate is all she makes out to be.' She blurted out the sentence before she could change her mind. The silence surrounding her pushed her on. 'For instance, she knows more about archaeology than she's letting on. That saying about not finding things,' Eleanor said, addressing Kate, 'you don't pick up a saying like that from a chance hearing.'

'What has that got to do with anything?' Kate argued back, 'and what business is it of yours?'

All hope of Kate being reasonable slipped away.

'It's nothing personal. I'm just trying to prove the point that you all have things in your lives that could have an implication on this case. They just haven't found it yet,' Eleanor said.

Eleanor saw Darryl put his head in his hands. Her doubt turned to embarrassment.

'Carry on,' said the DI.

Eleanor hesitated with a sense of digging herself deeper into the hole she was standing in.

'Then there's Oli, who has done nothing but scowl at me from the first moment we met. There's clearly some anger issues there, but to be honest, I don't think I want to know what they are, but it may be well worth your while finding out,' Eleanor added directly to DI Hutchins.

'Come on then, while you're at it.' Mr Nelson folded his

arms defensively. 'I'd love to hear what you have to say about me.'

'I have to admit,' Eleanor said tentatively as Darryl left his seat and moved towards the glazed doors. She was certain he was purposefully avoiding her eyes. 'I was wondering, what exactly did you need to talk to Maureen about after lunch? Did you need to be in the kitchen at that time? It looked very busy to me, and so for you to just go in and ask questions—'

'I am a very busy man, I'll have you know,' he interrupted her. 'There is more to this job than just watching everybody else go about their business.'

'I'm sure there is, but I was wondering, couldn't it have waited?'

DI Hutchins put up a hand to stop Mr Nelson from retaliating. Much to his disgust. Eleanor was glad she did. She didn't really want another argument, and she wouldn't be voicing these opinions if it weren't for DI Hutchins's insistence.

Once they had both calmed a little, the DI said, 'You missed Rochelle.'

A small squeak came from Rochelle; her eyes were still red and swollen from crying.

'I'd say Rochelle is the only one who couldn't possibly have done it. She sat in that corner the whole time, and I'd be surprised if that hasn't been confirmed by the CCTV. And yet...'

'And yet what, Mrs Garrett?' DI Hutchins asked.

As a last desperate attempt to prove to her colleagues that she wasn't just being argumentative for the sake of it, Eleanor turned her focus on the DI's own methods.

'And yet, you insist on making this poor girl sit here shoulder to shoulder with a murderer somewhere in this room.'

DI Hutchins raised an eyebrow. 'And you got all that on

your first day here. I have to admit I'm impressed. Except for one thing. How about you?'

A loud '*ha*' came from Maureen's direction.

'You've given plausible accounts for everybody except you,' DI Hutchins went on. 'That's interesting in itself.'

'What possible motive could I have? I've never seen him before today.'

'Did you know, Mrs Garrett, that the guilty party is often very keen on casting blame elsewhere? Anything to take the focus off themselves.'

Chapter Fourteen

Darryl knew Eleanor had a propensity to throw accusations around, but she had only ever done it in private before. Her intentions were good and her loyalty to Larry was admirable, but to do so by antagonising all his work colleagues was exasperating. Nervous energy had pulled him to his feet, and he left the uncomfortable edge of the display unit where he had been perched. Wanting to remove himself as far as possible from the scene, he only made it to the glazed door and gazed out the window, just as Larry had done a short while ago. A longing to be outside and walking away had risen in him. A longing he was sure had resonated in Larry. But trapped by a feeling of inevitable condemnation.

As Eleanor kept on, Darryl wanted to pull her away; somehow keep her quiet. It hadn't taken long for him to realise the significance of Larry's keys. Larry didn't have a cat. In fact, he believed Larry was allergic to cats, so he would not be taking in any furry felines. As for discussing a cat that morning? Definitely not. But they had been talking about the stolen artefact hidden in his house. It was clear to Darryl that Larry had known he would be suspected as soon as the police discovered his connection with the victim. He had been lucky enough that the box wasn't found all those years ago. Could he chance it again? And if they found it now, after denying its whereabouts for all these years, Larry would have no defence. They wouldn't be interested in hearing the truth. The police would consider Larry a thief, along with his father. On Larry's removal from the gift shop. Darryl had resolved to head directly to Larry's house and find it. If only Eleanor would stop so they could get out.

When he turned back to the room, Eleanor was floundering a couple of feet away in front of him. The DI's remark had clearly insinuated Eleanor's guilt, carefully avoiding directly accusing her. He knew she hadn't committed murder, but she wasn't doing herself any favours. He reached forward and slipped his hand into hers, and gently pulled. When she looked at him, her face reminded him of a startled rabbit; wide eyes in a pale face.

'You'll all be able to leave soon,' DI Hutchins announced to the room. 'I'm just waiting for a couple more things—'

'Like what?' interjected Mr Nelson with an irate undertone. 'Surely you can't be watching the CCTV again.'

'We're just being thorough. You have nothing to worry about unless you've something to hide. It won't be long now but I'm sure it goes without saying,' the DI turned and spoke directly to Eleanor, 'we *all* want to find the truth of what happened here.'

'Everything's going to be alright,' Darryl whispered, hoping to calm Eleanor. 'You have nothing to worry about.'

'I know *I* don't. It's Larry I'm concerned about,' she implored.

'He's been through all this before. They cleared him then, and I'm sure they'll see sense at some point very soon and they will clear him again.' He tried to keep his tone reassuring, even if he wasn't sure he believed it himself.

'But that just makes it worse,' Eleanor said, much louder than Darryl would have liked. 'If he's been through it once, why should he have to go through it again?'

'I know, I know,' he tried to reassure her. Unfortunately, he also knew that Larry was lying.

Everyone suddenly looked towards the doorway at the sound of fast, determined footsteps coming down the corridor. DS Johnson hurried in and spoke quietly to DI Hutchins. Her demeanour didn't change while she took in the information, other than the now familiar raise of her eyebrows, and she gently nodded.

'Well, that's very interesting,' she said finally.

The room was silent. Eleanor assumed everybody else was hoping DI Hutchins would reveal what was so interesting, too. Taking a couple of steps closer to Eleanor, the DI continued.

'It seems there may be a motive for you after all, Mrs Garrett.'

'What do you mean?' she asked nervously, squeezing Darryl's hand.

'My DS here has been looking at more CCTV footage, in particular, the events of this morning leading up to the incident.'

A cold chill ran down Eleanor's back.

'You told me you had never met the man before, and yet, when my DS looked further back, there you are having quite a heated discussion with the gentleman.'

'Well, yes,' Eleanor stammered. 'I meant I had never met him before today. I don't *know* him.'

'Would you be so kind as to explain?'

Eleanor tried to ignore the frown of curiosity on Darryl's face, but it was no good. With everything else that had happened that day, she had forgotten to tell him about the argument.

'He – he was shouting at a child,' she said, as if this information would explain everything. Her glances snapped quickly between Darryl and DI Hutchins.

'Your child?' DI Hutchins asked.

'No, he was part of a school party.'

'So you attacked an elderly man who was shouting at a stranger's child,' DI Hutchins summarised.

'I didn't attack him,' Eleanor said, outraged at the implication and trying her best to ignore the loud *ha* that came from Maureen.

'According to the CCTV, it looks like you had to hold yourself back. "Almost struck him" were the words my DS used.'

Breathlessly, Eleanor took a moment to take in what the DI had said. 'I had no intention of hitting him. That's crazy. I spoke up for the boy. Nothing more than that.'

The room was silent. Once again, everyone's eyes were on Eleanor. She looked around her wildly. The intimidation of silence doing more than shouting ever could.

'He was excited, and running around the shop, like several of the school party that had come in,' she explained to the room, her voice cracking at the high pitch. 'Unfortunately for him, he ran into the path of this bad-tempered old man who immediately started shouting at him. And, he grabbed him,' Eleanor pointed at the DI as though proving her point was valid. 'That's not acceptable to go grabbing a child.'

'Quite the good Samaritan, aren't you?' Maureen mumbled.

'I try to be,' Eleanor retaliated at the sarcasm. 'Don't most people try to be helpful if they can?'

'Not in my experience, no. And I'm curious, you got Sahara sacked on your first day here,' Maureen went on. 'That was being helpful, was it? Like I said before, vindictive.'

'I may not have put it quite like that,' DI Hutchins said, now raising a hand, attempting to quieten Maureen. An attempt that failed.

'I think you can safely assume,' Maureen said, turning her focus to the DI while ignoring the raised hand, 'that you've found your motive.'

Eleanor stood with her mouth open. Her mind numb.

'Maybe it's time to take this conversation to the station,' DI Hutchins intervened.

'What?' Both Eleanor and Darryl exclaimed together.

'That's crazy,' Darryl said. 'She tried to help the man, not kill him.'

'I'm not arresting her,' she said to calm him. 'I'm just inviting her down to the station to help with our enquiries.'

'Why?' Eleanor asked. 'I didn't do anything. Nobody else here even tried to help him. I tried to save his life and yet it's me you're arresting?'

'I'm *not* arresting you, Mrs Garrett, I'm—'

'I know why you're doing this,' Eleanor spoke over her. 'It's just to prove a point, isn't it? Just because I said you were giving up at the first hurdle. Blaming the first person who came along who just happened to have had an unfortunate past. It's astonishing to think it would be because you believe what this woman is telling you.' Eleanor shot an angry glance towards Maureen. 'Well, I won't come. I'm not going.' She turned the handle on the door behind her, leading outside. 'I want to go home.' The door had been locked earlier and so she strode across the shop floor towards the exit.

'And now I *am* arresting you. Johnson, would you do the honours?'

DS Johnson stepped forward and took out his handcuffs. 'You do not have to say anything—'

'You can't do this,' Eleanor implored.

'But it may harm your defence—'

'No, you can't do this,' she continued to scream, panic screeching through her voice.

'Actually, I can,' DI Hutchins said.

Chapter Fifteen

The same look of shock on Eleanor's face was probably mirrored in Darryl's own expression as he watched in silence. He didn't want to leave her to the clutches of the police and hesitating, he balled his fists hopelessly while he watched her being handcuffed and led away from the gift shop. He held back the profanities he wanted to scream at them. He wanted to fight, fight for her freedom. But he knew that whatever he said or did now wouldn't make the DI change her mind and bring Eleanor back, and would ultimately only make things worse. Now he needed to make a decision. His initial instinct was to follow Eleanor to the station. He had to be there for her as soon as they came to their senses and released her. But there was still the box to find. Time was short, and he only had a vague idea of where it was hidden. If the police truly still suspected Larry, then searching his home would be high on their priority list. Once they had been given permission to leave the shop, Darryl headed straight for his car. Though in his mind it felt like treachery, he knew what he needed to do.

He struggled with his conscience, not liking where this was taking him. He'd become an accessory.

Eleanor's humiliation only grew as she walked into the police station, acutely aware of the cold steel of her handcuffs against her skin. They directed her to stand in front of a desk. Her clothes and hair clinging to her, wet from the rain.

'Hello,' the woman behind the desk said to her in a tired but friendly voice. Her fair hair pulled back tight in a bun for maximum practicality.

Does she really think she's going to be my friend? Eleanor ignored her, enraged at the woman's attitude.

'Your name, Garrett,' she said, looking at a computer screen. 'Is that spelt golf, alpha, Romeo, Romeo, echo, tango, tango?'

Eleanor chewed her bottom lip. Why should she be helpful to these people who won't even take the time to do a full investigation? After a moment's pause, she nodded brusquely.

The woman turned her attention back to the constable who had brought Eleanor in.

'Time of arrest?' she asked.

Eleanor's shoulders stiffened further at the word *arrest*.

'Eighteen fifty.'

'What's the offence?'

Trying to save a life is considered an offence now, is it? But Eleanor held her tongue.

'Suspicion of murder,' the constable said.

'I'm supposed to have committed murder.' Eleanor blurted over the officer's answer, unable to hold herself back any longer. 'I didn't murder anyone,' she said through gritted teeth. 'I tried to save him.'

Their eyes flicked in her direction, but nothing more. Eleanor's insides burned with fury.

'Circumstances, please,' the woman continued.

'I didn't kill anyone,' Eleanor pleaded. 'This is all a big mistake.'

The woman behind the desk stopped and looked kindly towards Eleanor. 'I am the custody sergeant here, and I will decide whether this detention is authorised. But I need to hear the circumstances first.'

Eleanor opened her mouth to speak. She was more than happy to explain the circumstances if it meant she could go home, but the sergeant cut her off.

'From the constable here, I'm afraid.'

Eleanor closed her mouth again like a gaping cod, disbelief enveloping her. Any explanation coming from the police would be biased to their own wants and needs. Not the truth.

'Evidence has come to light—' the constable began, but Eleanor interjected.

'What evidence? I haven't been shown any evidence.'

The custody sergeant stared at Eleanor with a furrowed brow, but Eleanor continued.

'They haven't shown me any evidence,' she implored, using every inch of effort to reply in a more calm tone. 'They said I went to hit the man, and really, do I look like someone who goes around hitting old men?'

The sergeant looked back at the constable and jerked her head towards the back of the room. They both moved towards a room a couple of metres behind the desk, leaving Eleanor to seethe. A constable standing over her shoulder like a guard.

'There is no evidence because it didn't happen,' Eleanor shouted as the door closed between them, her anger finally getting the better of her.

'Go on, girl. You tell 'em.'

Eleanor jumped at the sound of a drunken man's voice from behind. He was also wearing handcuffs and had just entered, staggering forwards to lean on the counter to stop himself from falling. He sidled up to Eleanor.

'Got a fag?'

Eleanor turned her head away at the stench of alcohol and nicotine that came from his breath and his clothes.

'Come on now, Scampi. Leave the lady alone. You know you can't smoke in here, anyway.' An officer put his hand on Scampi's shoulder and gently directed him to the side of the entrance hall.

'Why not?' Scampi persisted.

The officer remained quiet and led him towards some hard-looking plastic chairs sat in a row by the wall.

Scampi looked back at Eleanor, stumbling as he turned. The officer caught him as he fell and assisted him into one of the seats. Though three or four metres away, Eleanor could still smell his distinct scent.

'Cheers,' the old man said. 'Have *you* got a fag?' he asked the officer.

Eleanor turned away. Looking down, she choked on the thought that she and Scampi were considered one and the same in the eyes of the law. Associated simply by the steel around their wrists. Pulling her eyes away from the handcuffs, she shifted her focus back for any sign of the constable and custody sergeant returning. Now they had someone with a fresh eye looking at it, they must surely come to the realisation that this was a mistake. Nothing short of a farce.

Hardly able to breathe, she waited for those few long minutes that felt like hours until she would be able to have these ridiculous handcuffs taken off and be sent home.

The door opened, and they both walked back silently to the desk. The custody sergeant sat back down at her computer and continued typing. Her nails clicking on the computer keyboard.

Eleanor held her breath. Waiting for that moment she would be told she could go home.

Finally, the custody sergeant stopped typing and said, 'Do you understand why you've been arrested?'

Eleanor stared back, gaping once again. 'I haven't been arrested,' she whispered in reply. Shock stealing her voice.

'Mrs Garrett, you have been arrested on suspicion of murder—'

'I didn't murder anyone—'

'I understand you refused,' the custody sergeant spoke over her protestations, 'to attend for an interview after evidence was found—'

'There is no evidence,' Eleanor's voice became louder as her fury burned.

'That's right love, you tell 'em,' Scampi shouted from his chair where he sat slouched, looking as though he was about to slide off at any moment.

'This is all one big mistake,' Eleanor continued, trying her best to ignore him.

'They never believe me neither, love,' Scampi continued. 'It's all a mistake, I tell 'em.' His loud, raucous laughter filled the room.

'I'm going to organise your detention,' the custody sergeant said to her firmly but calmly, over the top of Scampi's interjections, 'so that you can be interviewed regarding this information. You will then have the opportunity to give an explanation. Do you understand?'

Eleanor stood silent for a moment, open-mouthed. The sergeant moved on.

'Now, any jewellery?'

Eleanor's hand moved instinctively to the necklace hidden beneath her shirt that Darryl had given her just a couple of months earlier. Her wedding ring safely looped onto it. Reluctantly, she stood motionless while an officer removed the necklace then dropped it into a clear plastic bag as though it was nothing more than a cheap plastic ring won at a fairground. It's significance stripped away.

'Could you please stand against the ruler so I can see how tall you are? Mrs Garrett?'

Voices faded around her, even Scampi's continuous cackle as he drunkenly amused himself at her expense.

'Mrs Garrett!' Eleanor suddenly realised the sergeant was calling her. As though in a dream, her eyes drifted till she made contact with the sergeant's, and her voice came further into focus.

'There's a ruler on the wall behind you. Could you please stand against it? I need your height.'

Eleanor, moving in slow motion, looked at the wall behind her. Her feet felt heavy as she moved towards it. A tear rolled down her cheek; patronised and treated like a child.

'Thank you,' the custody sergeant called across to her. 'I need to do a quick risk assessment. Any history of self-harming?'

What kind of question is that? she thought, but she didn't have the energy to argue. She simply answered, 'No.'

Keyboard clicks and then the next question.

'How do you feel now?'

Eleanor stared at her. *Numb. Frustrated. Angry.* 'Fine,' she said.

Chapter Sixteen

Darryl reached Larry's house within half an hour. He sat in his Land Rover on the driveway and looked up at the tall, handsome Victorian terraced building. Original features in abundance that any archaeologist would have been proud of. He hesitated. Not only should he be at the station with Eleanor, but also the thought of hiding stolen property sat uncomfortably with him. But so did abandoning a friend when they needed his help, especially when there was something he could do about it. Something more constructive than sitting in the corner of some room, being ignored while waiting for the police to come to their senses. Right now, his time was better spent trying to stop his friend from being targeted any further.

The decision made, he climbed out of the car and strode up the driveway. He jogged up the four steps that led to the porch and the front door, determined to see this through.

Larry's house was immaculate. A narrow mahogany table with long, spindly legs stood to the right of the wide hallway displaying an oak bowl for keys and a large marble fragment of a Roman relief. As he placed Larry's keys in the bowl, he could hear Eleanor's voice in his head.

'This isn't the sort of place I would have considered Larry's bachelor pad to be at all,' she had told him on their first visit. 'It's so clean and tidy.'

To Darryl now, it was also quiet. Too quiet. Without Larry there, the house was eerily amiss. He set his mind on one job and one job only and got straight to work. Trotting up the stairs to the attic, he entered a room that looked more like a home-cinema than a bedroom. A blackout blind on the window kept the room dark, and he switched on the light. Coloured LED lights circled the room. This is more the bachelor pad Eleanor would have imagined, he smiled to himself.

The floorboards were old and worn, with three rugs positioned around the room. One on either side of the bed, and a larger one in front of the largest TV screen he had ever seen. It had to be at least 100 inches. He started by walking the length of the room, listening and feeling for any telltale creak, or the slightest of movements. Many floorboards creaked, and at first, his heart raced with each one, believing he had found the spot. But after closer inspection, none gave the slightest sign they could or had been removed without needing some considerable force. As time went on, beads of sweat appeared on his forehead, intensifying his growing exasperation. He took off his jacket and threw it on the bed. He didn't want to hurry the job and risk missing that small sign that may reveal the concealed hiding place, but at the same time, he needed to get back to Eleanor for when she is released. *Because she will be released,* he kept telling himself.

The thick rugs hid any sign of movement or sign of disturbance and needed to be moved. First, he pulled the large one in front of the TV out of the way and continued his search on his hands and knees. Once he was satisfied with his search, he haphazardly replaced the rug in his haste and moved on to the one beside the bed, furthest from the window. Under the second rug, he found it. Definite movement. The piece of oak floorboard was around twelve inches long and definitely loose. He looked around for something he could use to prise the board. With nothing in sight, he pulled his car keys out of his pocket to use, and tried not to damage the floorboard any further. The sight of the small, narrow wooden box fitting perfectly between the floorboards took his breath away. He reached in and found he needed to tilt the box on its side to remove it from its dark hiding place. The box was beautiful in itself. A deep red mahogany with gold-coloured clasps. A small keyhole was in the centre of one side. He remembered Larry's keys. There was a small key attached to his fob that Darryl was sure was the right size. He now cursed himself for leaving the keys downstairs when he entered. As he climbed back onto his feet, he heard a noise downstairs. He paused. He couldn't be certain of what he had heard. Then the sound again. Glass breaking. Two floors up, he could easily have been mistaken, he convinced himself. Or maybe it came from next door. Frozen, he heard a door creak open and paranoia set in. The front door hadn't creaked like that. Someone was breaking in through the back door. The excitement and relief he had felt at finding the box suddenly vanished. He carefully crept to the bedroom door. Once he reached the top of the stairs, he was certain he could hear movement inside the house. Only a thief would break in; a thief with impeccable timing. Knowing that Larry wouldn't be home and news of his father's past coming to light. A coincidence or somebody looking for the stolen artefact? The implications of that thought led him to another. The real murderer was there. In Larry's house.

Eleanor stood in a grey over-sized sweatshirt, a pair of matching trousers and her socks. They had taken away the rest of her own clothes for forensic analysis. She stared at the ceiling, blinking away the tears, while some stranger rubbed the end of a small swab against the inside of her cheek. She had no option but to comply; no matter if she felt violated. All hope of making them see their mistake was gone. She followed orders, sent from one place to another. No longer a human being, simply a label. Unfortunately for her, her label said murderer.

After DNA swabs had been taken, Eleanor followed the woman out of the small room, barely big enough for the two of them and all the equipment it stored, and through a door that led to a long corridor. The first thing that hit Eleanor as she entered was the smell. A pungent odour of feet that turned her stomach. A long line of doors ran down one side of the plain white corridor, each with a small hatch at head height. She suddenly realised she was walking towards her cell. The room she would spend the next few hours in, longer if they continued to refuse to see the truth.

Chapter Seventeen

Darryl froze at the top of the stairs on the first floor landing. The house had gone quiet. His mind raced in the silence. Had the intruder found what they wanted and gone? Or would they suddenly appear at the bottom of the stairs, turn the corner any moment, and see him hovering? The scrape of a drawer opening drifted up the stairs and Darryl released the breath he only now realised he had been holding. He slowly began the descent down the stairs, each creak as loud in his ears as a crash of cymbals. Luckily, the intruder's rummaging seemed to disguise any sounds Darryl made as they continued their search.

The rummaging stopped and Darryl froze again, three steps up from the hallway. As he looked down at his hands, he realised he had been clutching the box the entire time. Not exactly useful as a weapon and it was an obvious assumption that it was the box in his hand that they were searching for. Keeping it with him maybe wasn't such a good idea. He didn't want to risk returning upstairs to hide it; this could be his one chance to catch the real murderer. He looked around him. Neither the shallow bowl of keys nor the marble fragment were large enough to hide the box. He even considered the coats hanging on hooks behind the door, but their pockets wouldn't have been big enough to fit the box inside. A stupid idea. He also didn't have time to find out as hurried footsteps moved towards the kitchen diner at the back of the house, and then cupboards opening and closing. Hurrying, he placed the box on the stairs, tucked in as tight to the banisters as possible. He could only hope it was out of sight unless ascending the stairs. And that was exactly what Darryl intended to prevent from happening.

Finally, he reached the bottom of the stairs. Though he hadn't found a good hiding place for the box, the marble fragment had given him an idea. It went against every archaeological bone in his body to use it in this manner, but right now, it made the perfect weapon. Fitting nicely in his hand and holding it high, he crept towards the now quiet kitchen. Thankful for the silent tiled floor of the hallway beneath his feet. Entering the kitchen, his eyes darted around the room, searching for the mysterious intruder. The small broken window pane where they had reached inside and unlocked the back door, allowing easy access, was directly ahead. He peered around the front of the large fridge freezer as the room opened out into the large newly renovated kitchen diner that was stretched across the back of the house. He saw no other sign of an intruder. No more sounds of searching. Darryl's disappointment seeped in at the realisation that he may have lost his opportunity. He stepped further towards the opening that led back into the lounge, all the time listening carefully for any sound. But there was nothing but the thumping of his heart pounding in his ears. The circular layout of the ground floor meant that the intruder could easily have made their way back towards the staircase. But the creaking of the stairs would have alerted him if that was the case. Darryl was suddenly falling forwards. A hard thump on the back of his head had sent him flying. He landed splayed on the tiled floor. The artefact sliding from his fingers and breaking on impact.

Eleanor held her head in her hands, pulling at large clump-fulls of hair between her fingers while tears ran silently down her face. Bangs, yells and expletives from another cell rang in her head like a clock tower bell, reverberating and ringing out long after the strike. Eventually, she ran out of tears. Exhausted, she pulled herself up onto the bed and laid there quietly. She wrapped herself in the thin blanket that laid coarsely next to her skin compared to her own soft and warm blankets at home. As she closed her eyes, the scene played out in her head with all the vividness and drama of a movie. How she'd flinched as her knife had scraped along the plate when she'd cut her scone. Ordinarily, this wouldn't have bothered her, but she'd dreaded calling attention to herself, not wanting the man to turn and see her. She had looked up in panic, only to see his lack of courtesy as he ignored Kate when she arrived with his order, still intent on watching what everybody else was doing. He had watched Larry march out the tea-room. She had found it strange at the time, but now she understood Larry's distracted behaviour. She scrunched her eyes tighter in an attempt to block out the persistent noise and the lingering stench around her. Soon, despair turned into anger.

Larry had given her his keys knowing what would happen as soon as the police realised the victim was his father. How predictable they were. They gave no thought to his poor kitten that would have been left to fend for itself had she not given his keys to Darryl. Anger raged through her that not only was Larry going through the same ordeal as her, but he was having to endure it for a second time. She could understand them wanting to ask a few questions; the victim was his father after all. But dragging him off to the police station was outrageous. Their job finished. Or so they must have thought. Until Eleanor had landed in their lap with so-called means, motive, and opportunity.

Motive? She thought in disgust. *What possible motive could I have for killing him? You don't kill someone in cold blood after a petty argument that happened half an hour earlier.*

So consumed with her thoughts, she hadn't noticed that the banging had ceased. She jumped as it began again, as suddenly as the realisation and determination that she would have to find the culprit herself if she wanted to stay out of prison. Taking a deep breath, she turned her mind to visualising the events of that afternoon. Following each person's movements, slowly and methodically, one by one.

She hadn't left the jam for a moment until she had exited the kitchen. There was no way anybody could have tampered with it while she was there. Of this, she was certain. Pulling the blanket tighter around her shoulders, she tried to shut out her current surroundings and visualise who was in the kitchen when she'd left.

First, she visualised the jam, sat in its shallow ramekin in front of her just before she had left the kitchen. Kate was in the tea-room. And, although she hadn't been able to see what was going on behind her, she had been aware of sounds and movement. Directly behind her was the scraping of plates. The remnants of lunchtime meals being emptied into the waste disposal unit by Oli, before being loaded into the dishwasher. Eleanor flinched as a louder than average boom came from the woman two cells down. In her head, Eleanor allocated the sound to Oli, banging dishes and cutlery as he worked. A lame attempt to remove herself from her reality. Forcing herself back into her imagination and memories, she focused again on sounds, this time for Maureen. In the far corner of the kitchen, she was over Eleanor's shoulder. Complaining and waging a one person warfare defending her scones. No doubt, Mr Nelson was being sympathetic, trying to calm her, but Eleanor remembered the close call he'd had with Kate on both entering and leaving the kitchen reminding her of how he hadn't given a convincing argument as to why he was there at that time at all. She wished now that she had listened to their conversation, but eavesdropping wasn't something she would usually do.

Lastly, Larry was on her right side. The clatter and tinkle of broken glass and china being collected had finished. He was now mopping up the remnants of his coffee and Kate's water. She could remember seeing him, as she glanced his way, with the mop in his hand, when she exited the kitchen.

Now she had placed each of them, she visualised each one in turn, collecting some of the broken glass fragments, and then stirring them into the ramekin of gloopy jam. Of course, it would have been easy for Larry. He was the one clearing up the glass. Unfortunately, the police would also come to that conclusion all too easily.

Oli was only a couple of steps away from the jam counter. Everyone else was either on the other side of the room, or busy elsewhere. He would have had time to take those few steps before Kate returned to the kitchen. Also, as far as she knew, there was no evidence that the broken glass was Kate's. Oli could easily have broken a glass while he was clattering and banging, and no one would be any the wiser. In fact, with all the noise that was going on, that could have been true for any of them.

As Eleanor turned her focus to Maureen, a wave of fury rose inside her. Maureen had goaded her. It was because of her that she was in this cell. She took a deep breath and refocused on her aim, pushing her anger aside. Maureen and Mr Nelson had been together in the far corner of the kitchen. That could be problematic for Eleanor's theories, but not impossible. Maureen could have moved to the jam counter after Mr Nelson had left. Or, knowing his keen disposition to help out, he may have stopped to speak to Oli, or Larry, giving her more time with the jam before Kate returned to the kitchen. Similarly, Mr Nelson could have left Maureen intending to leave the kitchen, but stopping via the jam on the way. Both Larry and Oli would have had their backs turned.

An extra strong whiff of urine entered Eleanor's nostrils, forcing her to remember where she was once again. Screwing up her nose and trying to cover it with her sleeve, she focused on the last of her suspects, Kate. *He's had a go at me every time he's been here.* Those were her words, but what did she mean by *had a go at?* Belligerent snipes and orders like he had done today, or were they really upsetting scenes? Her own encounter with him had left her shaken. Having to deal with that kind of animosity regularly could be distressing, to say the least. Putting the glass in the jam before taking it through would have been very easy. *She* had broken the glass in the first place. Had that been her intention all along? Larry had just given her a convenient excuse; making her jump and dropping her glass. And one more thing, it had been Kate that had told her he likes lots of jam. She had thought nothing of it at the time, but could that have been to make it easier to cover the telltale traces of glass?

Her exercise left her with the resigned belief that any of them could have done it. She pulled the blanket up over her head. Screwing her eyes tight, she tried to shut out the noise while she considered one more thing. Someone in that room had not only resorted to murder, but had also calmly denied it and let their colleague take the blame.

Chapter Eighteen

Lying flat on the kitchen floor, Darryl shook his head in shock. The markings on the floor tiles shifted slightly in his vision; his breath snatched from him. For a moment, he struggled to remember where he was until the front door slamming reminded him with a jolt. He clambered up from the floor, reaching for the sore patch on the back of his head that only served to slow him down further. Trying to ignore the throbbing in his head, he staggered out of the kitchen and down the hall. He opened the front door and, even though the rain was falling from dark clouds, he blinked in the seemingly bright light. He stumbled past the Land Rover, and skidding on the gravel drive, he reached the end of the driveway, where he arrived on a street that had very few people. Frantically searching his surroundings, he held his head in his hands, trying to will away the throbbing. He had no time for pain; he couldn't miss this opportunity to catch the killer.

In a residential part of town, the street was composed of the everyday lives of people. A couple of families with pushchairs pushed their way through the rain towards the town at one end of the street, and a seventies housing estate at the other.

Toddlers cried or laughed, though to Darryl it made no differ-ence, it was just noise. Elderly couples meandered, well equipped for the squally weather. But nobody looked flustered. Nobody was hurrying along the street with their head down, hoping they wouldn't be seen.

The alternative was that he was hiding. Cars were dotted either side of the wide avenue and large oak trees lined both sides of the road. Plenty of places to hide. His frustration grew as his search looked more and more useless until he thought he saw Kate. He couldn't be sure. Her head was down and the hood on her pale blue raincoat was pulled up as she hurried along on the opposite pavement towards him.

'Kate,' he called in a desperate hope, but either she didn't hear his call or he was mistaken. It was only when she looked up to cross the road that Darryl almost laughed with relief and he caught her eye.

'Did you see anyone running down the street?' he called across the road.

She looked confused. Maybe she hadn't heard him properly. He waited impatiently for her to cross the road as she dodged between the cars.

'Did you see anyone on the street just now?' he asked as she approached him. 'Anybody running, or – or – they looked like they had been running?'

'I didn't see anybody like that. I was just – I was just going into town.' She took a step back, away from Darryl. 'And, to be perfectly honest, I don't know why I'm even talking to you.'

'What?' His laugh was one of confusion, not amusement.

'After everything Eleanor said earlier today.' Kate turned brusquely away and left.

Darryl took a step after her, but stopped. It would have been of no use. He wasn't able to make any excuses for Eleanor. He knew she was only trying to help a friend, but he had to admit, she went about it in a very unhelpful manner.

He heaved a heavy sigh of frustration. Time was running out, and the truth was, his assailant could still be there, hiding behind one of the thick tree trunks that were easily large enough to hide a person. Or crouched behind a car laughing at him from their hiding place. It soon became clear it was a pointless pursuit. Furious with himself for not only letting him get away, but not even getting a glimpse of who it was.

'Are you alright?'

Darryl suddenly halted his frantic search, coming face to face with an elderly woman peering at him from under her butterfly covered umbrella.

'You look a little perturbed, dear. Are you alright?' she asked again when Darryl didn't answer.

In truth, everything was the opposite of alright. First his friend had been taken away for questioning, then Eleanor was arrested, while the actual killer was still free and had nearly knocked him out. He rubbed the sore patch on the back of his head again.

'Fine,' he answered. 'I was just looking for—' He couldn't think straight. Not even enough to make up an excuse for standing in the middle of the pavement looking like a lunatic.

The woman leaned forward and placed a hand on his arm. 'Get inside out of the rain. You're getting very wet, dear.' She shivered as though the rain was running down her neck and then she continued down the street, huddled under her umbrella.

Darryl looked down at himself. His shirt was soaked through, his jacket was still lying on the bed in the attic room. With a last hopeful sweeping look around him, he returned to the house. The front door was still open from when he had flung it wide in his chase. He remembered the sound of it slamming as he had laid flat on the floor. *Such a clever arse, aren't you?* he thought spitefully. *You even purposefully shut the door behind you, so I'd have to stop and open it, slowing me down.* Seeing the empty table in the hall and remembering the broken marble relief in the kitchen, a wave of guilt swept over him. His eyes then moved to the stairs. The box he had placed on the stairs was gone. Frantically looking around him, his eyes stopped at the back door, which was now open. Suddenly, everything fell into place. He admitted the box hadn't been well hidden, but for someone running past at speed from the direction of the kitchen, it wouldn't have been noticed. But the attacker hadn't left the house at all. He had slammed the door shut in the hope that Darryl would assume he had run that way. The open doorway to the lounge was only a couple of steps from the front door, and ducking through it would have been easy. All the time Darryl had been searching out in the street, the killer had found the box and made his escape out the back, the way he had come. As if Darryl wasn't furious enough with himself for losing his assailant, he now also felt humiliated at being tricked so easily. Cursing didn't seem to do justice to the situation.

Chapter Nineteen

DI Hutchins sauntered through the interview room door. What looked like a young, timid, uniformed officer followed close behind.

'Sorry to have kept you waiting,' she said.

I'm sure you are, Eleanor thought sarcastically. She didn't look as though she was in any hurry to deal with Eleanor, but Eleanor bit her lip, not wanting to antagonise her any further.

After an officer had arrived at Eleanor's cell and escorted her to this bleak, empty room with nothing other than a table with two chairs on either side, she was then told to wait. And wait, she did. Looking around her, she had seen enough detective programmes to recognise the recording machine on the table and the two-way mirror on the wall. The room was a dull beige, with marks and gouges etched into the walls, the only outstanding characteristics that set it apart from any other room. Left on her own, her imagination had wandered and she had visualised the possibilities of what could have made those marks and gouges. Fights breaking out? Chairs being thrown? And the anger behind those fights or chairs. Angry at being caught, or, like herself, at being unjustly arrested.

Finally, DI Hutchins had arrived with the same disinterested look about her as she'd had at the Minstrel-wood site.

'Now, there are a few bits I need to go through with you before we start, and then could we go over everything you said earlier today.' DI Hutchins said.

Eleanor noted she said the question as a statement.

After the preliminaries of turning on the recorder and other formalities were dealt with, Eleanor went through everything she had spent the last few hours running through in her head with the unnerving feeling that the DI was watching her rather than listening. Leaning back in her chair, her legs were crossed and her arms folded. Her chin almost disappeared into her chest. Eleanor was so certain she was about to fall asleep, she was waiting for the woman's eyes to droop.

She made a point to highlight Mr Nelson's lack of a satisfactory explanation for his presence in the kitchen during that time, as well as Kate's clear directive to ensure the victim was served plenty of jam, therefore making it easier to hide the glass. It almost came as a shock when Eleanor finished her explanations and the DI spoke.

'And what about you? With everyone in their places, tell me, did you have the time and opportunity to remove glass from the bin, or even break a different glass, and mix it into the jam? As you say, Oliver Kenward would have had his back to you, Larry Chambers, too, if he was mopping up at this point, or at least focused on the job at hand. Maureen Bradbury and Daniel Nelson were absorbed in their conversation on the other side of the room, and – remind me again, where was Katherine Reeves at this point?'

'In the tea-room,' Eleanor said quietly through pursed lips. 'So, yes, I guess I would have had the time to do it.'

'The time and the opportunity,' DI Hutchins mused to

herself, but loud enough for the remark to be picked up by the recorder and taken in by Eleanor.

She paused, staring at Eleanor as though waiting for some reaction. Maybe she hoped Eleanor would feel intimidated enough to throw her hands in the air and confess. But Eleanor had nothing to confess, and her frustration and anger only grew. As the DI had just confirmed, time and opportunity, but they still hadn't produced this so-called evidence, giving her a motive. Why? Because there was none.

Finally, DI Hutchins smiled and said, 'You told me earlier that today was your first day working there, and yet you seemed very sure of Mr Larry Chamber's innocence. How well do you know him?'

'I know that he was hounded by the police after his father was arrested,' Eleanor snapped.

'You must have known him for a long time, then?' the DI replied, pointedly ignoring the malice behind her remark.

'My partner knows him better.' Eleanor tried to rein in her temper.

'Mr Darryl Westwood?'

Eleanor nodded.

'They work together at the Minstrel-wood site, is that right?'

'Yes. They've known each other for years. But I believe that was the phrase *Larry* used earlier.' Her temper rose again at the memory of him leaving the room, flanked by two police officers. 'Like father, like son. Is that the theory? People aren't capable of thinking for themselves.'

Eleanor fidgeted uncomfortably in the silent pause that followed while DI Hutchins watched her intently.

'Mr Chambers has finished helping us with our enquiries for the time being and has left,' the DI said pragmatically.

'Looks like you were a bit too quick to judge, then.' Eleanor could see the smile behind her eyes and her sarcasm felt justified.

'Too quick to judge?' DI Hutchins gazed up at the ceiling thoughtfully until Eleanor interrupted, finally losing her patience.

'So, tell me, why was I arrested? I'll tell you why. Because I was the easy suspect, that's all. It's me or him. It couldn't possibly be anyone else. And now you've let him go, you're left with me. Job done. I hope you're proud of yourself.'

'Mrs Garrett.' The DI's voice was loud and firm. 'I'm trying to gather all the information before I come to any decision, especially that of charging somebody. I would actually say it's you who's being too quick to judge.'

Eleanor was speechless, fury raging inside her.

'You see, some would say it's all a matter of psychology,' the DI went on. 'You've been trying so hard to convince me that somebody else committed this crime that I can't help but wonder why.'

'And that's why you arrested me? Because I was trying to point out other options?'

DI Hutchins laughed, which infuriated Eleanor more.

'You refused to come with us. That's why I arrested you. I had hoped not to go down this route, but I'm afraid you brought all this on yourself. So far, out of everyone in that room, you had the best opportunity, the easiest means and the strongest motive, so we need to speak with you even if—'

'Strongest motive?' Eleanor interrupted, 'I stuck up for a small child. How is that a strong motive for murder?' Eleanor clenched her fists, her breaths short and sharp.

'And you lied when you told us you didn't know the victim,' the DI spoke over her.

'I didn't lie. I don't know him. I had an argument with him that morning. That doesn't mean I knew him.'

DI Hutchins simply stared back at her. She leaned back in her chair as though she had no interest in what Eleanor had to say.

'You said you had CCTV evidence,' Eleanor went on, infuriated by this woman's lack of enthusiasm. 'Well, where is it? I haven't seen any CCTV, let alone evidence against me.'

DI Hutchins glanced at the officer sat by her side. He pulled out a tablet, and with a couple of taps, he then placed it on the table in front of her.

'I'd like to show you the CCTV footage from this morning,' the DI said quietly and calmly.

The screen showed a black and white, grainy image of Eleanor approaching the old man just before the argument that morning. A knot tightened in her stomach at the sight of him gripping the small boy's arm.

'It's quite an old system and the quality's not the best,' the DI said, ' but we can still see quite clearly what's going on.' She paused the screen, her finger hovering over the button. 'Is that you, Mrs Garrett?' she asked.

'You know it is,' Eleanor said.

DI Hutchins set the video going again, but still her finger hovered. Halfway through the argument, she paused the video recording again.

'Could you please tell me what you're doing at this point?'

Eleanor peered at the screen, but it couldn't have been right. She had pulled her hand back, level with her ear, and it looked as though she was about to hit the man.

'I – I –' Eleanor's mind had suddenly gone blank. All her anger and frustration drained from her body in a single moment.

'To clarify for the recording, the footage shows Mrs Garrett lifting her hand as though about to strike Mr Chambers.' DI Hutchins pressed the play button and resumed the recording while continuing with her commentary. 'before seemingly bringing herself under control and returning to the argument.'

Mr Nelson walked into the scene on the screen, and the recording was paused again.

Eleanor shook her head, unable to take her eyes off the frozen screen. 'No. No, I wouldn't do that.'

'You did do that. We have the evidence on the screen. You have confirmed that this is an image of you, and you can clearly make out where you have raised your hand, ready to strike.'

'No. It's not true.' Eleanor reached across to rewind the scene, but the younger officer tried to stop her. DI Hutchins stopped him and nodded, allowing Eleanor to continue. She touched the button on the screen. It rewound ten seconds and played again. Again and again, she rewound the scene and watched it as this incredible and impossible scene played out in front of her. On the fifth time, she stared numbly at the screen as she left the footage to play. She watched the figures in front of her: the teacher taking the boy away; the intervention of Mr Nelson; the whispered conversation with Sahara at the till. Suddenly, her hand flicked again on the screen and the reason suddenly came back to her.

'The fly,' she said, almost in tears at the relief.

'The what?'

'Look, I do it again,' Eleanor rewound the scene and watched with DI Hutchins as she swiped at the fly that had been buzzing round her head. 'There was a fly. It had been buzzing round my head for the last half an hour or so. I was swiping at a fly, not Mr Chambers.'

'A fly?'

'Yes, a fly.' She couldn't hold back her tears any longer as the relief consumed her. She was going home. 'It wasn't the first time, either. Mr Nelson had spoken to me earlier about them.

He told me that I'll need to get used to them, so I'm sure he'll remember.'

'We'll need to corroborate your story,' DI Hutchins said, 'and at this time of night, that might be difficult.'

'So what are you saying?' Eleanor clenched her fists as she tried to stop her hands from shaking.

'It's getting on for ten in the evening,' DI Hutchins said as she gathered her things together. 'I guess I'm saying you may be staying the night.' With that, she left the room while her colleague dealt with the formalities of ending the recording, and Eleanor sat unable to speak.

Within minutes, she had gone from absolute fury to disbelief, followed by ultimate relief, before returning to anger once again. All the time the police were questioning her, the real killer was still free.

Chapter Twenty

Darryl stood in the hallway, dripping onto the red and black tiled floor. His wet clothes were cold as they stuck against his skin. A familiar chime signifying the half hour drifted through from the grandfather clock that stood proudly in the lounge. Darryl glanced up at the time; half-past eight. It had already been over two and a half hours since the police had taken Larry to the station.

He pushed himself on to complete one last job. Clearing up to make sure that if the police did arrive, there was no evidence that he had been there. And yet, the thumping in his head made it difficult to focus on anything, let alone decide what to do first. Adrenaline had been the only thing that had kept him going, blocking out the pain.

With his energy gone, he hung his head, defeated. A trail of wet footprints had followed him into the hallway. Decision made, he slipped off his boots and moved towards the stairs to find a towel. His first few steps made him rethink his decision as his head pounded with the movement. First stop, kitchen. His limbs moving on autopilot, he avoided looking at the broken marble fragment on the floor and found a bag of frozen peas. Ice covered the bag on the outside from where it had clearly not been used for some time. Larry had never been the most enthusiastic of cooks. He winced as he bashed the bag against the counter to loosen the solid lump of peas inside, when a noise from outside made him stop. His thoughts returned to the threat of the police turning up. Eager to continue his search, he gave up loosening the peas and wrapped the bag in a tea-towel. He held it against the large lump that had raised on the back of his head, swearing at its touch.

He climbed the stairs as fast as his head would allow, stopping off at the bathroom for a towel and dried himself as best he could. He carried on up to the loft to replace the floorboard and rug.

Exhausted, he sat heavily on the floor, letting out a small grunt at the jolt and taking hold of his head in both hands. He took a moment to breathe deeply to steady himself. Eventually, he picked up the floorboard and leaned across to replace it. All thoughts of the police suddenly disappeared. In the darkness, he saw an envelope that had been hidden underneath the box. Reaching in, he found there were two. One was new, with a hand-written address, and, peering inside, he could see it contained a hand-written letter. History in the making came to his mind. Nobody writes hand-written letters anymore. The other envelope was yellow and brittle with age, and contained a folded sheet of newspaper. Larry hadn't mentioned anything about envelopes. Just the box. Intrigued, he hauled himself up off the hard wooden floor and sat on the edge of the bed to examine what he had found. First, though, he returned the tea-towel wrapped bag of peas to his head. They had loosened in the bag, and when replacing it, he found it fitted better around the stubborn lump on his head.

The newspaper page had been roughly torn down one side. As it was dated from years ago, Darryl presumed it had some relevance to Larry's father's arrest, and after a moment's search, he found it. A small article that contained little information about the man himself, but focused on the hoard that had been stolen from a museum and then found in his possession. According to the article, nobody could understand how the hoard, originally from Ancient Greece and dated around 1000 BC, came to be discovered in a field just outside the small town of Sellinsborough. One artefact, though, was never recovered. A priceless necklace that was believed to have been stolen to order and therefore sold immediately after the theft.

He refolded the article, put it back in its envelope, and then turned his attention to the letter. He didn't usually make a habit of reading other people's mail, and he hesitated, tapping it against his knee. He had already come this far to help his friend. Being hidden under the floorboard with the box and newspaper article meant there was a high probability that it had something to do with his father. And, as Larry had trusted Darryl to find and retrieve the box, he leaned towards feeling justified in opening it, especially if it contained something that could help Larry. Justified or not, he had to make a decision. He opened the letter and read.

My dearest boy,

I am writing to you in the hope that we can talk and work things out. I am pleading with you. Coming to the end of my life has made me see my mistakes, and losing you is the only one I care about. I must make things right before it's too late. I can see now that it was wrong of me to ask you to take on such a responsibility. You must believe me when I tell you that it wasn't part of the original plan. You know how much I tried to convince the police they were wrong, but they wouldn't believe me. But with your help, I will finally be able to free us both from all of this.

I will be going to the Minstrel-wood site again on September 14th. Please meet with me. I want to take any possible blame from you, and I will be able, at last, to make things right.
Love always
Dad

A siren suddenly blared from outside the house. Darryl quickly moved to the window and lifted the blind. An ambulance was trying to make its way down the busy street. His focus back on his situation, he returned the letter and newspaper article to their respective envelopes and replaced the floorboard and rug. Deciding against putting the envelopes in his jeans pocket, which were still damp from the rain, he picked up his jacket from the bed and put them in the inside pocket. It didn't take much to realise this letter could further implicate Larry. There would be no doubt that he knew his dad was going to be at the site that day, and that Larry probably knew about the where-abouts of the stolen artefact and had been lying to them the whole time.

He returned downstairs where the last few stairs forced him to come face to face with the empty hallway table. Cursing himself again at losing the box and the attacker, the fact remained that Larry's artefact was still on the kitchen floor. More to the point, still in pieces on the kitchen floor. The sight of the marble relief, itself broken in two and separated from its stand, was heart-breaking. With everything else Larry was going through, he didn't need Darryl adding to his problems. Not knowing what to do with the broken pieces, he laid them on another tea-towel on the dining table. He returned the peas to the freezer and looked around him for one last check. How was he going to explain this to Larry?

He pulled the front door closed behind him as his phone

rang. Eager to hear from Eleanor, he pulled it from his pocket to see Larry's name on the screen.

'Larry, mate, where are you?'

'Still at the station. They've just released me. I've been trying to get hold of Eleanor, but her phone's just going straight through to voicemail. I don't suppose there's any chance she gave you my keys, is there?' His voice was flat and unemotional.

'You mean so I can feed your new kitten?' Darryl said satirically, trying to bring a little light into the situation and feeling a sense of relief as this lifted the risk of the police turning up. 'Unfortunately, Eleanor was arrested just after you left. You'd have been proud of her, though. She was putting up quite a fight for you.'

'I'm flattered, and not what I would have expected, to be honest. I never really thought she took to me.'

'I learnt early on,' Darryl said. 'she's nuts, but her heart's in the right place. But don't worry, she'd already given me your keys. I got the message and I've—' Darryl suddenly thought about whether anybody could be listening in to the conversation. 'I've fed your cat,' he continued. Somehow he had to explain that after finding the box, he then lost it again, but that wasn't a conversation for over the phone. 'I'm at your place now. I'll come pick you up.'

'No, it's fine. I'll meet you at the car park across from the police station and get my keys. But then I'll walk home. It's not that far. Besides, I'm sure you'd rather be here for when Eleanor gets out.'

'I'll meet you at the car park and drive you home,' Darryl insisted. 'No arguments. If Eleanor's out in the meantime, I'm sure she'll understand.'

Chapter Twenty-One

Eleanor had been returned to her cell, where she sat waiting. For what, she wasn't sure. To be told she could go home? To be charged with murder? Although her realisation of the fly buzzing round her head had been the reason she had struck out, doubt still plagued her. She no longer saw the wall that sat only a few feet away. Only an enormous expanse of nothingness stood in front of her. Her anger simmered gently within her exhausted body.

After what seemed like several hours, her door opened, and DI Hutchins appeared.

'We have corroborated your story—'

'My story,' Eleanor interrupted with disdain and turned away from her.

'- and you may go home.'

Eleanor looked up suddenly. She hadn't dared hope to hear those words.

'As I'm sure you realise,' the DI continued, 'you are still under investigation, but for now at least, you may go home.'

Fighting back tears of relief, Eleanor jumped as the raucous lady from two doors down shouted again for her release. Eleanor's frustration and humiliation rose again.

'I don't know how you could even imagine that I deserve to be here,' she snapped as she stood, ready to leave. Time alone with her thoughts had only made her resentful.

The DI moved and stood in Eleanor's way as she attempted to walk out the door. 'What do you mean, "deserve to be here"?'

Eleanor nodded her head in the direction of the noise. 'I would imagine she's probably here for good reason.'

'And you think you weren't?'

'Of course not. I'm innocent.'

DI Hutchins laughed loudly before reining herself in. 'That's a coincidence. She says she's innocent too. Should we believe her?'

'No, probably not,' Eleanor answered quickly, without thinking. 'Well, she doesn't act as though she's innocent,' she continued, feeling her remark may have needed clarification.

'Why?'

DI Hutchins's short, sharp question took Eleanor by surprise. Although the woman was loud and raucous, that didn't make her guilty of anything illegal. Eleanor suddenly remembered Darryl's words when he called her a snob. Maybe he was right. When Eleanor didn't answer, DI Hutchins leaned casually against the wall, blocking Eleanor's exit.

'In my younger days, I used to watch old cowboy films with my dad,' she said, smiling at the memory. 'I can remember asking him one day, "How do you know who the good guys are from the bad?" Do you know what he said?'

Eleanor, wondering where this was going, shook her head.

'He said, "The good guys wear white hats, and the bad guys wear black."' She laughed again. 'Can you believe that?'

Eleanor wasn't sure if DI Hutchins expected her to laugh with her, but she wasn't exactly in a laughing mood.

The DI turned directly to Eleanor, her expression now serious. 'Unfortunately, real life's not that easy. Everybody seems to wear multi-coloured hats these days. Or no hat at all. Sometimes good people do bad things and bad people do good things. And that's where we come in.

'You told me earlier, in the interview room, that you think I'm not interested in finding out the truth, and, I have to admit, others before you have commented on what they perceive as my lack of enthusiasm. I may not be rushing around, Mrs Garrett, and why should I when younger legs can do the running around for me? But just because my resting expression is one of disinterestedness, that doesn't mean I am. This is me taking everything in. Do you really think I don't take my job seriously? Take murder seriously?'

Her pause made Eleanor's skin crawl. Humiliated by her own judgements.

'In my experience,' the DI continued after her brief pause. 'I've often found there's usually somebody who's far too keen to provide the answers I need. Some helpful do-gooder or someone who considers themselves an amateur sleuth, or, as I said earlier, somebody who is trying to distract from the truth. I do have to admit, I enjoy those little arguments that occur with just the right word mentioned in the wrong place.'

'You created those arguments on purpose?' Eleanor exclaimed.

'That's when you usually find out the truth about people. Not when they're being all nicey, nicey and cooperative. But when tempers fly and they begin to understand exactly what's at stake. The thing is, we don't know what colour hat you're wearing until we ask questions, and I can only hope that one day you come to understand that we are simply doing our job, and our job consists of asking questions. Of *everyone*. So, my question for you right now is, what makes you so special?'

Eleanor turned her eyes towards the floor. 'Nothing,' she mumbled.

~

A few minutes later, Darryl pulled up in the car park, where Larry was waiting huddled under a tree. His shoulders were hunched and his jacket pulled tight around him. The rain was beginning to let up, but still, as Larry climbed into the car, Darryl saw he was wet through. His vacant expression was one Darryl had seen many times on Eleanor when they had first met after the deaths of her husband and son. Numb and unaware of what was going on around her.

During the journey back to Larry's house, Darryl floundered and flustered as he explained what had happened. Larry remained silent throughout. Staring out the side window of the car, only adding to Darryl's shame. Larry usually had some silly quip ready for most occasions. He would rather Larry screamed at him than the silence that confronted him. It wasn't until after Darryl apologised that the box with the stolen artefact had been taken that Larry finally spoke.

'Are you kidding? Why are you apologising? You're lucky to get away with your life.'

Darryl was left speechless by Larry's outburst.

'Don't you see? It must have been the killer,' Larry went on. 'Someone from the tea-room found out about the connection between me and Dad and immediately came round to my house to look for the artefact.'

'We can't know that for certain,' Darryl said. 'Maybe they just grabbed the box as a last resort and ran. The box was locked so they wouldn't have known what was inside it, and better not to leave empty-handed after going to the trouble of breaking in.'

'It would be one hell of a coincidence. No.' Larry shook

his head with conviction. 'They knew what they were looking for, which means it must have been someone who was working with him at the time to have been able to recognise the box. Like I said this morning, I put it under the floorboards and left it. It was the same box that Dad gave to me all those years ago.'

'Then, maybe we should go back and tell the police what's happened, if you're so certain that this must be the same person,' said Darryl.

'And tell them what? That I *did* have the stolen artefact after all? Even though I've just been denying it for the last few hours. Not to mention when they questioned me years ago about it. But could I say anything without getting Dad into more trouble?'

'You're right,' Darryl conceded. 'Plus, I've no proof that anyone was there at all, other than this huge lump on my head. They'd probably think I'd made it up and I'm just trying to get the two of you off the hook by claiming the killer's still out there.'

Darryl turned onto Larry's road and saw a figure walking hurriedly out of Larry's driveway.

'That's Kate, isn't it?' It wasn't easy to tell as she was walking away from them with her face hidden, and the hood of her raincoat covered half her head. In fact, Darryl only guessed it was her because he had seen her earlier wearing the same pale blue coat.

'Could be.' Larry gave a slight shrug, as though the movement was too much for him. 'I don't really feel like seeing anyone, though. I'm glad she's leaving.'

'Do you know her?' Darryl waited opposite Larry's house for a break in the traffic before he could pull into the driveway.

'Why?' Larry asked.

'It's just strange. She hasn't been working at the site for long.

How does she know where you live? You haven't been trying it on with her, have you? You do know she's engaged.'

The corners of Larry's mouth didn't even twitch at Darryl's attempt at light-hearted banter.

'No.' His voice was void of any emotion. 'She lives in the estate at the end of the road. It's the quickest route into town.'

Darryl pulled into the driveway and stopped the engine. They sat a moment in silence; Darryl not wanting to rush him.

'I'll need to get my car,' Larry continued finally in the same banal tone.

'We can sort that tomorrow.' Darryl glanced at the time on the dashboard. It was already nearly half past ten. Surely Eleanor would be released soon. Nevertheless, he wasn't sure if leaving Larry on his own was a good idea. 'Do you want me to come in?' he asked.

'No, I think it's best if I have some time on my own.'

Silently, Darryl was relieved, but Larry still sat in the Land Rover, not making any attempt to leave.

'I'm so sorry, Darryl,' he said finally.

'What are you sorry for?' Darryl asked incredulously.

'That you were nearly killed—'

'You're exaggerating,' Darryl interrupted.

'That Eleanor's all caught up in this—'

'It's not your fault the police are idiots. They'll see reason soon enough. There's no point you worrying about that.'

There was another long, uncomfortable pause before Darryl hesitantly asked, 'What did they want?'

'Just to go over everything *again*, but I have to admit, once they had seen the files from last time, they soon realised they were making a mistake. Of course they've said I'm being *released under investigation*,' he stressed as though the term was comically dangerous, 'but that's just them covering themselves and trying to put pressure on me.'

'More than likely, I hate to think how Eleanor's holding up.'

'I'm really sorry,' Larry said again. 'She shouldn't have to—'

'It's not your fault,' Darryl insisted, while Larry's eyes filled with tears.

'You were right,' Larry said, turning away from Darryl, hiding his face. 'About regretting not speaking to my dad before he died. I only hope I might have come to that conclusion myself before he died, if someone had let his cancer run its course.'

'I'm sure you would. You're a sensible bloke. Or so I've heard it rumoured.' Darryl tried again to lighten the atmosphere a little, though probably more for himself than for Larry. In truth, he knew now wasn't the time for comedy. And Larry simply continued staring blankly out the front window.

They sat for another minute in silence.

'Are you sure you don't want some company?' Darryl offered again as he glanced at the clock. He wasn't so certain that Larry did want to be on his own. 'Even if it's just—'

'No, I'll be fine,' Larry interjected. 'Thanks for running me home.'

He climbed out of the car and walked towards the front door. He only turned to look at Darryl as he closed his front door, giving a half-hearted wave of thanks as he did.

Darryl closed his eyes and fought the urge to scream in frustration. His friend's dad murdered. His partner arrested for that murder. How ridiculous can you get?

His phone rang, and he hurriedly took it from his pocket. It was Eleanor. At last, something was going right; they must have released her. But he couldn't shake the sense of dread from another awkward conversation. If she had taken Sahara's thieving so badly, how would she take the fact that Larry not only had his dad's stolen artefact all this time, but that he had also lied to the police about it?

Chapter Twenty-Two

'Come and get me,' Eleanor growled down her phone, fighting back her tears.

'You're out,' Darryl exclaimed. 'I've just dropped Larry off at home. I'll be straight back.'

'How is he? They told me they'd let him go,' she said, desperate to focus on something other than her own past few hours.

'OK, considering. I'll tell you about it when I see you.'

His tone was sharp, and she had the feeling he wanted to get off the call quickly. Knowing Darryl, he was probably trying to protect her from how Larry was really feeling. She arranged for him to pick her up at the nearby car park. Hanging around at the police station was out of the question.

She sat huddled on a bench on the edge of the car park next to a large playing field. Staring into the darkness, numb from her ordeal. Subconsciously aware of the occasional late dog walker that passed by and a small boy playing on his own in the playground. Its only source of light was the little that spilled over from the streetlights surrounding the car park where the roads shone, wet from the recent rain.

The sight of the Land Rover arriving jolted her back to reality. Darryl charged out of the car and headed straight towards her as she walked along the gravel path between the playground and the car park.

'What did they say? Are you OK? Why did they make up that story about you hitting the man? Where are your clothes?' Darryl's questions came fast and furious, with no pause for an answer.

He enveloped her in his arms as if he never intended to let go. Overwhelmed, Eleanor was torn between releasing her pent up frustration in tears and collapsing into his arms, or rallying her anger into action. After indulging in his safety for a moment, she then practically pushed him away as if saying, *Now, let's get down to business.*

'First of all, let's deal with Larry. How is he?'

'No,' Darryl said firmly, holding Eleanor by the shoulders and staring directly into her eyes. 'Let's deal with you.'

Eleanor stared back for a moment before shaking her head. 'I don't want to talk about it right now, and all you need to know is that I don't want to go back there,' she whispered. 'We have to find out who did this.'

Darryl pulled her close again, and they stood quietly for a moment until Eleanor, again, pushed him away.

'Please, tell me about Larry. I need to focus on something else. If his dad was killed because of something in his past, then Larry may know more than he thinks.' Darryl hesitated and so Eleanor persevered. 'Please, how is he?'

Begrudgingly, Darryl said, 'He's OK.'

Eleanor knew there was more to it than that.

'He's shocked, he's dazed, just as anyone would be in his situation,' Darryl clarified. 'But he'll be OK.'

'I don't think I've ever felt so angry.' Eleanor clenched her fists and strode over to the car just a few steps away. 'I know they're just doing their job, but I feel so victimised. I can only imagine how he must feel.'

'The worrying thing is, he just wanted to be left alone, and that's not like him.'

'Do you think we should go see him?' she asked.

'I offered, but, as I said, he just wants to be on his own. We'll go and see him tomorrow. Give him a chance to let it all sink in. There's also something else I need to tell you,' he continued awkwardly.

Before he could continue, a woman's shout interrupted him.

'Leave me alone.' Her voice was low and hoarse. She looked in her forties with dull, unclean clothes. She staggered down the gravel path that led past the car park towards the playing field. Weaving from side to side, trying to stay out of the bushes that bordered the path. A nearly empty bottle of vodka in her hand. A girl ran up behind her, pulling on her arm. It only took a moment to realise the girl was Sahara.

'Leave me alone!' the woman yelled. 'He's fine. Stop hassling me.' She pushed Sahara away with such a force she fell to the ground.

Immediately, Eleanor and Darryl ran to help her up off the ground, only for her to pull her arm away from Eleanor's grasp as soon as she realised who it was.

'Do you really think I want your help? Get lost.' She brushed the muck from her hands down her trousers and marched after the drunk woman.

Sahara's response shook Eleanor, though she didn't really expect anything else. But she wasn't just angry, she was spiteful.

'Hey, Sahara,' Darryl called after her. 'We're just trying to help.'

Sahara stopped suddenly and doubled-back. 'Help? Is that what you said? Help? She got me fired.' She pointed viciously at Eleanor.

Eleanor's temper was high from being interrogated by the police for hours, but she took a step back, humbled by Darryl's intervention even though she knew he didn't agree with what she had done.

'She was just doing what she thought was right,' he said.

'Well, maybe she should find out all the facts before making that decision,' Sahara spat.

'I had all the facts,' Eleanor said, trying to stay calm. 'I saw you with my own eyes steal money from the till. You were then found with that money in your pocket. I can't see what other facts there could possibly be.'

'I wasn't stealing. I would never do that.' Sahara took an aggressive step towards her, but Eleanor had had enough of being pushed around.

'So, how did you end up with that note in your pocket? Your back was turned to the camera, but not to me. I saw you take that money from the till.'

'I didn't steal it.' Sahara took another step towards her and Darryl forced his way between them, blocking Sahara's path.

'Calm down,' he told them both, gently but firmly.

'I thought you were a friend,' Sahara snarled at him.

'Why don't you tell us what happened?' His voice was quiet and calm.

'You didn't give me that luxury at the time.' Sahara's face was red with anger.

Darryl took a deep breath. 'Don't blame us for what Nelson did,' he said calmly. 'He was the one who was so quick to fire you.'

'Yeah, but only 'cause of her.'

'You were stealing,' Eleanor stressed.

'I wasn't stealing. I was only borrowing.'

'Borrowing? You were going to give it back, were you?' Eleanor failed to hold back her sarcasm.

'Yes, I always do,' Sahara insisted.

'I knew it,' Eleanor said excitedly. 'I knew it wasn't the first time you'd done it. So, you're saying that you were going to return the money on the exact same day that the head office reports a thief?' She ignored the look of frustration from Darryl.

'It's true. Mr Nelson even knows I do it.'

Both Eleanor and Darryl were shocked into silence. Sahara suddenly squeezed her lips together as though she had said too much.

'We have – we had a sort of arrangement,' she continued quietly. 'I don't want to get him into trouble, though. He tried to help us.'

'Told you so,' the drunk woman was weaving her way back along the path towards them. 'He's fine,' she spat as she passed Sahara.

'Mum!' Sahara called and was about to chase after her again when the sound of a small child crying made her turn back to the play park.

Eleanor and Darryl, curious, followed her and saw that she was crouched in front of the small boy that Eleanor had seen earlier playing on his own.

'It's OK,' she said to the boy as she gently wiped the dirt off his hands and knees with her coat sleeves. 'Wow, you must have been running so fast that your feet couldn't keep up.'

'As fast as a superhero?' the boy asked her.

'Faster,' Sahara told him.

The boy's face lit up with a beaming smile. His fall forgotten, he ran off again as though nothing had happened.

'Stay in the light,' she called after him. 'That's Toby, my little brother,' she explained, watching the boy running mindlessly round the park. 'Mum struggles and sometimes gives in. She's an alcoholic, to put it bluntly, and sometimes there's no money left for food. I just take what I need to be able to feed

Toby. He doesn't deserve to starve because our mother can't cope.'

A wave of shame swept over Eleanor as she watched the small boy running happily around the roundabout. He appeared unfazed by the cold, even though he was only wearing a pair of shorts and a t-shirt that was clearly too small for him. 'How long have you been living like this?' she asked.

'She started drinking soon after my other brother, Mitch, was killed in a hit and run two years ago. I don't blame her. She just couldn't cope. Neither could Dad. He just upped and left one day. Haven't seen him since.'

'That's awful. I'm so sorry.' Eleanor's words were hardly audible. She knew all about the pain of losing a child. Taking respite from that pain in the form of alcohol was understandable and, she had to admit, there were times she had succumbed temporarily herself.

'Yeah, well, you should be.' Sahara returned to her antagonistic manner. 'Thanks to you, I've lost the only means I had to feed him.'

'What do you mean by Mr Nelson knew?' Darryl asked curiously.

Sahara hesitated. Finally, she turned away from watching her brother Toby and continued in a low murmur.

'He caught me about a year ago. It was the first time I tried, in fact. I was desperate. Toby hadn't eaten for I don't know how long. When I explained the situation and that I intended to put the money back once I got paid, he completely understood and let me continue. "Just keep it quiet,"' she said, standing tall and putting on Mr Nelson's efficient mannerism, '"and be more careful," was all he said. "Make sure nobody sees you again, and that includes me." After that, we never spoke of it again.'

'Maybe if we go back and talk to him, he'll—' Eleanor implored, but Sahara cut her off.

'Now that the police know, too? That's hardly likely.' Sahara turned back to watching her brother.

'Why didn't you ask for an advance on your wages?' Eleanor's gaze followed and watched the boy, now on the climbing frame, trying to lift his short leg over a bar that was too high for him.

'I didn't even know there was such a thing, not till a couple of months later when I heard Oli asking for one. When I asked, though, he refused. Instead, he said he preferred to turn a blind eye to my borrowing. It was less paperwork that way and would be better for both of us. But because you made such a big deal out of it, in front of all those people, he had no choice but to sack me.'

'I'm so sorry,' Eleanor said again. Her words feeling inadequate.

'Well, sorry isn't going to feed Toby this evening, is it? I need to go and find Mum. See if she's got any money left after her drinking binge this evening. She won't know nothing till she wakes up in the morning and he's not eaten for hours.' Sahara walked away.

Before Eleanor could change her mind, she blurted, 'Come back with us.'

'You what?' Sahara turned back to them. The expression of disdain had returned.

Eleanor looked at Darryl questioningly and was pleased to see him nodding in agreement.

'Both of you,' she went on. 'Come back with us. We'll give you a good hot meal. We have a spare room you can stay in. And we'll bring you home in the morning. You said yourself your mum won't know anything till morning.'

'No. You're just feeling sorry for me, and I don't like pity. Nor charity neither.' Sahara turned and began to walk away again.

'You're right,' Eleanor called after her. 'I am feeling sorry for you because it's my fault you're in this position now. Please, let me do this, if not for you, at least for your brother.'

Sahara stopped and looked back at her, frowning.

'I know it's not a long-term solution,' Eleanor went on, 'but at least we can help tonight.'

Sahara shifted uncomfortably from one foot to another.

'As you said, it's getting late,' Eleanor persevered. 'We can give you breakfast in the morning, too. I bet you haven't eaten either, have you?'

'I'll need to leave a note for Mum,' Sahara said eventually. 'Just in case she decides to care about us for once and wonders where we are.'

'Of course,' Eleanor blurted with relief. 'We'll stop off at your place on the way. Whatever you need.'

Chapter Twenty-Three

Eleanor watched Sahara and her brother for a moment as they sat together on the sofa. It was now past midnight and she had taken their dinner through for them on trays. Sahara had been changing channels on TV, trying to get Toby to decide what to watch while they ate, when Eleanor came in the room. But Toby was more interested in throwing himself against the large, comfortable cushions on the sofa. She had heard his giggles long before she'd arrived at the room. As soon as he saw Eleanor enter with their meals, though, he sat with a calm expectancy. His eyes lit up at the sight of the spaghetti bolognese on his plate. Eleanor had been concerned he would complain as she remembered the endless cajoling and coaxing around mealtimes with her son, Chris. Chris would never have eaten spaghetti bolognese. But she guessed things were very different for Toby. It had been so long since he'd eaten anything, he was more than grateful.

With remorse running through her, Eleanor smiled at the scene as she closed the lounge door quietly behind her. She returned to the kitchen and joined Darryl at the table for their own meals. The spaghetti was the quick and easy choice for this late at night, but now, neither of them felt particularly hungry.

'I really messed up there, didn't I?' Eleanor dropped heavily into her chair.

Darryl paused with his fork and spoon in his hands and looked up at her from his meal.

'It's OK,' she continued. 'You don't need to say anything.' She picked up her own fork and began picking at a piece of carrot in the Bolognese sauce. 'I know you were right, and I was wrong. I still believe stealing is wrong, but I could have dealt with it very differently.'

He tentatively nodded and returned to twisting his spaghetti in the bowl of his spoon.

'I have to help her get her job back. Or find her another one. I've made everything ten times worse in every respect.'

'Don't be ridiculous,' Darryl said, putting his fork and spoon down on his plate, the food never making it to his mouth. 'Come on. Let's look at what we've got.'

'A starving family, stolen property, and apparently a motive for murder for a man I've never met before. It's not looking good.' She was tired from mulling over what had happened that day and the only thing she had got from it was a headache.

'If you look at it that way, I guess it doesn't look good, but what we do know is that someone else broke into Larry's house and I think we can all agree that person was specifically looking for the original stolen artefact.'

'There could be another reason,' Eleanor mused, still picking at her bolognese.

'It's a bit of a coincidence that someone just happens to break into his house at that precise moment, and didn't bother taking anything else even though Larry has some nice stuff,' said Darryl.

'But that's just it. Why now?' She gave up with her meal

and laid down her fork. 'Let's say, for them to have recognised the box, it must be somebody who knew Mr Chambers senior from the past,' she continued.

'Larry believes it could be that they didn't know the connection between him and his dad until today.'

'Even though they had the same name? It wouldn't have been hard to work out.' Eleanor frowned.

'Maybe. There are a lot of people called Chambers, though. Are you going to check all of them?' Darryl suggested.

'I suppose only if you're specifically looking for him, and then you'd already know the connection. And if you know the connection, it brings us back to why wait till now to go looking for the artefact?'

'Maybe, like me, they thought the police would search his house again and they would only have a small window of opportunity to search it first. I'm sure the police have much more effective methods of searching for things nowadays than they did back then. And,' Darryl sat back, letting out an enormous sigh, 'I think we both agree that whoever it was is also the murderer.'

Eleanor agreed, but there was still one thing that her curiosity couldn't shake. 'What I don't understand is why kill a man who's already dying? That just doesn't make any sense. Can I see the letter again?' She pushed her plate aside to make space to read the letter.

Darryl reached for the envelope that he now had in his back pocket, along with the newspaper article. 'Just as well these were *under* the box, otherwise they would probably have been taken, too.' He passed it to Eleanor, leaving the envelope with the article on the table.

She opened the letter and quietly read it again, her brow furrowed deeply with thought.

'"I must make things right before it's too late." It sounds like he really did want to reconcile with Larry. "It wasn't part of the original plan," I bet it wasn't,' Eleanor mocked.

'Not when the plan was always to sell the stuff and live happily ever after. He only turned to Larry for help when he knew the police were on to him.' Darryl picked up his fork and spoon and began picking at his meal again.

'So, why was he trying to convince the police they were wrong? Surely that means he was trying to tell them he was innocent, doesn't it?'

'Larry said he always protested his innocence and, I have to say, from what Larry told me about his dad this morning, he didn't trust him at all. The alleged reconciliation was just another ruse to try and get the artefact back for himself.' He lifted his fork, ready to eat, but seeing it seemed to change his mind. He put it back on his plate and he, too, pushed it aside.

'I can't believe the audacity of the man,' Eleanor said incredulously. '"With your help I will finally be able to free us from all of this,"' she read aloud. 'After everything he had put his son through, he's still asking for Larry's help. And really, what help can Larry give him?'

Thoughtful silence filled the room once more, their meals growing cold to one side, until Eleanor spoke again.

'I can't get away from the fact that he was dying,' she said exasperatedly. 'Not only is it odd that someone would kill an already dying man, but also it wasn't like the man himself would have the time to enjoy the benefits of the stolen artefact or of the money if he sold it. I'm inclined to think he did plan to hand it in. Clear his conscience and make some kind of reconciliation between father and son before he died. At the end, here,' she pointed to the bottom of the letter, 'he talks about taking the blame and making things right.'

'After a lifetime of lies, though, you can understand why Larry found it hard to trust him.'

'One thing's for certain, this letter doesn't help us in working out who killed him.'

'So, at the moment,' Darryl said, 'we think it's somebody who knew Mr Chambers way back when, but didn't know that Larry was his son until today.'

'I think that's the only theory that fits the facts. Well, it's somewhere to start, anyway. Maybe it would help if we knew more about this missing artefact. When and where it was stolen. Maybe we can find a connection with one of the others who is working at the site now. I wish I could see it,' Eleanor said thoughtfully.

'No need to rub it in. I can't believe I lost it,' Darryl grumbled and punched his knee in fury.

'Wherever it is, at least it's no longer in Larry's house,' Eleanor tried to console him.

'I have to admit, I'm surprised at how well you've taken the news.'

Eleanor looked at him quizzically.

'That Larry *did* have the stolen artefact and even lied to the police about it.'

'I'm learning that my judgement isn't always the best,' she said with a quick nod of her head towards the lounge. 'Besides, that fact has nothing to do with who killed his father and he's still a friend who needs help. We need to know who would have had some connection with his father in the past. Maybe we can find out some more about his dad in here.' She pulled over the other envelope and took out the newspaper page.

Darryl shuffled his chair round closer to Eleanor, and they read the article together. Even though it wasn't long, they were able to glean some information from it. The crux of the story was that the Sellinsborough hoard had been recovered except for one item and the thief, Mr Albert Chambers, was pleading his innocence, claiming he was framed. The rest of the hoard would be returned to Sellinsborough museum, and they also listed a few other archaeological sites, such as Beesford, Steeplewich, and Telsham, where Mr Chambers had worked and where other items may have gone missing.

'I see what Larry means about his untrustworthiness,' Eleanor said. 'All this time he's been pleading his innocence and yet Larry had the proof that he did it.'

'Well, he *did*,' Darryl grumbled again.

He pulled his phone from his pocket and went about tapping and swiping the screen moodily. 'I've found the museum ... there's the hoard,' he said, tapping his phone further. 'And ... here we go, the Sellinsborough necklace.'

He held out his phone to show Eleanor. The image on the screen showed a beautiful, elaborately detailed necklace made of gold with amethysts and emeralds. Darryl had shown her many archaeological artefacts during their time together, but nothing like this. His interests tended to lie with items that showed how everyday people lived. This necklace was elegant and flamboyant. Even Eleanor could tell it wouldn't have been worn by a commoner, but by a person of much higher standing.

'That looks heavy,' she said, always thinking practically.

Darryl nodded. 'I don't think comfort was considered. Wealth and status was what it was all about.'

'OK, we know when the hoard was stolen, so Mr Nelson, Maureen, and Oli are the only ones old enough to have been around then. That only cuts out Kate.'

'She could have some other association.' Darryl rose from his chair and carried their untouched dinners over to the kitchen counter. Even though neither of them had eaten for hours, it was clear they had no appetite. Instead, he poured himself a glass of apple juice. 'A parent, older sibling? We can't rule her out just on age, but at least we know where to start.' He silently asked if Eleanor would like a glass. After she declined, he continued. 'We also have something else of great value that will help us solve this.'

'What's that?' she said, her voice full of doubt.

'You.' He lent against the counter and drank a mouthful of his juice. 'You were there the whole time and I'm pretty sure you probably saw something that just didn't click at the time, but if you think back, something may jog your memory.'

Eleanor groaned with frustration. 'I've been doing nothing but thinking over all the events again and again. It was a useful distraction while I was in my cell,' she said, fighting back tears at the memory. 'But there's nothing. I couldn't come up with anything that could shed new light. And none of this explains why somebody would murder a dying man.'

'Never mind that, let's do this systematically,' Darryl returned to the table and sat. 'We'll go through them one by one.'

'I'm tired. What's the point of going through it all again?'

'Because I don't particularly want a friend of mine going to prison for a murder he didn't commit, and I'm pretty sure you didn't do it either.'

Chapter Twenty-Four

Eleanor had been over the events of the day so many times her brain ached. And though the last thing she wanted to do was to go over it all again with Darryl, she knew he was right. For both Larry's and her sake. As it seemed like the police weren't even *looking* elsewhere, their only hope was to find the real killer themselves.

'OK,' she conceded. 'Let's go through it again.'

'We also still need to get the spare room sorted,' Darryl added tentatively.

She put her head in her hands from exhaustion.

'Don't worry about the spare room,' he said. 'I'll get that done.'

'No,' Eleanor rallied, standing from the table. 'Let's get it done now. We can think while we work.'

'Just one more thing before we go.' Darryl pointed to the kitchen counter. 'Why do we have a plastic badger in the kitchen?'

Eleanor gave a much needed burst of laughter. She explained how she had put it in her pocket earlier in the day and then placed it on the side to remind her she needed to return it to the shop. Now it sat there, its unblinking stare serving as a constant reminder of the day.

They left the kitchen together and, passing the lounge door on the way, they heard laughter coming from inside. She couldn't stop the wave of guilt that surfaced, but at least Sahara and Toby were enjoying their stay.

Eleanor and Darryl had been renovating the house over the last few months and much of it was still full of unopened boxes. Luckily the spare room was one that had at least been organised into the semblance of a bedroom rather than the store room it had previously been. All that needed to be done was to make the bed, but the effort of getting clean bedsheets, and then making the bed was too much to bear thinking about.

'So, who first?' asked Darryl as they climbed the stairs.

Once again, Eleanor thought about the events of the day.

'There was one thing that *could* be seen as suspicious,' she said tentatively. 'I told DI Hutchins this, too, but she didn't seem interested. It's probably just a coincidence, anyway.'

'Let's hear it. Then we can decide.'

'I stress *could*, mind you.'

They arrived at the linen cupboard, where Eleanor began pulling out the necessary items for making up the bed in the spare room and loading them into Darryl's obliging arms. 'When I first realised there must have been glass in his food,' she went on, 'I rushed back to the tea-room to find that the table had already been cleared. Mr Nelson was in the kitchen, clearing it away. The question is, was he just being his normal efficient self, or was he trying to get rid of the evidence?'

'Good,' Darryl said encouragingly, though not convincingly. 'Anything else?'

'Also, he told me that he would "handle everything",' she stressed the words, adding speech marks in the air, 'after my argument with Larry's dad.'

'Well, that sounds good and suspicious to me,' Darryl said. 'I thought you said you couldn't think of anything.'

'Nothing definite. Either of those could have been innocent.' She closed the cupboard door.

He begrudgingly agreed. 'But I'd say he's a good contender. He has definitely worked at other sites. Have you seen all those pictures he has all over his office wall?'

'I had no choice but to see them,' Eleanor groaned.

Darryl laughed at her expression. They both knew how proud Mr Nelson was of his photographs.

'Who's next, then?' he asked as they walked along the corridor to the spare room and entered.

'Maureen, Mo, or whatever you want to call her. She's a bit of a live wire. Kate had to pretty much hold her back when he ordered his scone.'

'I know she's spritely for her age, but really? She must be at least in her sixties.'

'And that makes her old and decrepit, does it? In fact, she's seventy two and proud of it.' Eleanor yawned. Her tiredness was dragging her down. 'I hope I'm like her when I'm that age.'

Darryl gave her a curious look as they pulled out a sheet over the double bed and fitted the elasticated corners over the mattress.

'OK, I don't mean I want to be *like* her, but to be as fit and able as she is.'

'You want to be fit and able to break in to other people's houses and start fights over scones?' Darryl laughed.

'You're missing the point,' she said exasperatedly, throwing a pillow at him.

Darryl gave an enormous sigh and dropped onto the edge of the bed. 'I hate to admit it, but I can't even rule her out as the one who hit me over the head and escaped over the garden wall.'

'Off the bed,' Eleanor instructed, and Darryl jumped up like a naughty child. 'Is she likely to have had a previous acquaintance with Larry's dad?'

'Nothing so obvious as our dear Mr Nelson, but that's something we'll need to find out.' Darryl helped lay out the quilt over the bed.

'So, that's two. What do you know about Oli?' she went on.

'Not much,' Darryl shrugged. 'No, actually, I know nothing about him. I don't think I've ever even heard him speak. He's always just there. At the dishwasher. And that's it.'

They each took hold of a corner of the quilt and the cover, then began the process of sliding the cover over the quilt.

'He's old enough to have known Larry's dad from before his time in prison,' Eleanor said thoughtfully.

With the quilt cover now on, Eleanor began securing the buttons. She knew this was a part Darryl didn't like. He couldn't seem to get the knack of doing buttons up inside out, as he called it. So, to see him standing, thinking intently instead of helping, didn't surprise her.

'One problem, though,' he said after a moment of silence. 'I seem to remember he had a walking stick.'

As soon as he said it, she remembered the stick. How his knuckles were white from his tight grip on the handle as he'd moved from the kitchen to the tea-room, soon after Mr Chambers had died.

'Whoever hit me over the head at Larry's place was too quick on their feet to need a stick. I would hope I'd have noticed the clonk of a walking stick on the hard floors, too.'

'Are we ruling him out, then?'

'I think we're going to have to, at least for now. He's not a priority, put it that way.'

The buttons done, she threw a pillowcase to Darryl, and they both picked up a pillow each.

'The last one is Kate, but she's too young,' Eleanor smiled at the sight of Darryl struggling to fit his pillow inside its case as if trying to fit a square peg into a round hole.

'Forget motive for the moment. Could she have done it?' Darryl asked.

'She certainly had the time and opportunity, just like the rest of us. In fact, anybody else would have risked being questioned as to what they were doing with the jam, but she wouldn't. She's the one who smashed the glass in the first place. And, of course, she told me he likes lots of jam.'

'Sorry?'

'When I offered to dish up his butter and jam, she told me he likes lots of jam; making sure I put plenty in the ramekin. And she...'

'Yes,' Darryl said curiously.

'Immediately after it happened, we all went out to the patio. She was, or so I thought at the time, comforting Rochelle. But, she was asking her all these questions like if she had seen anything, or if she saw anybody adding anything to the jam. But the poor girl was distraught. She wasn't in any fit state to be answering these kinds of questions.'

'Ok, so she has bad timing?' Darryl asked.

'What if she was asking to find out if Rochelle had seen *her* adding anything to the jam?'

The bed now made, they both sat on either side, and continued their conversation.

'That definitely sounds suspicious. I don't know her very well, she hasn't been there long. She was outside Larry's, too, which I thought was odd.'

'When?'

'She was coming out of Larry's drive when I was taking him home,' he explained.

'You don't think—' Eleanor began, but Darryl interrupted, clearly understanding Eleanor's thoughts.

'He says not, but I wouldn't put it past him. She was also there after I was attacked.'

'Attacked!' Eleanor raised her eyebrows. 'Isn't that a little melodramatic?'

'Not from my position, no. They could have killed me.' He rubbed the back of his head from the memory, flinching at his touch.

Eleanor leaned across the bed and took his hand as a sign of comfort.

'Anyway, she was walking on the other side of the street when I ran out of the house, too,' he went on. 'It didn't occur to me that it could have been her. She was walking towards the house and didn't have the box with her. Larry said, too, that she lives further down that street and it's the quickest route into town if you're walking. So she would have had a legitimate reason for being there.'

'Could it have been her? Could she have seen the box on the stairs on the way out, grabbed it, and then hidden it under a car or in a bush or something and then double-backed so you'd see her without it?' Eleanor asked.

'She could have,' he said. 'I suppose it's not out of the realm of possibility. I didn't think about it at the time. But then why would she go back later?'

'Another question to answer. But if it was her, how would she have recognised the box and know that it contained the necklace?'

'She wouldn't have unless someone had told her about it previously.'

The door to the bedroom creaked open and Toby's face appeared from behind it.

'Hello, Toby. Have you finished your dinner?' Darryl asked.

He nodded, but looked too shy to speak.

Though the pain of losing her own child still seared through her, her maternal instincts took over. She couldn't let him just stand there awkwardly. She rose from the bed and went over to him. Crouching next to him, she spoke gently, 'What can I get for you now?'

'A drink.'

'A drink? And how do you ask nicely for a drink?'

'Can I have a drink, please?' he mumbled.

Eleanor pretended to gasp in surprise. 'That was so nicely asked for. Of course, you can have a drink. Would you like water or milk?'

His eyes widened at the mention of milk.

'I'm guessing you'd like milk, then.'

He nodded shyly.

'Would you like it warm?' she whispered.

He nodded again, but this time, he was unable to hold back his enthusiasm and flapped his arms. Eleanor raised her eyebrows as though expecting something else from him.

'Yes, please,' he said with a broad smile.

Eleanor longed to take hold of him and hug him, but she knew it wouldn't fill the hole in her heart.

'We need to go back downstairs to the kitchen, then.' Her voice cracked as her throat tightened.

Darryl quickly rose from the bed. 'Would you like a piggy-back?' he asked Toby.

Eleanor was grateful for the distraction. With some struggle and a lot of giggling, Toby finally managed to climb onto Darryl's back. They left the room and Eleanor took a moment for a couple of deep breaths. She forced a smile and followed them down the stairs to the kitchen. Darryl galloped round the kitchen, much to Toby's delight, while Eleanor warmed some milk.

'Fanks,' Toby said as Eleanor handed him the glass.

'You're welcome,' she struggled to say.

He took a mouthful of the drink before turning away to leave the room. At the door, he put his glass down on the floor. She watched curiously as he turned back, ran to her, and threw his arms around her. She froze at this outburst of gratitude, hardly able to breathe. Once again, Darryl came to her rescue.

'You'd better get back to your sister,' he said, coaxing Toby away. 'She'll be wondering where you've got to, and it's way past your bedtime.'

Toby went back to his drink, carefully picked it up off the floor, and walked back to the lounge.

'Good boy.' Sahara's voice drifted from the lounge. 'Did you remember to say thank you?'

'I did, I did,' he cried excitedly.

Eleanor couldn't hold back her tears any longer. Darryl held her silently while her guilt, her exhaustion, her grief, and all the emotions she had kept bottled up from during her time in custody finally came flooding out.

Chapter Twenty-Five

The next morning, Darryl received a text from Mr Nelson saying the site would be closed due to the ongoing police investigation, and that neither of them should go in to work.

'Now what?' he said, showing Eleanor the text.

'It's not really surprising, considering the circumstances, I suppose,' she said, 'But I can't live in limbo, worrying that the police are going to knock on our door at any moment and take me back into custody.'

Her pale face frightened him, but he felt useless. 'I don't know where everybody lives, only Larry. He might know, as he's been working there longer than me. I'd like to drop in on him, anyway. See how he's holding up.'

'Of course,' Eleanor agreed.

'Great.' Darryl started to get out of bed.

'But... would it be better to speak to Mr Nelson first? And then, anything we can't find out from him, we can ask Larry.'

'I don't know where he'll be,' Darryl said, exasperatedly. 'I don't—'

'I thought something like this might be the case, and I know I haven't known Mr Nelson for long,' she went on, 'but it wouldn't surprise me if he will still be at the site, ever efficiently running the place. Even if it is closed.'

Darryl gave a knowing smile. 'And as he is top of the suspect list right now...' he conceded. 'We'll go to the site first.'

'I'd also like to ask him why he would tell Sahara to steal from the till,' Eleanor said. 'Even if she did pay it back, it would surely have been much easier, not to mention more ethical, to give her an advance when she needed it.'

'Maybe,' Darryl said thoughtfully, 'it would be a good thing if he wasn't there.'

Eleanor looked at him quizzically.

'If he's not there,' he explained, 'we might be able to get in and search his office.'

'Sounds like a win - win situation.'

'And then on to Larry's?'

Eleanor nodded as the sound of laughter drifted along the corridor from the spare room. Her smile confirmed his own thought. But we need to take Sahara and Toby home first.'

Eleanor spent much of her morning revelling in the task of cooking an extra large breakfast for them all. Although Darryl had the suspicion that she was doing it out of guilt, he wasn't going to turn it down. Besides, he was glad to see her smiling and enjoying their giggles. It was the first time he had known her be able to cope with the company of a child so close to her son's age without breaking down.

The four of them sat together at the kitchen table eating and laughing until their plates were cleared. Sahara and Toby returned to their room to pack up their things, and they all made the journey back to Chartford Brooke. Darryl and Eleanor dropped their guests back home, and then continued on to the Minstrel-wood archaeological site.

'The car park is busy considering the site is closed,' Darryl said. Four vehicles were already in the car park, including

Larry's still left from yesterday, and a police car. Darryl recognised the other two as those of Mr Nelson and Maureen.

'Two out of three's not bad,' Eleanor said as they climbed out of the Land Rover.

Darryl faltered at the catch in her throat and noticed she was playing nervously with the tie that hung loosely from the waistline of her coat.

'Are you OK?' he asked.

Her eyes flicked towards the police car parked next to the gateway that led through to the main reception.

'They're not here for you,' he said reassuringly. 'They would have come to the house first if they were looking for you, wouldn't they?' Her face was white and with his hands cupped around her shoulders, he could feel them trembling.

'Maybe they did,' she whispered. 'Maybe they were at the house while we were dropping Sahara and Toby off at home.'

'Then surely they would have called to find you.'

'To let me know they're after me? Give me the chance to escape?' Something caught her eye behind him and she stiffened. Turning to look, he saw two uniformed officers exiting the main building and walking directly towards them.

'They've come to take me back,' she squeaked.

'They're still investigating,' Darryl said firmly. 'Remember? That's why the site's closed and that's why they're here.'

Eleanor continued staring at the officers. Darryl watched out of the corner of his eye as they came closer down the long pathway that led from the main building to the car park. Only fifty metres away now.

'Eleanor!' Darryl could hear her shortness of breath, feel her shoulders juddering as she attempted to breathe. 'Eleanor, look at me.' He gently squeezed her shoulders. 'Look. At. Me.'

He forced himself into her line of sight as the officers almost reached the gate. She tried to back away as the officers came closer, but he held her firm.

'Breathe. Deep breaths and look at me,' he said gently. He couldn't see where the officers were now, but the sound of the crunch of their shoes on the gravel path was loud enough to know it was close. 'Deep – breaths.' He breathed deeply himself, hoping she would mimic his action.

'Excuse me,' Darryl's heart jolted at the voice behind him.

Maybe she was right, and they were here for her. He turned slowly, keeping Eleanor behind him. Unable to speak, he smiled at them.

'The site's closed,' the taller of the officers said.

Darryl let out the breath he had unconsciously been holding.

'Yes,' he said. 'It's closed,' he repeated awkwardly. 'Thank you – that's fine.'

The car clunked as it unlocked, and the officers climbed in, the doors slamming behind them. Darryl turned back to Eleanor.

'It's closed.' He laughed with relief.

For the next few minutes, they stood together, comforting each other while the police car made its way along the long, meandering road back to town. Her reaction had scared him. It had been reminiscent of her nightmares following the deaths of her husband and son. They were becoming less frequent, but no less intense. This wasn't how he wanted her to live her life.

He could feel her breathing slow and her shoulders collapsed as the panic left her.

'I can't go back,' she whispered.

'And you're not going to. That's why we're here. Are you ready to move on?'

Her shoulders juddered one more time as she took another deep breath and nodded.

The site seemed eerily quiet as they headed towards Mr Nelson's office. The shortest route to the office was through the gift shop exit, but today it was locked. Instead, they entered through the main museum entrance. A car pulled up in the car park as the door closed behind them. Kate climbed out and began the long walk towards the tea-room.

'And there's the third,' Darryl announced, though Eleanor seemed oblivious to his attempt at a light-hearted comment.

Though entering through the museum took a little longer, a shortcut meant they could miss most of the museum. With no visitors or staff in the corridors, the usually busy and productive area was deserted. On reaching Mr Nelson's office, they knocked and found him hurriedly rearranging the piles of uniform in the stationery cupboard. He hastily closed the cupboard door behind him on seeing them.

'Darryl, Eleanor, did you not get my message?' he asked in an unusually higher pitch than normal. 'I'm relieved to see you're out, though, Eleanor. I was quite worried for you when I got the call from the police last night asking about flies, of all things.'

Flies? Darryl thought. Eleanor had only told him the police's so-called evidence was nothing more than a misunderstanding, but he really hoped she would explain about the flies.

'What an ordeal it must have been for you,' Mr Nelson went on.

She nodded, but quickly changed the subject. 'I feel I should apologise for what I said yesterday.'

'No need to worry about that. It was a very stressful situation for all of us, and let's face it,' he said, pulling his shoulders back, standing tall, and jingling the keys in his pocket, 'some people are better able to cope with stress compared to others. I hope they didn't keep you there all night.'

'I picked her up last night, thankfully. Soon after they

released Larry, in fact,' Darryl said, seeing Eleanor was playing anxiously with her coat tie again. Twisting the end into a tight coil round her finger.

Mr Nelson blinked with shock at this news. 'I have to admit, I'm surprised by that. Of course, I never thought it was you, Eleanor, but Larry? I know he's your friend, Darryl, and I'm sorry to say it, but I can see the possibility.'

DI Hutchins's comment of the guilty being the first to cast blame drifted through Darryl's mind. Mr Nelson was just digging himself in deeper.

'Oh, and your tools, Darryl,' Mr Nelson continued, as though suddenly remembering, 'I collected them last night after you left. They are in the staff room. I didn't think you'd want them left out in the rain. Larry's are there, too,' he added as an afterthought.

'Thanks, that's really good of you,' Darryl said, his mind racing as he tried to find the best way to ask about Sahara's borrowing arrangement. Awkwardly, he went on, 'We saw Sahara last night—'

'Well, I guess we'll be off then,' Eleanor suddenly interjected. 'Don't let us disturb you. You are obviously very busy.'

Darryl's heart sank. She clearly didn't feel up to it anymore. As Mr Nelson had shown, there were likely to be questions and remarks regarding her own encounter at the station.

'Was that Mo's car in the car park?' she asked. 'It might be a good opportunity for me to apologise to her, too.'

'Yes,' Mr Nelson drawled. 'Insisted on coming in. Said she'd make use of the time to do a long overdue stock-take of the main storeroom. She's absolutely right, of course. Taking advantage of this quiet time is the best thing we can do, and it's only a relatively small area that's actually cordoned off. It's exactly the same reason I'm here. But beware, she needs careful handling, that one.'

They were about to leave when Mr Nelson asked, 'What did you come in for?'

Darryl and Eleanor stared back at him blankly.

'Surely you didn't come all this way just to apologise to me. You didn't even know I was going to be here,' he continued.

'My bag,' Eleanor said quickly. 'They rushed me off so quickly yesterday I left my bag in my locker. We saw that you were here and thought you might like an update on the situation.'

'Yes, thank you. It's good to see you made it out alive.' He laughed as though Darryl and Eleanor would appreciate the joke. Eleanor threw him a look that made him realise they didn't.

Chapter Twenty-Six

'That was a quick exit,' Darryl said once they had closed the office door behind them.

'Whatever he was doing when we entered, it wasn't something he wanted us to know about,' Eleanor whispered.

'Yeah, I got that impression, too,' he said.

'He hadn't shut the safe door properly either,' Eleanor went on, 'and he doesn't strike me as the kind of man who would leave a safe door open when he's over the other side of the room. I think it may be worth our while searching the office before we question him. Let's see what we can find out from Mo, Maureen, whatever her name is. Kate will probably be with her by now, too. We can talk to them both at the same time.' A sideways glance towards Darryl caught him smiling at her. 'What?'

'Nothing,' he said, but his smile grew. 'What was all that, asking about Mo? Don't you trust that I know her car?'

'Of course I do. But if we're going to be hanging around, waiting for Mr Nelson to leave his office, we need a good excuse for doing so. Otherwise, we risk him asking too many questions if he sees us still here.'

With a new sense of empowerment, Eleanor finally felt in

control. Her reaction to the police car had scared her. But, she was not going to return to the empty vastness of an uncertain future without a fight.

They retraced their route back to the main entrance of the museum; grateful for the necessity of avoiding the tea-room. Darryl hoped to stay clear of any more painful memories for Eleanor. Although, looking at her now, she was confident and determined. Her panic attack in the car park seemed a distant memory. Any doubts he'd had on whether Eleanor was up to investigating, were soon forgotten.

They exited the building and, hidden round the back, away from visitors, they arrived at a pair of large red double doors. They heard the cacophony of loud music from inside long before they reached what was effectively a large tin shack with peeling paint and patches of rust.

As the thumping pop music reverberated behind the closed doors, Eleanor's face twisted into a grimace.

'No, that's her,' Darryl said, correctly guessing Eleanor's unspoken question. 'She loves a lot of different types of music. She's not fussy really, just so long as it's loud.'

He opened the door, and the music blared. Old strip lights flickered here and there, choosing where to shed their light. Although clean and tidy , there was still a feeling of disorder with scribbled signs on ripped paper stuck to the shelving with Sellotape and peeling at the edges. The smell of flour and spices lingered mustily in the air. Ingredients filled half the space, while the other half seemed to store what wouldn't fit in the museum. Being away from public view, the historical ambience that the site strived for was lost in this ramshackle practical space with stainless steel shelving against every wall; the same shelving creating every aisle. It didn't take long before they came across Maureen as they wandered through the huge store. She was bending over, her head lost from sight towards the back of a two foot deep shelf and hidden behind large bags of flour.

'Hi Mo,' Darryl called as they walked towards her.

Mo didn't seem to hear, but considering Darryl hadn't even heard himself over the loud music, it was hardly surprising.

'Mo,' Darryl called again, louder as they got closer.

'What do you want?' she shouted back, not looking up from the shelf.

'We were wondering how you are,' Darryl said.

'It was quite a traumatic day yesterday,' Eleanor added. 'We were concerned.'

Maureen looked up abruptly at the sound of Eleanor's voice and stood, staring directly at her. She pulled a remote control from her electric blue cardigan pocket, pressed a button and the music stopped.

The sudden quiet was a shock and Darryl tried not to let his relief show.

'Traumatic for you, maybe,' she said. 'I didn't kill a man. Still,' she went on with a shrug, 'you did us all a favour, so I don't suppose it counts.' She grinned widely with the look of a mad scientist about her; her grey hair flying wild and unruly. She picked up a clipboard from the shelf, the edges of the papers curled, and carefully examined the contents.

'I didn't kill him—' Eleanor began, but Darryl interrupted.

'Is Kate here?' he said, ignoring the look of annoyance that flew his way from Eleanor.

'No, I'm not expecting her either. Why are you here, anyway? The site's closed.' Mo looked at them suspiciously.

'There are just a couple of bits we needed to pick up,' Darryl said.

'What, like her P45?' she nodded towards Eleanor. 'I don't

suppose murderer is what you want on your CV. But I don't suppose anyone will hold it against you. Other than the police, of course.'

Darryl laughed loudly, over-compensating for Eleanor's irritation. 'You really didn't like the man very much, did you?' Darryl cut her off before she had the chance to retaliate, her face growing redder with each remark.

He knew Mo well enough to know that she was joking. She had reached the age where she didn't care what others thought of her and that, combined with a strange sense of humour that many people took offence to, she came across as outspoken and direct. Darryl had always found it amusing.

'No, I didn't like him' she replied. 'I don't care what people say about me, but I'm not having people insult my scones.' She turned her attention back to the contents of the shelf.

Darryl took hold of Eleanor's hand and squeezed. Thankfully, she took the hint and remained quiet, though he could see she was struggling with holding herself back. 'Did you never want to speak to him about it?'

'Of course I did. Have you ever known me to back down?' She laughed at the thought.

'No, I can't say I have,' he mumbled.

'The thing is -' Maureen suddenly stopped rummaging through the shelf, '- Kate knew that and didn't want me to make a scene. She never told me he was there until after he'd left.'

'You knew yesterday,' Eleanor spat out.

Darryl gave her a quick look of warning, and she continued with a small light-hearted laugh.

'He was so loud with his demands,' she tried to continue jovially, 'everybody heard him come in. Did you plan on talking to him yesterday?'

'I did. But I was in the middle of my next batch of chocolate fudge brownies when he came in and it was inconvenient, but I was going to go out and give him a piece of my mind as soon as I was done. Unfortunately for me, someone got there before me,' she said, giving Eleanor a knowing look. She turned back to the shelves and continued her searching.

Darryl was grateful that Mo had looked away, although he had a suspicion she knew exactly what the look on Eleanor's face was at that point. Silently, he tried to calm her. Though he was worried she seemed to be losing her patience with him, too.

'Did you know him before?' Eleanor asked through gritted teeth and a forced smile.

'Before what? Before you killed him?'

Darryl laughed loudly. 'Before he started visiting here?' he cut in quickly. A silent argument went on between them behind Mo's back while she answered with a non-committal sound that could have been taken either way.

'To have taken such a strong dislike to the man,' Eleanor said, still trying to sound cheery, 'it seems strange for that dislike to be just about scones, almost trivial.'

That was it. Exactly what Darryl had been dreading. He screwed his face as Maureen once again stood and turned till she was looking Eleanor in the eye.

'Trivial?' She turned to Darryl in disbelief before returning to Eleanor. 'Are you calling my scones trivial?'

'No, of course not,' Eleanor laughed wildly. 'I'm not calling the *scones* trivial, just the subject. They're very nice scones. I was just thinking that a dislike of scones is – is – a harsh reason to hate the man so much.'

'Very nice?' Maureen repeated in a whisper. 'Very nice? Award-winning scones, these are. A little better than *very nice*. Or maybe your culinary skills far outstrip mine and my poor efforts are pale in comparison.'

'That's really not what I'm saying—'

'Darryl, please, take me away from this place,' Maureen

looked pleadingly at him, grabbing hold of his arm. 'It's full of philistines.'

Darryl laughed distractedly and warned Eleanor away with a stern look. 'I'll see what I can do, but it won't be today.'

Although her face was screwed with anger, he was glad to see Eleanor walk away, further along the aisle.

'How long have you worked here, anyway? You must be sick of the place.' He needed to get back on the subject of work. Anything other than her scones.

'Too long, that's for sure. I don't like to think about it.'

'You could always retire. Surely then you could get away.' He glanced towards the door, hoping Kate would walk in at any moment and help tame the situation, but there was still no sign of her.

'And what would you be suggesting by that?'

Darryl hopped nervously from one foot to the other. He didn't want to blow it now. 'I just mean it's something for you to look forward to—'

'You're saying I'm old.' She looked at Darryl with the same cold stare she had given Eleanor. She suddenly burst into laughter. 'Of course I'm old. Should have retired years ago, but I've always been too restless. I don't want to stop and put my feet up, heaven forbid. I want to get out there and live.'

'I bet you have lived, too,' Darryl said conspiratorially.

'Things that would shock you. The parties, and what goes on at those parties, if you know what I mean,' she said with a twinkle in her eye. 'Still, I've no time for that now.'

'But what about work?' he persevered, glancing towards the door, and then to Eleanor, who was inspecting something interesting on one of the shelves. Her colour had returned to normal. As far as he could tell under these lights.

'Those parties were my work, if you know what I mean.'

Darryl's cheeks warmed, and Maureen laughed loudly at his embarrassment.

'Surely, this isn't the first archaeological dig you've worked at?' he continued with another glance towards the door.

'I work in the kitchen. I don't know anything about archaeology. I leave all that up to you. You chaps flit in and out of the kitchen; so much tea and coffee it can't be good for you. Never hanging around for even the tiniest bit of conversation. Except Larry, of course. He's always up for a bit of fun. You will help him, won't you?' She pleaded. 'He doesn't deserve this. And as for that odious man being his father, I can hardly believe it. They are so far apart in every respect, it's - it's – just unbelievable.' She stopped abruptly. 'Are you expecting someone?' she said.

Darryl was stunned into silence for a moment.

'No, why would you think that?'

'Because you keep looking toward the door as if you're hoping somebody's going to be coming through it.'

'I thought I saw Kate arriving in the car park and just assumed she would be coming here to see you.'

'She's what?' Mo exclaimed. 'I told her not to come in.' She thought for a moment. 'You asked about Kate earlier,' she whispered with a sideways glance towards Eleanor. 'Now, I don't mind what you get up to. It's not for me to judge. But you might want to be a little more clandestine about it when your lady's around. Take it from me, it's for the best.'

It took Darryl a moment to understand what Mo was insinuating.

'Oh no, no. there's nothing like that going on.' He could see Eleanor's shoulders juddering with silent laughter a few meters away.

'That's down to you. I'm just giving you a few words of

wisdom from my years of experience.' Maureen sighed fondly at the memory of her years of experience.

'I just expected her to walk in, that's all. Nothing more.'

'Well, I have to say I'm not really surprised at the fact she's here.'

'What do you mean?' asked Darryl.

'She's always so keen, wanting to stay behind at the end of the day to help finish up. Coming in early, even though she's not needed. It's not right. A girl of her age should be out there partying.' Maureen gave a jiggle of her hips and shimmied her shoulders. 'Well, she's too late, anyway. I'm leaving soon.'

'Maybe I was mistaken. My eyesight's not the best these days.'

Darryl pulled his hands away as Mo tried to pull him into her dance. Eleanor was now thoroughly enjoying the spectacle.

'Tell me about it,' Maureen groaned.

'It's always so busy in that kitchen. I don't know how you cope with it. Why was Nelson in the kitchen at that time?' He tried his best to make his questions sound nonchalant. 'It seems crazy.'

'He's always in and out whenever it suits him. He likes to know the lunch numbers before the afternoon tea lot come in.'

'Is that it? Can't that wait?'

'You'd think, wouldn't you? But then he starts going on about preparations for the half-term holiday and walks out the kitchen, leaving me staring at the rota - what the hell?' Mo was suddenly distracted by Eleanor inspecting some large bags on one of the lower shelves. 'What do you think you're doing? Get away from there?'

Eleanor jumped back, holding her hands in the air as though Mo had held a gun to her. 'Just looking.'

'Oh really? What is all this? Why are you asking me all these questions?'

'We're trying to help Larry, just like you asked,' Darryl floundered.

Mo frowned at them both suspiciously. 'Do you think I'm stupid? You think it was me.'

'No, no,' Darryl and Eleanor stumbled over each other.

Clearly not impressed, Mo pulled the remote out from her pocket again and, pointing it directly into Eleanor's face, began the music again. Ignoring their protests, she abruptly shifted the topic, signalling the end of their conversation. 'My granddaughter gave me this,' she shouted over the music. 'Her favourite band. She thought I might like it, too. She was right, they're pretty good. And besides, on this tin roof, it drowns out the noise of the rain.'

'It's stopped,' Eleanor mumbled sarcastically.

Mo stared at her coldly. She pressed another button on the remote. The volume turned up a notch.

'I'm sorry I can't hear you,' she shouted. 'So if you don't mind, it's time for me to shimmy while I count.' She turned abruptly back to the shelving.

As they left the store room Darryl could sense Eleanor's coldness.

'Great, now we're not going to be able to get anymore from her,' she mumbled.

'Did you hear much of what she said?' Darryl asked tentatively.

'It was hard not to. She's not exactly a quiet lady, is she? Why did you tell her we're helping Larry? It's obvious then that we were questioning her.'

'She asked me to help him. I didn't expect her to get so touchy—'

'Are you trying to protect me?' Eleanor cut in. Coming to an abrupt halt, she turned to confront him.

'What do you mean?'

'I know I had a moment of ... panic in the car park. But I'm OK. I don't need you to protect me.'

'It's just that you wind her up,' Darryl said.

'I wind *her* up?'

'You know what I mean. Nelson said it himself. She needs careful handling and—'

'And I'm like a bull in a china shop.'

'That's not what I'm saying at all. I didn't want her upsetting you just as much as you upsetting... I mean... you might just say the wrong thing and then...'

'What, like you didn't? And we didn't find out anything of any help.' She gave a cold stare and turned on her heel, striding back towards the museum entrance.

'We can presume,' Darryl went on tentatively, trying to keep up with her long forceful strides, 'she didn't work at any other archaeological sites, but who knows who she met at those parties.'

'And if Mr Chambers senior was anything like Mr Chambers junior, he could well have been at those parties, and very much enjoying himself.' Eleanor snapped. 'We can't rule her out yet.'

A thought made her slow her pace. 'It was interesting what she said about Kate, though.'

'You mean her eagerness for being here?' Darryl nodded. 'And where is she now if it's not to help Mo in the stockroom?'

'What if she's the thief?'

'Of the box?' Darryl asked, confused.

'No, here at the site.'

'I thought that was just a misunderstanding with Sahara.'

'Not necessarily. Would head office even notice if the odd ten pounds or so goes missing and then gets replaced? What if Kate is stealing, but Sahara was just conveniently caught?'

'It's certainly a possibility.' Darryl took advantage of the quiet and asked, 'Am I forgiven?'

'No,' she answered with a smile in her voice. 'I'll forgive you once we've caught the killer.'

'I don't suppose you found anything of interest on the shelves?'

'A few bags of scone mix,' Eleanor laughed.

Chapter Twenty-Seven

As Eleanor and Darryl turned the corner of the main building, the rhythmic thumping of the music's bass beat still resonated from the storeroom. Darryl's hand suddenly grabbed hold of Eleanor's arm, bringing her to an abrupt halt. They had narrowly avoided Mr Nelson leaving the building and heading towards the reception block.

'Now's our chance,' she said excitedly.

They entered the building, and it was Eleanor's turn to stop Darryl in his tracks. Hurried footsteps echoed down the empty museum corridor. They followed quietly and arrived at the office just in time to see Kate entering.

'Are you looking for Mr Nelson?' Eleanor asked in a rush, not wanting to miss the opportunity to search the office. However, her suspicions of Kate intensified instantly.

Kate jumped, shocked at hearing her voice. 'You gave me a fright. I didn't realise anyone else was here.'

'We've just seen him going towards the reception block,' Eleanor continued.

A look of recognition swept over Kate's face. 'Oh – OK – I'll make my way there, then,' she said harshly. 'Why – what are you here for? Come to make more trouble?'

'I'm sorry about yesterday,' Eleanor said, and Kate reluctantly met her eyes.

'I'm glad to see they let you go,' she said coldly.

As Eleanor opened her mouth to apologise further, Kate interrupted her.

'Well, I'd better go find Mr Nelson,' she said sharply and hurried down the corridor, away from them.

Eleanor and Darryl continued nonchalantly down the corridor, past Mr Nelson's office.

'If Kate had wanted to see Mr Nelson,' Eleanor whispered, 'she'd have had plenty of time. It's odd she turns up now when he's popped out. And where's she been all this time?'

'I'm sorry to say it, but it would support your theory of her stealing from the company,' Darryl replied.

Once they were certain Kate was out of sight, they quickly double-backed to the office.

'Did I hear Mo say that they don't get to talk to you archaeologists much? That also strengthens my suspicion that she's lying about where she heard that phrase from.'

'I think you may be reading too much into that. I'm not even certain it is specifically an archaeological phrase. You just heard it first said by an archaeologist,' he said as they reached the office door.

'It just seems odd to lie about something like that. If she does have an archaeological background, it could connect her to Larry's dad.'

Even though she had just seen Mr Nelson walking away from the office, Eleanor's nerves still tingled as Darryl slowly and quietly opened the door. Watching carefully that Kate hadn't double-backed, she closed the door softly behind them. She left

Darryl to scan over the photographs on the wall while she went to the stationery cupboard and started looking through the spare items of uniform where they had seen Mr Nelson rummaging earlier. Although, it didn't take long for her to conclude that there was nothing there except what should be, she was still surprised at the dishevelled state he had left it in. Did they interrupt him trying to hide something, or was he moving something already hidden? She turned her attention back to the room. Darryl was still looking closely at the photographs on the wall opposite her. She was now standing exactly where she had stood yesterday when Mr Nelson had given her the fresh shirt. Something was different, but she couldn't put her finger on it.

'There are only three here from before or around the time Larry's dad was arrested,' Darryl said, seeing that Eleanor was now looking at the wall. 'These three here. All the others are relatively new.'

The three pictures in question consisted of groups of men and women, most in shorts, t-shirts and wide-brimmed hats to keep the sun off while they worked. They stood in the ruins of a building in two of the photos, and the one directly in front of her looked more like an empty field with a squared off muddy patch next to them. Beneath each photograph was a small plaque stating the place and the year.

'This one's changed,' she said, pointing directly ahead of her.

Darryl moved to the photograph she was pointing at.

'Since yesterday? The plaque says it's Beesford from thirty years ago, but-' he took a closer look at the image, '-this photograph is of Nanbridge.'

'It's a field. How can you tell that?'

'I recognise the church tower.'

Eleanor came closer to the photograph and, in the distance, there was a church tower peering out above a hedgerow.

'And if it is Nanbridge, that site was only discovered five or six years ago,' Darryl continued. 'Can you remember the picture that was there?'

She tried to envisage the scene as she saw it yesterday. She remembered her boredom when Mr Nelson had shown her the photographs at her initial interview. Though she had smiled with politeness, it was through a stifled yawn. Now, she wished she had listened closer to his ramblings of where these places were, and the significance of each.

'No, I can't. But I know it wasn't this one,' she said finally.

She looked wildly around her until she saw a paper shredder tucked behind the desk in the corner of the room. She ran to it and emptied the contents onto the table.

'Surely he wouldn't be that stupid,' Darryl said.

The expected strips of letter paper were abundant, but luckily there were also strips from a photograph.

'Clearly, he is that stupid,' he went on.

'I suppose we did interrupt him, but...' she pulled a face, fully aware that this foolishness couldn't be justified.

'You keep searching and I'll sort out this photograph.' Darryl began rummaging through the strips, pulling out the photograph and replacing the paper strips back in the shredder compartment, out of the way.

Eleanor turned her attention to the desk. Not a thing was out of place. No random bits of paper strewn across it, or post-it notes with odd jottings and reminders. The top drawer contained the usual stationery items you'd expect; pens, pencils, paperclips, etc., all neatly arranged in their own sectioned compartments. The second drawer contained one cardboard file marked *For My Attention*. She flicked through the papers inside. A purchase order form from Maureen for kitchen ingredients, a couple of holiday request forms, and the papers for Sahara's dismissal. A fresh wave of guilt swept over her and she hastily pushed the pages back in the folder, as though pushing away the memory of what she had one. She returned the folder to the drawer and tried the bottom one. It was locked. She tried the filing cabinet. Again, locked. The safe. Locked.

'He's excessively tidy,' she said. 'There's not much here to look at and most of it's locked.'

'Mmm?' Darryl was focusing intently on the strips in front of him and clearly not listening to her.

'Do you have something there?' she asked.

Most of the shredded bits of paperwork were back in the shredder, but there were a few that Darryl had fitted together and were still on the desk. He was currently trying to take a photograph on his phone of two specific strips, while trying to keep them together and flat on the desk.

'Come and look at this,' he said.

He expanded the image on his phone and Eleanor was about to walk out from behind the desk when the door swung open. They both stared in silence as Mr Nelson walked in with a large, seemingly empty holdall.

'What are you doing here?' he said. His face immediately turning red with fury.

'We were waiting for you,' Eleanor said, trying to sound as casual as possible.

'Behind my desk? What do you think you're playing at? Get out from behind there. You're already under suspicion with the police. Come on, get out from behind my desk. Maybe they'd like to know about you snooping around in my office, too. Get out, now.'

'That might interest them,' Darryl said, 'but I bet they'd be more interested in this photograph.' He moved to one side, revealing five strips laid out, forming one half of the original photograph still lying out on the desk. 'That's you at the front of the group, isn't it?'

Mr Nelson quickly glanced down at the top of his desk. The neatly arranged strips showed a group of archaeologists, just like many of the others. His eyes flicked between Eleanor, Darryl, and his desk.

'And I may be wrong, but isn't that Larry's dad?' Darryl continued.

Mr Nelson was silent.

'Sorry, can't you see? This one right here.' Darryl pointed to a man three from the left in the back row. 'I've expanded it on my phone, if that's any help. The resemblance to his son is incredible, don't you think? Especially Larry from a few years ago when I first met him. He's getting a bit of a paunch nowadays.'

The only sound from Mr Nelson was the rattling of his heavy breathing as panic set in.

'And the name on the plaque where you removed this photograph from,' Darryl continued in a casual tone, 'I know I've heard that name before. Beesford, Beesford, where do I know that name from?' he mused. 'Got it.' He clicked his fingers in an ostentatious manner. 'That was one of the names that was mentioned in a newspaper article from when his dad was arrested. They gave a few of the sites he had worked at. Sites that may have had artefacts go missing.'

'That proves nothing,' Mr Nelson said defiantly.

'That in itself doesn't, but you told the police you didn't know him. And, clearly, from this picture, you did.'

'Just because we worked on the same site for maybe a couple of weeks doesn't mean we were close friends. I didn't even realise he was in this photograph.'

Eleanor joined Darryl with a disbelieving look. 'Why would you have tried to destroy it, then?' Eleanor asked.

'What I mean is, I didn't realise until – until I saw it when we came for a clean shirt, you remember, Eleanor,' he stammered.

'Yes, I remember. I also remember you saying you were going to wait at the entrance gates for the police to arrive, and yet you'd only just left after I had changed and was ready to return to the patio with the others. What were you doing all that time?'

Mr Nelson stammered, making no coherent sounds.

'Removing one photo to replace it with another?' Eleanor suggested. 'Hoping the police wouldn't see a connection between you and Mr Chambers?'

Mr Nelson's red face didn't know which way to turn.

'Mr Chambers,' she repeated. 'He threatened you, didn't he?'

Mr Nelson faltered, taking a step backwards towards the door. Both Eleanor and Darryl automatically stepped forward and rounded on him.

'After my argument with him,' she clarified, 'he said something about *telling the truth*,' she waved her hand in the air, not remembering the exact wording, 'and asked you if that's what you'd like. I assumed he was threatening to give a bad review of the site, but that wasn't it. It was more personal than that, wasn't it? He was actually threatening you.'

'Well, OK, yes, I knew him, but it was from a long time ago. But I've no idea what you're going on about with threats and reviews and what-have-you.' He gave a half-hearted laugh, but Eleanor could see right through it. With the holdall in one hand, he started to play nervously with the keys and coins in his trouser pocket.

'So, what truth could that be?' she continued, trying to ignore the jingle jangle she found so irritating. 'We all assumed that his "truth" was that he was going to own up about having the missing artefact. He couldn't have done it before without getting Larry into trouble for hiding it, but that only concerns Larry. So, what truth would affect you? It was you,' she said with a gasp. 'You were what? Accomplices?'

'Now Eleanor, I think you're taking things a bit far.' Mr Nelson's burning face had turned white.

'I think she's raised some very valid points,' Darryl said. 'And then there's this.' He held up a few strips of the paper that he had laid on the table. 'I recognised the logo immediately.'

'I – I—' Mr Nelson suddenly threw the large holdall at them and dived towards the door.

Chapter Twenty-Eight

The large, empty holdall did no damage as it collided with Eleanor and Darryl, other than leaving them momentarily stunned. But it slowed them enough for Mr Nelson to slip through the door and close it behind him, his keys already in his hand. Just as Darryl gripped the handle, they heard the distinct click of the lock sliding into place. Eleanor scrambled to find her phone in her bag, cursing the lack of police when she needed them while Darryl yanked at the door. It was soon clear it wasn't going to move.

Eleanor remembered seeing a letter opener in the top drawer of Mr Nelson's desk.

'Here,' she called as she tossed the replica roman sword across the room.

'Thanks,' Darryl said with a frown and inserted it into the gap between the door and the frame.

There was a snap, and Darryl jolted.

That didn't work then, she thought as she turned away, trying to focus on the voice from the emergency services that crackled through her phone. She began explaining their situation to the lady on the other end of the phone, who was calmly trying to stop Eleanor from shouting at her. Eleanor continued trying to make herself heard over Darryl's banging and swearing while he grabbed objects from the cupboard to use as leverage until, eventually, there was a loud crack as the door frame split and the door popped open. Darryl ran. The sound of his footsteps echoed through the museum corridor. Eleanor struggled to keep up, her voice juddering as she ran, shouting down the phone to get a message to DI Hutchins that they were chasing the real killer.

'We need the police now,' she shouted in desperation.

Just outside the main door, she pulled up short. She had assumed Mr Nelson would have headed directly to the car park, but it wasn't hard to work out why there was no sign of him. A police car was pulling up into the car park, with another car behind it.

'Don't worry, you're here,' Eleanor said, down the phone and hung up.

She quickly scanned the horizon and saw the two men slipping on the wet grass as they ran up the slope leading to open fields. Waving her arms frantically in the air, she desperately tried to get the attention of the officers who had just arrived, anxious to pursue the two men. DI Hutchins climbed out of the second car and, after a brief discussion that looked like orders being shouted at them, the two officers set off in her direction at a run. Now she was certain they had seen her, she joined in the chase. She was glad to see Darryl had rapidly closed in and she caught sight of them just in time to see Darryl leap into the air and land on Mr Nelson. They both fell to the ground, disappearing from view on the other side of the ridge, hidden at the top of the slope.

Eleanor raced behind and finally reached the top to see them rolling around on the ground.

'Stop,' Mr Nelson screamed. 'I surrender.'

Darryl had Nelson by the shirt collar, sitting astride him. His fist pulled back ready to strike.

'Why? Why did you do it?' he growled.

'We all like the nicer things in life. Don't try to convince me that you believe otherwise.'

'But murder?'

Mr Nelson's screwed up angry face dropped in panic. 'No, no, I didn't kill anyone.'

Darryl gave a disbelieving laugh. 'You've already admitted to us you knew him. What happened? Double-cross you, did he? Did your accomplice turn on you? Wouldn't tell you where the most precious item of your stolen hoard was hidden?'

'No, that's not it,' Eleanor intervened as she joined them, breathless from the run. 'That wouldn't explain why he killed him.'

'I didn't,' he implored. 'I didn't kill—'

'But it does explain the setting up of Sahara.'

Both Darryl and Mr Nelson turned to look at her. Darryl with a look of confusion, Mr Nelson's of shock.

'It worked before, so why wouldn't it work again? You planted those artefacts on Mr Chambers—'

'I—'

'You framed him—'

'I—'

'Just like you did with Sahara. You conveniently looked the other way, knowing that one day you'd be able to use her as a scapegoat, because it's been you stealing, hasn't it?'

'I—'

'Not just the odd ten pounds as and when she needed to feed her brother, but I bet if we spoke to head office we would find that it's been a lot more than that. But that wouldn't matter. Once she's been found guilty of any kind of stealing, nobody's going to believe her if she says it was only a small amount that she always paid back.'

'I was right, too. Nobody did believe her.' Mr Nelson spat. Proud of his deception.

'We did.' Darryl pulled him closer and growled at him, two inches away from his face. He pulled the man to his feet. 'Once she had the chance to explain, we believed her. No wonder you sacked her so fast. And to think, she was worried about getting you into trouble.'

Eleanor glanced behind her. The two police officers running up the track towards them weren't far now.

'He was going to tell the police that it was you who framed him,' she said hurriedly. 'And you'd do anything to avoid going to prison, even murder.'

'No. No, I wouldn't. It wasn't me. He wasn't my accomplice,' Mr Nelson spat. 'He had worked out what I was doing and hid the necklace, realising that I was about to steal it. He was going to try to catch me in the act and turn me in. Unfortunately for him, I knew what he was up to and instead, I took other artefacts from the hoard and framed him. I got him sent to prison before he had the chance to do the same to me.'

Eleanor could see in Darryl's face that he was thinking the same as her. This insufferable man spoke proudly of what he had done. That he had destroyed the relationship between father and son. Destroyed a marriage. Destroyed the life of a man willing to sacrifice everything to stop the theft of a precious artefact.

'He told me he still had the necklace and was going to hand it in, explaining everything to the police,' he went on. 'I knew it would only be a matter of time before Larry returned it to him, but I had intended to be long gone by then and I wanted to make sure I found it first. I searched Larry's bag after you left yesterday and it wasn't there.'

'That's why you collected our tools?' Darryl intervened. A look of realisation appeared on his face. 'Did you search Larry's house yesterday? Was it you that hit me over the head?' Darryl raised his fist again.

'You weren't supposed to be there, I'm sorry,' Mr Nelson blustered. 'But I didn't kill Albert. You have to believe me. I didn't kill him.' His voice becoming more and more panicky as the two officers came running up the slope behind them.

They took over from Darryl and began the formal arrest procedures.

'I couldn't have done it. I was with Maureen the whole time I was in the kitchen. Ask Mo. I didn't—'

'I am arresting you on suspicion of murder...'

The rest was lost under the noise of Mr Nelson's shouts and screams of protest. They struggled to hold Mr Nelson as he fought to get away. Eleanor and Darryl stood and watched the continuous struggle as they made the long walk back towards the car park, passing DI Hutchins on their way as she sauntered up the hill. Happy to let the younger officers do the hard work.

'You're quite the little investigators, aren't you?' she said. 'I've been looking into your background and this isn't the first time you've caught a killer.'

'Maybe you should have been looking into his background,' Eleanor mumbled.

'We have been, Mrs Garrett. In fact, we were already on our way here to find Mr Nelson when your call came through.' Looking pleased with herself, DI Hutchins turned and began her amble towards the car park.

Pushing the DI's remark from her mind, Eleanor turned her attention to Darryl. 'Are you OK? You're bleeding.' She pulled a tissue from her coat pocket and wiped the blood that was trickling down his face.

He looked down at himself; grazes on his knuckles, mud and grass stains on his clothes.

'I think I'm going to need a bit more than a tissue.'

He pulled her close and hugged her, but she fought to get away from his muddy body. Laughing as she pushed herself away, relief consumed her.

'We got him,' Eleanor said as she fought back the tears that followed the laughter so readily.

'We got him,' he repeated. 'It's OK. You're not going back to prison. I'm getting good at this catching game,' he continued, clearly trying to lighten the mood.

'Well,' Eleanor said with a twist of sarcasm, 'you didn't need to do much. Being an office-type, he wasn't really suited for out-running anyone. If I hadn't been making the call to the police, I'm sure even I could have—'

Darryl looked at her disbelievingly. 'An office-type,' he repeated, cutting her off.

'I am very impressed by your restraint, though. I would have hit him.'

Darryl stood tall, projecting an air of exaggerated authority as he pushed his shoulders back confidently.

'That comes with experience. I wouldn't expect you to understand the finer points of diplomacy within a combat situation.'

Both laughing, he pulled her in again.

'By the way, what was on those strips of shredded paper?' Eleanor asked.

'I've been asking for ages about more funding to increase the excavation out by the mosaic. He's always said he hasn't heard yet.'

'But he had,' Eleanor guessed.

'He had. And we got it, too. Except it looks like he must

have fiddled it somehow to go into his personal bank account rather than the site's.'

They continued to watch the struggling Mr Nelson as he was taken closer to the police car. Eleanor became more relaxed with every step.

'He's not very good at covering his tracks, is he? How did he manage to get away with it for so long?' she asked.

'By blaming other people, apparently. I wish I'd asked him where he put Larry's box. I reckon there's still a chance Larry can get out of this with his and his dad's reputation still intact.'

'I suppose it was a bit difficult to bring up the topic of hidden stolen property while the police were around. But...' Eleanor's words trailed off thoughtfully.

'But?' Darryl repeated.

'He seemed pretty keen for me to get away from his desk. Maybe...'

'Do you really think he would have brought it here?'

'The bottom drawer of his desk was locked, or there's the safe. The police may have already searched his office yesterday, making him think it was safe. Then why not here, especially if he thought they were too interested in Larry or me? And that's probably why he'd got the holdall. Ready to pack up everything and disappear, just as he said he'd planned to do.'

'Well, they might look again now, knowing he's the killer.'

'We'd better be quick, then,' Eleanor said cheekily and they set off towards the office.

Mr Nelson and the officers had almost reached the car park when they saw Larry climbing out from a taxi. They stopped to watch the events unfold as the realisation of what was going on dawned on him. Even from such a distance, they could almost see the cogs turning in his brain.

'I think we'd better get down there,' Darryl said, panic in his voice. They both set off, sprinting towards them.

Chapter Twenty-Nine

Larry's voice travelled in the wind. 'You?... Why?' Fury written across his face.

Darryl sped up, pulling ahead of Eleanor. His fears became a reality when Larry flew at Mr Nelson. The officers on either side were now attempting to fend off Larry while still trying to hold on to a panicked Mr Nelson. DI Hutchins stood back, shouting at Larry to stop or risk being arrested for breach of the peace. But he didn't stop. Not until Darryl arrived and forced him to. He grabbed Larry's arms and pulled him backwards, away from his target.

'He killed my dad.' Larry's voice was low and venomous.

'I know, but this won't help,' Darryl cried in desperation. 'It will only help to get you arrested, too. Let the police deal with it now.'

Larry was strong, leaving Darryl unsure of how much longer he could carry on.

In frustration, Larry let out a piercing scream while desperately trying to break free from his friend's hold.

'No, no, I didn't,' Mr Nelson pleaded.

'Nice act,' Larry spat at him, 'but it's not going to save you.'

'Please, I didn't kill him. I admit to everything else, but I didn't kill him,' Mr Nelson continued as the two officers attempted to get him into their car.

Relieved that Larry had finally stopped struggling, Darryl was now comforting Larry more than restraining him. He had buried his face into Darryl's shoulder, his sobs muffled. With Eleanor's arrival, Larry pulled himself away and attempted to compose himself, sniffing and wiping his face on his sleeve.

'What are you doing here?' Darryl asked. 'I'd thought this would be the last place you'd want to be.'

'I – I needed to get my car. No,' he shook his head. 'It was more than that. I felt I had to come,' he said through his sniffs. Eleanor passed him one of the tissues from her pocket as he continued. 'This was, after all, the last place my dad was alive. The last place I saw him. And,' he hesitated as he choked back his tears, 'you're going to think me such a hypocrite, and I hate to admit it, but you were right. Now he's gone, I feel like I should have made more of an effort. He tried so many times for a reconciliation but I was too stubborn. I—' His words broke off, unable to speak.

'It's OK.' Darryl put his arm around his friend's shoulders. He was happy to give what little comfort he could.

'What about you?' Larry shrugged, trying to give the impression that everything was OK. 'What have you come back for? Don't tell me you've been doing your own little investigation again.'

'We were,' Darryl said with exaggerated pride, 'and, as you can see, very successfully, too. Even if I say so myself. He won't admit to killing your dad, but that will come, I'm sure.' Darryl hesitated, knowing how hard Larry would take the next piece of news. 'He admitted to framing him, though.'

'What? You mean Dad was innocent this whole time?'

Darryl nodded. 'He did take the necklace, but it would seem

he took it to keep it safe, knowing that Nelson was about to steal it.'

Larry shook his head, clearly unable to take in what he was being told.

'I don't believe it.' His eyes were frantically searching the space around him, as though he would find the answer to an unknown question. Seeing Eleanor, he continued, 'I'm so sorry you've been caught up in all this.'

'You've no need to apologise to me,' Eleanor said. 'I'm just glad we got the actual killer.'

'I'd like to say thanks, though, for trying to save him. Let's face it, not many people would have tried.' He stood quietly for a moment. His focus wandering into the distance. 'I can't believe he's gone.'

They stood in reverie for a moment before Larry spoke again. 'Was it Nelson who broke into my house, too?'

'Yeah, I should have given him an extra punch for that,' Darryl said, rubbing the back of his head where the lump had only slightly lessened.

'Why?' Larry whispered before suddenly becoming angry and his outburst returned. 'Why did he do it? Just for a piece of junk?'

'Well, it was hardly junk,' Darryl said.

'Compared to a man's life? My father's life?'

Darryl thought it best not to say anymore, especially with the look he got from Eleanor. Maybe now wasn't the best time to argue with Larry's thoughts being so irrational.

'A piece of junk that he didn't even know where it was. And where is it now? What has he done with it?' His face burned red with anger.

'We were about to check his office,' Eleanor intervened meekly. 'He was certainly doing something suspicious in there earlier.'

'Do you mind if come along? If I can do anything to help put this man away for a very long time, I'll be more than happy to try.'

'Of course,' they said together. With no hesitation, both of them were more than willing to give Larry the opportunity to do something positive that would strengthen the case against his father's killer.

The walk back to the office was mostly in silence. Out of respect, or perhaps due to the weight of the day's events, Eleanor didn't know. But still, she couldn't stop thinking about Mr Nelson's pleas. He had sounded sincere. Or was it just another act? But it came as no surprise to her when they heard noises coming from inside the office as they approached. The door was slightly ajar, with large splinters from the fractured door frame jutting into the room. Swinging the door open wide, Eleanor wasn't surprised to see Kate was searching through the cardboard file from the second drawer, just as she had done earlier. Kate looked up suddenly at the sound of the door opening and dropped the file quickly onto the desk, causing the shredded strips of photograph and letter to waft across the desk. Her face went white as the three of them stood there looking at her.

'Still looking for Mr Nelson?' Eleanor asked curiously, her mind was whirring again. After all, Mr Nelson was adamant that he didn't kill Mr Chambers.

'I—'

'He's gone,' Larry told her. 'The police have already taken him away.'

'The police—' Kate sounded surprised. She looked directly at Larry. 'Was it him? Did he murder—' she broke off suddenly. 'Larry, I'm so sorry. I never thought he would be capable of doing something like that—'

'Why are you here?' Eleanor interrupted with a scowl.

'It's OK, Eleanor,' said Darryl with an embarrassed laugh. 'You can stop suspecting everyone now.'

'What?' Kate exclaimed. 'You thought it was me?'

'I believed it could have been anyone.' Eleanor wasn't so sure she could let her suspicions go so easily. There were still some unanswered questions for Kate. Behaviours that needed explaining. Eleanor's doubts were seeping in while she pushed the thoughts of Darryl's suspected paranoia aside.

'Why were you hounding Rochelle with questions so soon after the death?' Eleanor was aware of the two men turning to her with curious looks at her harsh tone.

Kate was taken aback by the question, too. 'I —'

'Were you worried that she had seen you doing something you shouldn't have been?'

'Eleanor, I think—' Larry said gently, but Eleanor cut him off and continued her interrogation.

'It was clear that she was too traumatised by what she had just seen happen to be asking those kinds of questions.'

'I was trying to help,' Kate snapped back. 'I thought she might find it easier to speak to a friend than to a stranger, especially when that stranger is a police officer.'

Now it was Eleanor's turn to be taken aback. This was not an option she had thought of and she could understand Kate's reasoning.

'I - I'm sorry,' Eleanor stammered. Though still trying to save face, she continued, though less harshly. 'So, what are you doing here, searching through Mr Nelson's desk?'

'You've got me there. I can't deny that one. I...' Kate hesitated, glancing at Larry and clearly not wanting to say any more.

'You may as well come clean,' Larry told Kate. 'He's confessed to everything.'

'I knew it,' she gasped and dropped into Mr Nelson's chair.

'What do you mean?' said Eleanor, her head flicking back and forth between Kate and Larry in frustration.

'You were right. I'm not who I said I was,' said Kate. 'My fiancé used to work here. Louis.'

'Wasn't that who worked with—' Darryl turned to ask Larry.

Larry nodded. 'We were working together before Darryl arrived,' he clarified for Eleanor. 'That's who Darryl replaced.'

'Nelson fired him,' Kate spat. 'One of the artefacts he had excavated went missing before he had a chance to record it.'

'I've been trying to help Kate find out who it was,' Larry confessed, his tone sheepish. 'I'm sorry I didn't tell you. I swore I wouldn't tell anyone. It wasn't difficult to keep Kate's identity a secret because I was the only person who knew her.'

'There were a few people we've been trying to keep an eye on,' said Kate.

'To begin with, we thought it was Isla, the cleaner,' Larry said. 'I had seen her hanging around at the time. But it turned out not to be her.'

'It wasn't Harriet either.' Kate laughed gently at his mistake.

'That's right, Harriet. Sorry, my brain's not working quite right at the moment.' He self-consciously bowed his head and stared at the floor.

'Of course.' Kate got up from the chair and came round to Larry. She threw her arms around him. 'You don't deserve this.'

'Who is Harriet?' Eleanor asked Darryl quietly.

'That's who you replaced in the gift shop.'

'Sahara told me she had left after being accused of stealing by one of the archaeologists.'

Kate nodded. 'That was Louis. He's never been the most tactful of people. When he confronted her, she denied it, and strongly. When Louis spoke to Nelson about it, he was accused of stealing it himself. He was told to leave immediately or have charges brought against him.'

'Just like he did with Sahara,' Eleanor mumbled shamefully.

Kate looked at her curiously and Eleanor responded with a brief, 'Remember in the gift shop when he told her to leave now and there will be no further action? And now we've heard the full explanation, she didn't deserve that.'

Kate nodded. 'That poor girl. I always gave her a lift, being so out of the way here. We've often talked and, no, you're right, she didn't deserve that.'

Eleanor's simmering guilt forced her on, bringing the subject back to Kate. 'Is that why you got the job here, to find out what happened?'

'Finding out who was the actual thief was the only way Louis could move forward,' she nodded. 'He hated the thought that he was considered a thief. I had my suspicions of Nelson and we've been looking back at his past jobs with help from some of Louis's old archaeologist friends. We found out that the odd item would go missing, but nothing could ever be proved. After a while, he would then move on to another job.'

'What were you hoping to find here?' Eleanor asked.

'I don't know, anything that may help me prove that he is a thief. But it looks like that pales into insignificance compared to murder,' she said sympathetically towards Larry.

'At least the police have got him now,' Larry said, avoiding everyone's eyes.

Eleanor noticed the return of the manly shrug she had seen from him earlier. Trying to be strong, especially in company.

'Then I'm done.' Kate broke the awkward silence. She suddenly beamed at the implication of what she had been told. 'It means Louis doesn't have to live under this cloud anymore.' She gave Larry another big hug. 'Thanks for everything, Larry. If you ever need us, you know where we are. Call any time. But, excuse me. I need to give Louis the news.'

And with that, she ran out the door along with Eleanor's

theories. Eleanor was deflated so suddenly she could hardly breathe. *Paranoia, then,* she thought.

Remembering why they were there, and to hide her face that had reddened from shame, she went round to the other side of the desk. The bottom drawer was still locked. While Darryl showed Larry the strips of photograph of his father still lying on the desk, she searched the top drawer for something to help break it open. Different sections kept each item organised, but there was nothing that could be used to prise the drawer open. The scissors were too big, the stapler too bulky.

'There's nothing here that's going to help open this drawer,' she said.

'He has a miniature sword letter opener somewhere,' Larry said. 'Won't that do it?'

'It's broken,' Darryl and Eleanor said simultaneously. She tried to avoid his disapproving stare as he walked around the desk to join her in her search.

'Here,' Larry said, reaching for the Leatherman in his back pocket and passing it to Darryl. 'Try this. Finally, I'm able to help with something.'

Darryl opened the blade and slid it into the gap at the top of the locked drawer. Eleanor was left staring at the cardboard file which Kate had left lying on the desk. Hesitantly, she picked it up and removed two sheets of paper from it. Folded them into quarters and slipped them into her pocket. On doing so, she found the plastic badger that she had placed there before leaving home. With everything that had happened that morning, she'd forgotten to return it. *Soon,* she thought to herself.

'What are you up to?' Darryl asked as he finally got the drawer open.

'Nothing,' she said with forced nonchalance.

To change the subject, she pushed in front of Darryl, forcing him round to the end of the desk. She pulled open the drawer and saw a beautiful red wood box. Mahogany, she guessed, though she was no expert. All three were silent as she reached in and lifted it out of the drawer. It was highly polished, obviously taken care of. It didn't look like something that had been hidden under floor boards for years, as Darryl had said it was. But then Larry had hidden the letter and newspaper page under there too, so he must have opened it sometimes, she surmised. As she lifted it out of the drawer, she looked up at the expectant faces of the two men, both standing in awe of what was in front of them. Darryl put the knife down on the desk, keen to take the box from her, but she didn't pass it to him. Something didn't seem right. She remembered the picture of the large golden necklace. The jewels encrusted into it. It had looked heavy, and Darryl had confirmed that it would have been. And yet, the box wasn't. Something was inside. Something moved as she had lifted the box. But it was small and light. She was sure it wasn't the necklace that she had seen in the image from the museum website.

Chapter Thirty

Eleanor stared at Larry. His eyes were on the box that she still held in her hands. She trembled at the sudden thought that had flown into her head. She looked back down at the box. The keyhole faced her. There were no telltale scratches or marks where Mr Nelson may have tried to force it open, yet it was still locked. The Sellinsborough necklace should still be inside if everything Larry had said was true. Her frantic brain struggled to find a reason for the necklace not to be there other than... She pushed the thought out of her mind. But then, could that also mean ... his own father? She held back the gasp that was longing to escape. Could he have killed his own father to prevent anybody finding out that he had already removed the necklace? Her chest ached as she looked towards Darryl. He had no doubt in his mind that Larry was as much a victim of this whole affair as his father. And until this moment, she had believed the same. But what should she do now? Removing Sahara's dismissal papers from Mr Nelson's file was one thing, but to let a murderer go free? *No,* she chastised herself. *I must be wrong. There has to be some other explanation. And even if he has taken the necklace, that doesn't automatically make him a killer.* All she had to do was find that other explanation.

'You guys are amazing,' Larry said, breaking the awed silence.

'What will you do with it now?' she asked, placing the box on the table. Her voice was trembling, but neither of the two men seemed to notice. She moved out from behind the desk, clenching her fists to stop them shaking. But she wasn't going to let him leave this room before she knew what was going on.

Larry shook his head. His expression was blank, giving nothing away.

'I don't know. It has just sat there under my floor boards for so long that I'd forgotten about it.'

'Not quite,' Eleanor said, trying to keep her intonation light-hearted.

Both Larry and Darryl looked at her curiously

'Darryl said the letter from your dad and the newspaper article were underneath it when he found it under the floor-board.' They both stared at her in silence, and so she continued. 'I just meant that you must have taken it out every now and again.'

'Nothing gets past you, does it?' Larry gave his cheeky smile, but tears lay behind his eyes. 'I wanted nothing to do with Dad, as much as I wanted nothing to do with his stupid box.'

'You're free to hand it in, now,' she persevered. 'With your dad passed, it's not able to do him any more harm.'

'Maybe,' he replied.

Was doubt seeping in with the catch in his voice?

'Maybe?' Darryl said incredulously. 'Mate, there really isn't any other choice. You can finally explain to the police that your dad took it to stop Nelson getting hold of it. You'll be able to get him put away for years and clear your dad's name.'

'Clear his name,' Larry repeated banally. 'What if they decide to arrest me for being in possession of stolen property instead? Then there's lying to the police, perverting the course of justice, blah, blah, blah.' His jokey attitude didn't make anyone laugh.

'Well, clearly you don't want to be telling them you've had it all these years,' Darryl said. 'That's just asking for trouble. Tell them you found it when clearing out your dad's flat.'

'But what good will it do?' Larry's eyes had wandered back to the box that was still laid on the desk. 'He's already dead. It won't bring him back, will it?'

'Nothing will ever bring your dad back. But, after all these years, it's time to do the right thing,' Eleanor said, silently praying she was wrong and that Larry would agree to hand in the artefact.

'This is all I have left of him now.' Larry reached across the desk and picked up the box as though it were as fragile as a glass egg.

'May we see it?' Eleanor tried not to let the desperation sound in her voice.

'I don't think that's a good idea,' he said, pulling it close to him.

'Why not? I'd love to see it.' She kept her voice calm and gentle.

'I'm sure the picture didn't do it justice,' Darryl said, sharing the same eagerness.

'You've seen a picture of it?' The blood suddenly drained from Larry's face.

'Call it research for our investigation,' Darryl replied. 'You know what I'm like about research.'

Larry screwed up his nose and shook his head. 'No. I – I'd like to get back. I'm suddenly feeling exhausted,' he stammered and shuffled a step backwards towards the door. 'I need – to decide what I'm going to do with it. I'll probably hand it in tomorrow, but it's a big thing. Maybe just a bit more time to grieve for Dad and I'll feel better able to pass it on. Yeah,' he said assuredly. 'That's what I'll do.'

He turned and started towards the door, but Eleanor stepped in his way.

'No,' she said flatly. 'You're going to show us what's in the box.'

He stared at her blankly.

'Eleanor!' Darryl exclaimed. 'I think you're—'

'I truly hope I'm wrong,' she interrupted. 'but it's not the necklace, is it?'

Larry burst into laughter. A laughter that tried to express bewilderment. 'What are you talking about?'

'Eleanor?' Darryl joined the confusion. 'What are you doing?'

Darryl's reaction was understandable. He wouldn't yet understand, but she had to hope he would trust her.

'You know now that we've seen a picture of the necklace,' she continued, still staring deep into Larry's eyes. 'It looks big and heavy.'

'Eleanor, I insist—' Darryl tried again, but she would not stop.

'Whatever's in that box is not big and heavy,' she spoke over him and even he went quiet as she paused to let the information sink in.

The only sound in the room was Larry's breathing, which had become erratic as his eyes flicked towards the door.

'You've already sold it, haven't you?' she whispered. 'And probably a few other items along the way, too, that you've managed to get off the various sites without recording them. You didn't see the cleaner or the gift shop lady hanging about when

Louis's artefact went missing, did you?' Confident in her supposition, Eleanor took a deliberate step towards him.

Larry's automatic reaction was a step backwards. 'Of course I did. I simply forgot which one. Anyone can make a stupid mistake like that,' he said, continuing to move backwards as Eleanor pressed forwards. 'Especially considering what I've gone through these past couple of days. I think I can be forgiven for forgetting—'

'You didn't forget, though, did you?' Although she focused on Larry, she kept a close eye on Darryl. His face was pale from shock, but from his silence, she was hopeful that he would soon understand. 'You didn't forget because it wasn't something you saw. You had made it up. You're less likely to make a mistake like that if you had actually seen it. But you didn't because *you* were the one who took it. I always wondered how you lived so well on an archaeologist's wage,' she went on. 'The nice car, the big house with all the trimmings. Darryl always joked that it was because you didn't have kids, but now, I'm not so sure.'

Darryl was now looking around him in a daze. She could only guess that he too was searching for some other possible explanation, just as she had done a few minutes earlier.

'Where did you find her, Darryl? She's lost it.' Larry had finally backed himself against the desk.

'Actually, I'm learning to trust her instincts. The floorboard it was hidden under was pretty loose. I'm sure if it had been that loose all those years ago, the police would easily have found it. How did it get so loose, Larry?'

Larry's only reply was a bewildered look on his face.

'Humour me and open the box, please.' Darryl joined Eleanor at her side, between Larry and the door.

'I don't have the key.' Larry laughed as though the situation was ridiculous.

'Yes, you do,' Darryl replied bluntly. 'I'm pretty sure it's on your key-ring with your car keys. Open it.'

Larry's shoulders dropped. He looked down at the box still in his hands and let out an enormous sigh. 'I – I'm sorry, Darryl, but I'm not like you. I love this job, but the money really sucks. Once you get to know the right people to sell to, it's not that hard.'

'How could you?' Darryl whispered. 'How could you do that?'

'But that's not all you've done, is it?' Eleanor was gambling, but she was certain she was right. 'From the tone of your dad's letter, you already knew the truth he was talking about. You knew your dad had taken the necklace to keep it safe and that he had been framed.'

Larry's eyes were becoming more erratic by the second, flicking between her, Darryl, and the box.

'You must have known your dad was in that photo ever since you started working here,' she continued. 'Mr Nelson was keen to show them off to anyone and everyone. Even me, who knows nothing about archaeology or these sites where they were taken.'

'Maybe I did.' He shrugged his shoulders. 'I can't remember. I didn't take that much interest in them. It's not a big deal.'

'So, how would he react if he found out that you had sold the artefact that he had entrusted to you?'

In a momentary pause, his eyes betrayed a flicker of panic as they shifted towards the door.

'I'd like to leave, please. Move out of my way,' he said firmly.

Eleanor had her answer. Mr Nelson had told the truth about being with Mo the entire time he was in the kitchen. She remembered Mo complaining that he had left the kitchen, leaving her staring at the rota. But her heart sank at the realisation that she had been right. There was no other explanation that she had been praying for.

'No,' she replied, firmer still. 'You were banking on the police finding that connection with Mr Nelson and then he would become their prime suspect.'

'To start with,' Larry whispered hesitantly, before clearing his throat and beginning again. 'To start with, I told Dad I'd hide the necklace, but I made it plain that I didn't like what he was getting me into. And I meant it, too.'

His tone was sincere, but Eleanor wasn't prepared to trust anything he said anymore. Instead, she let him speak out of respect for Darryl. This was going to devastate him. She could tell from his silence that he still didn't understand the full implications of what was going on.

'But ... ahh, you should have seen it ... it was beautiful,' Larry went on. 'And the more I looked at it, the more I thought about what good it could do.'

Darryl gasped in exasperation.

'Don't worry,' Larry added quickly. 'I sold it to someone who really appreciated it for what it was. I wouldn't have just let it go to any old person. I made somebody really happy, and they made me really happy by paying me for it. Let's face it, you know how happy that car makes me.'

'But it wasn't yours to sell,' Darryl growled. Larry's cheeky smile dropped as he realised that his light-hearted banter wasn't going to work now.

'It felt like mine to me. I couldn't exactly hand it in.'

'You could easily have handed it in,' Darryl said.

'But then Nelson would have had another chance to steal it, and Dad would have been sent to prison for nothing.'

'He trusted you.' Darryl's shoulders stiffened and his hands clenched into fists.

'To hold on to stolen goods. What kind of father does that?'

'So you sold it,' Darryl surmised.

'So I sold it. It wasn't hard continuing to be pissed off with him for leaving it with me in the first place. When he told me about his cancer, I thought he would never get out of prison alive. It was a worry when he did, and I just had to keep up the pretence till, well, you know. But he wouldn't let it go, and I had to hurry things along a bit.'

The full implication suddenly hit Darryl.

'No!' Darryl gasped.

'Don't be like that, mate.' Larry shook his head. 'He was dying anyway. Had months to live at the most. I did him a favour. Put him out of his misery. I didn't plan to kill him. Not until I was cleaning up the broken glass. It was obvious from his bellowing and his sniping that it would do everyone a favour. And when Nelson walked in to the kitchen, it just seemed like fate was on my side. I knew who Nelson was. I didn't need to see Dad in a picture. He had told me all about what was going on at the time.'

Darryl shook his head. The look on his face was pure rage. 'And you played me for a fool. Open the box, Larry.'

Larry, shaking at Darryl's anger, reached slowly towards his pocket, reaching for his keys. He turned suddenly and grabbed the Leatherman from the desk, the knife still open.

'Get out of my way,' his voice quavered with the growl.

Eleanor suddenly found herself being held back as Darryl took an automatic step back. One hand raised defensively while pushing her back with the other.

'There's no need for that,' Darryl whispered. 'Go now and we'll forget everything we know. You can leave quietly. Just promise me we'll never see each other again.'

'If only I could believe you, but you know as well as I do that your conscience won't let you do that. Now, move,' Larry sneered with a flick of his knife. 'Move behind the desk and get on the floor.' His voice was getting stronger with every demand.

But Darryl didn't move. Eleanor took hold of his arm and gently pulled him round the desk.

'It's not worth it,' she told him quietly and calmly. 'Please.'

'Take out your phones,' Larry ordered as Eleanor slowly coaxed Darryl round the desk.

Larry took hold of the cord for the landline phone on the desk and cut it. His knife slicing through it easily.

Darryl's face was rigid with anger and she was worried about what he might do. The knife in Larry's hand left them defenceless.

'You don't have to do this,' Eleanor said, reaching for her phone. She watched Darryl closely. His clenched jaw and his white-knuckled fists. She hoped he wouldn't try to retaliate. Instead, he carefully removed his phone from his jacket pocket, clearly hesitant to hand it over. 'We'll let you go,' she went on with relief.

'You got Sahara sacked for stealing ten quid. Do you really think I believe you'll let me go?' he sneered at Eleanor. 'Now, throw your phones on the floor, over by the door.'

Eleanor and Darryl tossed their phones over as instructed and positioned themselves on the floor. Squeezing into what little space there was while Larry made his way backwards towards the door. Never taking his eyes off the pair of them and never losing focus on the knife in his hand. Once he reached the door, he stamped hard on each of the phones with his heel. Eleanor held on to Darryl's arm as he flinched at the sound of the screen cracking with each blow. Aware that each smash was another insult to their so-called friendship. Larry glanced quickly out the door with his knife in his hand and the box tucked under one arm. Unable to close the broken door, he turned and ran. Once again, fast footsteps echoed up the corridor. Darryl scrambled to his feet, heading directly for the door. Eleanor was not far behind him and scooped the phones from the floor, hoping desperately for any signs of life. They needed help and everybody had left. Nobody was around to see them charging through the building towards the exit. With no other transportation for miles around, the car park was the obvious place for Larry to head. But Eleanor wasn't so sure they would catch him. Unlike Mr Nelson, Larry was fit and fast. Even Darryl would struggle to keep up.

Chapter Thirty-One

Darryl's anger fuelled his body as he chased Larry through the museum corridor that led to the exit while Larry frantically pulled display plinths and cabinets over in his path. Each one slowing Darryl as he either clambered over or pushed each one out of the way. Glass smashed around him, exhibits broke as they hit the stone flagged floor. By the time Darryl had reached the exit door, Larry was on the long path down to the car park, nearly at the exit gates. Every other car had gone except Mr Nelson's. The reception building would be locked and even Mo must have finished and left. And, with no means of communication, it was down to him. At least Larry was right about one thing. Darryl wouldn't let him get away with what he had done. He pumped his arms hard and pushed his legs to the limit as he ran through the constant drizzling rain to reach his Land Rover. Larry jumped into his car and the wheels churned up mud and stones as they accelerated out of the car park and down the lane. Darryl charged down the gravel pathway towards his own car. Eleanor wasn't far behind and reached the car just as he started the engine, dropping something into her lap.

'What have you got there?' he asked as he drove over the potholes in the car park at speed.

'I grabbed our phones on my way out, just in case there was any hope of using them. But he did a pretty good job of smashing them,' she said, frantically reaching for her seat belt while she bounced around.

'I didn't think we'd be calling for help,' he grimaced.

'It would have been nice to know we had some kind of backup. I'd even hoped Mo was still here, but—'

'Yeah, I'd clocked her car had gone, too.' Secretly, Darryl didn't want to call for help. In his mind, this was between him and Larry. His head hurt with so many thoughts spinning round inside. His friend had been stealing under his nose and he hadn't seen it? But then to go on and kill his own father. Compared to that, the feeling of betrayal Darryl felt could have been considered insignificant, and yet it hurt so much.

Every now and again, the undulations of the surrounding hills would temporarily hide the bright red convertible speeding away. Only becoming visible once they were over the top of the brow before dipping down again and he was once again out of sight. Darryl quickly scanned the area. At least he had the advantage of driving a suitable car for this terrain. But he wasn't thinking about the roads. The surrounding fields were going to be more useful.

'Hold on,' he yelled as he made a sudden turn into the field on their right.

Eleanor gave a squeal at the sudden movement. 'Where are you going?'

'Trust me, it's a shortcut. The lane doubles back to get to the bridge further upstream.'

Every now and again Eleanor gave little squeaks as they bounced across the uneven ground while she clung on to the door with one hand and the dashboard with the other. But the wheels gripped the terrain as he had hoped they would. The mud and rain were no obstacles for them. But they did create another problem. The windscreen wipers cleared the splattered windows only to leave large, brown smudged arcs behind them. The drizzling rain was not enough to clear them. He peered as best he could through the smeared windscreens, watching for the red Ferrari that contrasted sharply against the green surroundings.

Two extensive fields had provided a direct route to the bridge, and coming towards the other side of the first field, Darryl faced an old wooden gate. Larry's car continued to twist and turn down the narrow pot hole filled lane. But he was worried that Larry was still ahead. He put his foot down and drove directly at the gate.

'What are you doing?' Eleanor screamed, but she hardly had time to get the question out before he crashed his way through.

'It's the shortest route,' he said, focusing intently on Larry fast approaching the bridge.

'But there are sheep in this field.'

'Never mind,' he said as he steered around a stubborn ewe that refused to follow the others and move from the middle of the field.

'Never mind?' Eleanor repeated.

He ignored the harsh, questioning tone in her voice and continued on. She was still squealing in the passenger seat as he drove through another rickety wooden gate on the other side of the field, perpendicular to the bridge. He braked hard, and the car skidded to a stop in front of the bridge's entrance, blocking Larry's route. Larry braked. His car, not built for this terrain, skidded along the track. Eleanor let out a high-pitched squeal as his car came closer, sliding erratically along the road, until a tyre burst causing him to finally skid off the road and crash into a cluster of small trees and bushes.

Only Eleanor's heavy breathing filled the silence as everything became still. For a moment, they all sat in their cars, staring at each other through the drizzle and mud splattered windows. Slowly, Darryl loosened his grip on the steering wheel and opened his door. Not knowing what to expect, he kept his movements slow and measured. He slowly swung his door open, aware that Eleanor was doing the same, while never taking his eyes off Larry.

In a sudden movement, Larry's door swung open. He clambered out and ran. Darryl, his heart still thumping hard, set off after him. He chastised himself for thinking that maybe Larry would realise he had nowhere to go and would give himself up. He had to give him that chance. But secretly, Darryl was glad to see him run. He wanted the opportunity to catch him. Of making him pay for what he had done. For everything he had done.

Chapter Thirty-Two

Larry had run in the opposite direction from the way he had driven. He'd doubled back along the lane, crossed the road behind his car and leapt over a dry stone wall before Eleanor had even made it out of the car. Darryl was close behind him, but they were evenly matched and there seemed little hope of him getting any closer. Eleanor scanned the vast, bleak surroundings as she followed along the lane and felt the same feelings of hopelessness she'd had yesterday morning when she'd arrived for her first day at work. And yet now, there was a flicker of hope. The barren countryside meant that she could see the terrain laid out like a map in front of her. Minimal obstructions obscuring her view, only the drizzling rain. It took no more than a moment to see that the wall Larry had leapt over bordered a field dotted with sheep, sloping gently down towards the river. He seemed to be heading for a sparse clump of small trees in the far corner. So sparse, they barely hid the entrance to an old and rickety-looking footbridge. With Darryl still blindly chasing him through the field, she stuck to the road. Though it was a longer route as it ran along the edge of the field, it had the advantage of a better track. There was no denying the men were fitter than her, but they staggered and stumbled their way through the wet and slippery field, dodging their way round the sheep that had no interest in them running through their home, and frequently sinking shin-deep into the boggy terrain. Once at the corner of the field, she turned off the road and onto a path that led directly to the footbridge, skidding in the gravel as she did so. The stone and shingle was loose underfoot, but, full of determination, she sped up. If there was the slightest chance that she may cut him off at the entrance to the footbridge, it was worth a try.

She ignored the pain in her chest; her legs were so numb, she could no longer feel them and she just had to trust to muscle memory to keep them moving. Closer to the entrance of the bridge, she saw a sign. Old, rusty and dirty, but the yellow background still stood out as it was designed to do and highlighted the triangle with a large exclamation mark in the centre. She was almost there. Darryl was still a few metres behind when Eleanor reached the bridge. She only just had time to throw herself across the entrance as Larry manoeuvred his way through the clump of trees in the corner of the field.

'There's nowhere – for you to go,' she called as he continued closer. Struggling to speak; her chest ached from exhaustion. But he wasn't slowing down. In fear, she tried again. 'The bridge isn't safe.' Holding her hands up in front of her, she screamed, 'Stop!'

But Larry didn't stop and at the very last moment, she saw that he still had the open Leatherman in his hand. He grabbed her, skidding on the gravel as he twisted round to face Darryl, who was fast approaching from behind. A glint from the blade was all she saw as it came closer until she felt the sharp edge pushed against her neck.

'Let me go,' he gasped, his breathing heavy and erratic. 'Nobody needs to get hurt if you just let me go.'

Eleanor could hardly breathe as Darryl skidded to a halt, wide-eyed with panic.

'No, please,' he implored.

Larry gave a quiet smirk. 'I told you it was perfect for all eventualities.' He indicated the knife in his hand almost apologetically. 'But I have to admit, I never thought this would be one of them.'

Darryl took a step towards them.

'Stay back,' Larry yelled.

Eleanor flinched as the force of the blade pushed harder against her bare skin. Darryl halted once more, lifting his hands in surrender. As he did so, Eleanor felt Larry's tight grip round her shoulders relax a little.

'What happened?' Darryl pleaded. 'We were your friends. Do you really want to do this to a friend?'

'Do you really want to send *your* friend to prison?' Larry sneered back.

Darryl slowly began another step forward.

'You know I'll do it,' Larry warned.

Eleanor felt his limbs shaking as he squeezed her tighter. Again, Darryl retreated submissively. A sudden jerk around her shoulders pulled her backwards onto the bridge. It creaked as if in pain as they stepped on, finding their way blindly. She remembered seeing the bridge's broken and missing slats, the rusty old chains that were somehow holding it together. But there was nowhere else for Larry to go. He kept her close, while fear kept her silent.

'You don't want to do this,' Darryl called. His voice cracking in panic.

'I will if I have to. You're giving me no choice.'

'Really? Think about it,' Darryl took another step towards them.

'Don't,' Larry cried out.

Eleanor felt Larry's hold tighten for a moment until Darryl stepped back again. Such a tiny movement rendered her helpless.

'If I can kill my own father, – then I can kill her.'

His hesitancy was all Eleanor needed. Her anger rose within her until it finally took over from her fear.

'But not with a knife,' she spat.

'What difference does it make?' he sneered into her ear.

Suddenly, his foot slipped, and a slat broke with a loud crack. For one moment, he lost his balance, but he was quick to recover and adjusted his pace on the slippery and rotten wood. Moving with shuffling footsteps, he tested every inch before trusting it with his weight and dragging Eleanor along with him. But that one moment of instability gave her an idea.

'What difference?' she said. Contempt oozing from every word. 'Think about it. Could you really push that knife into me? Feel the resistance against your hand as you push it through my flesh?'

The thought made her sick, but her words were her only defence. Larry was too strong for her physically. Distracting him was her only hope.

'Shut up,' he snapped and pulled her forcefully further along the bridge.

Without warning, the bridge dropped. Only two or three inches at most, but the warning was there. It had probably been years since anyone had travelled across it and now, with the weight of the two of them, it seemed likely it could drop further. They fought to regain their balance. Battling against gravity and each other. It only took a moment's pause for the bridge to settle, and Eleanor released the breath she had subconsciously been holding. The bridge had steadied, but the threat continued.

As they set off again, Eleanor's foot found a hole where a

slat should have been and, feeling for more stable support around it, she resumed her assault.

'You weren't even there for your father's death. You walked away.' She forced herself to remember that time. The image she had tried so hard to push from her memory. 'You didn't see him struggling to breathe while he fought for his life. You didn't see the panic on his face as he felt the glass ripping at his throat.'

Larry pushed the knife harder against her throat till she didn't dare breathe.

'Just keep moving,' he growled.

Halfway across and the bridge swayed dangerously. A loud crack came from beneath their feet and Larry lurched sideways. Eleanor's arms flailed, as she tried to hold on to the lengths of chain that were once usable as handrails. However, she was sceptical about their effectiveness now, but she had no other choice. With Larry's focus taken by his fall, she tried to pull away from his grip, but it only tightened, pulling her down with him. She struggled to break free. Twisting her arm while desperately holding on to the bridge. But she was no match for him and it became clear very quickly that if he was going to fall, then she would go with him. She gritted her teeth as the rough chains dug into her hands while he hoisted himself back up onto the bridge. The event only served to intensify Larry's anger and determination, and he strengthened his hold on her. They both took a moment to catch their breath. She glanced over the side of the bridge and saw the remnants of their struggle ten feet below them, tumbling and twisting in the fast flowing water from the heavy rain they had been having for the past few hours.

'Don't try anything like that again,' he growled in her ear. 'Play nicely and we'll all get out of this.'

Eleanor looked ahead of her, avoiding the sight below, only to see Darryl tormented by his helplessness. Still standing on the riverbank, getting further away with each step she took. He had been shaking his head at her throughout her verbal attack on Larry, and she could only imagine what he must have been thinking at the time. He wouldn't want her to antagonise him. He wanted her to be a good girl and do as she was told. Of course, it would be in her own best interest; to keep her safe. But she was sick of people-pleasing, and where had it got her, anyway? Eleanor had no intention of giving up and she returned to her attack as the shuffle across the bridge became even slower.

'You're a coward,' she went on. Her breath so shallow she found she could hardly speak. 'Darryl said you spoke of your father with contempt, that *he* couldn't face up to the consequences of what he had done, but you're just the same. In fact, you're worse because he wasn't stealing for his own gain. You are nothing but a coward,' she spat.

'Shut up!' he pushed the knife harder against her neck once again.

'No,' Darryl screamed, reaching out at her squeal, his voice trembling. 'Please, don't.'

'I'll do whatever is necessary,' Larry shouted back. 'Are you willing to take that risk? You're going to have to let me go,' he sneered.

'What good is this going to do you?' Darryl went on.

'You know he's right, Larry, listen to him,' Eleanor implored.

Larry's desperation was seeping through. His grip tightened once more.

'If you don't stop, this will not end well for you.' His voice shook as he sneered into her ear.

This time, Eleanor didn't just feel the edge of the blade against her skin. She felt the trickle of warm blood as the knife dragged slowly below her jaw bone.

The cold-hearted act of drawing blood was the limit. Darryl

couldn't stand it any longer. 'We can sort this,' he yelled. 'Just don't hurt—'

'Sort it?' Larry yelled back. 'How? Let's face it, you're not going to let me go.'

'We will,' Darryl replied defiantly. Futility running through him. 'We'll let you go. Just leave Eleanor. Please, let her go, then run. We won't follow. I promise. We won't—' he couldn't finish the sentence for the lump in his throat.

'I wish I could believe you,' Larry said sorrowfully.

Darryl could just make out Larry's arm relax a little, and it dropped slightly away from Eleanor's throat. As he let out a deep sigh, a wave of relief washed over him. Larry had finally come to his senses.

'I wish I could believe you,' Larry repeated. 'I'll give you a choice. Catch me, or save her.' He swiftly raised his hand and brought the butt of his knife down hard on the back of Eleanor's head and pushed her into the water below.

Chapter Thirty-Three

Darryl immediately dived into the water. Vaguely aware of the struggle Larry was having to stay upright as the bridge swayed violently after Eleanor had gone over the side, Darryl's only thought was to rescue her now. Though only a few metres away, it felt much further as he battled to reach her. By the time he got to her, she was upright and treading water.

'I hate rivers,' she screamed. 'What are you doing here?'

'Rescuing you. Try to relax. I'll pull you in.'

'Don't worry about me. Get after him.'

Darryl was stunned at her reaction. 'But – but – he hit you.'

'With that stupid little penknife. What damage is that going to do?'

'You screamed,' Darryl persisted.

'I was pushed off a bridge.'

A yell pulled their attention as one side of the bridge broke and Larry was left dangling by one arm. He had almost reached the other side when the bridge had broken, only a few steps further, and he would have made it. Darryl and Eleanor looked at each other. Neither needed to speak. They both knew there was still the chance to catch him.

They swam to the bank and tried to find a way out. The edge of the river was a steep cliff-like rock face with few hand-holds. Bushes jutted out at intervals, somehow thriving in the barren rock. Darryl was the first to find a bush that was stable enough to take his weight. He pulled himself up and out of the water, and into the undergrowth of larger bushes and trees a short way out of the water line. From here, he was able to help pull Eleanor out of the water and to relative safety. She had already followed his lead and was right behind him.

Larry was still hanging from a hand on the lopsided bridge. It creaked with every sway as he used his body's momentum to swing from one hand to the next, along the rusty cable, making his way across the bridge, inch by inch. There was still a way for Darryl and Eleanor to climb and, though he had been slowed, Larry was still going to be the first to reach the field and once more be ahead.

Darryl hauled Eleanor up into the undergrowth of the bushes as Larry struggled to reach the end of the bridge.

'Where —' Eleanor choked through her words. 'Where — is he?'

'Up there,' Darryl said, looking up.

Larry was now trying to swing his body up and over the last hurdle of the broken bridge as it swung with his weight and momentum.

'Then – get up there,' Eleanor pushed him away.

'Are you sure you're al—'

'Go,' she screamed at him. 'Or I'll never forgive you.'

No matter what she said, she was still his priority. He had come too close to losing her too many times already. 'Stay here and rest,' he told her, but Eleanor waved him away.

'I'll be right behind you,' she gasped.

He took off up the side of the river bank, annoyed that she wouldn't listen to him; he could deal with Larry on his own. He pulled on the bushes to propel him up the steep slope. Though soaked from his swim and his arms covered in scratches from the sharp branches, his determination never faltered. He was almost at the ridge when he looked up and saw Larry disappear over the top and into the field above him, momentarily out of sight.

With an extra last push of effort, he reached the top. He scanned the horizon as he hauled himself over the edge and into the field. But in those few seconds, Larry had disappeared. Darryl ran towards a dry stone wall a few metres away that ran along the path leading from the bridge, down to the next field. The only place that could possibly be used as a hiding place. He jumped onto the wall that was only a meter high at its tallest. Fuelled by adrenaline, he scanned the surroundings, anticipating Larry's appearance and ready to resume the chase of his friend, the murderer.

But he wasn't there. He jumped off the wall into the field on the other side. Moving in a large arc, he studied the wall. There were no holes or crevices that could conceal him; no corners or bends he could hide behind. Not even any sheep. He could see for miles and yet there was no Larry. His frustration only grew along with his anger.

He returned to the wall and climbed back on top, continually scanning the area. The cars were still standing in the same position on the other side of the river. Sheep were wandering on to the road where he had crashed through their gate, but there was no sign of Larry. The vast open fields meant either Larry had run a lot faster than was humanly possible, or he had vanished into thin air. The only movement was Eleanor scrambling up from all fours after her climb up the bank and into the field.

'Where is he?' she called as he frantically searched around him.

Darryl shook his head.

'I don't understand it. He's just disappeared.'

'He can't have. There wasn't time.'

'I know but...' Unable to say anything to the contrary, Darryl held out his hands as though presenting his surroundings; bleak, desolate, and no sign of Larry.

Eleanor took in a deep breath as she gazed around her. Resolved not to let Larry get away with everything he had done. The bridge had joined the field at the top of a mound. No matter which way they looked, they could see everything for miles. The wall that Darryl had been perched on so precariously was the only hiding place for at least a mile, but she had seen him check both sides of the wall on either side. There weren't any trees or bushes in the field, only those that were down the edge of the steep slope where they had just come. But they were sparse and few and far between. They would have seen if he had tried to get down to the river that way. The gentle curve in the river meant that the bank on their side was visible for quite a distance.

Darryl had now gone in the opposite direction, away from the wall. His exasperated yell was a clear indication that he felt the same frustration she did.

'There's nothing here!' he screamed. 'No tree to hide behind, not even a large clump of long grass. This is ridiculous. There are no signs of life here at all, let alone a full grown man.'

Eleanor pushed aside the pounding in her head as she tried to catch his voice in the wind. The drizzling rain didn't help. Her entire body felt heavy and her legs were numb with cold. She sat heavily on the grass. The sudden jolt intensified the pounding in her head. She closed her eyes and, holding her head in her hands, she tried to ease the pain.

'Are you alright?' Darryl called.

'I'm fine,' Eleanor said, trying to sound as reassuring as possible. 'Just keep looking.'

'Maybe it's time to call in the police,' he said. 'After all, they would be able to find him a lot more efficiently than we can on our own.'

Though Eleanor hated the idea of it, he was right. Their search was futile. She looked out again at the vast emptiness surrounding her. *No sign of life.* Darryl's words brought back the memory that she'd had that very same thought herself only yesterday. But thanks to Sahara, she had discovered there were signs of life, just not the kind she had thought of. The wildlife, the red kites, the badgers. She pulled the small plastic badger from her coat pocket and looked around her with a new perspective.

From the top of the slope, both she and Darryl had seen an open, flat field, sloping gently down towards more fields until finally reaching a farm nestled at the bottom. But from her seated position, she could see the ground wasn't completely flat. Darryl was walking on a level, where he should have been walking down. She looked back at the plastic badger in her hand. *It's not what it looks like,* she heard the excited small boy saying in her head. Though he was referring to a castle pencil sharpener, maybe there was more here than it seemed at first sight.

'The badger sett?' she mumbled to herself, questioning the possibility. 'No,' she said defiantly. 'If we leave to get the police, it will give him the opportunity to escape. We've got to keep looking.'

Slowly and quietly, she moved round the hillock. The levelled mound dropped abruptly at a cliff-like section. A vertical face of compacted soil revealed a series of earthy brown holes with a faint scent of damp earth. Originally created as an underground sanctuary for badgers, but now? Could this place of safety be used for a grown man?

She looked up at Darryl, who had noticed her creeping along in the field. She quietly waved him closer, and he walked towards her across the top of the badger sett as she made her way further round the hidden mound. Darryl was now at least a metre higher than Eleanor, a drop that couldn't be seen from their previous position. Moving slowly further round the hillock, she crept even closer, almost afraid to breathe. Suddenly Larry leapt out at her. Mud smeared over his clothes, he had been tucked in to the edge of a hole as far as he could go. Clearly hoping his crude attempt at camouflage would hide him. She screamed as he knocked her flying backwards. A sharp pain in her side.

Chapter Thirty-Four

Finally. He was here. The scream from Eleanor as Larry had pushed her out of the way only made things worse and Darryl was full of rage again. He had knocked her to the ground and was trying again to escape. Darryl leapt off the edge of the hidden badger sett that had been dug so discreetly into the side of the field and charged at him. With his shoulder to Larry's back, he ran full force into him, knocking him to the ground. Although Larry tried to fight back, the incentive of staying out of prison was nothing compared to the anger that Darryl had in his soul. An anger that spilled from every pore.

His eyes were drawn to the glint of the knife in Larry's hand. That had to be his priority. With it came the lingering doubt of Darryl's success.

Eleanor tried to pick herself up from the ground where she had fallen, only to cry out as pain soared through her. She clutched at her side. It felt damp. Not the cold dampness from the river, but warm. Looking down, she recoiled as she saw the blood. She untied her coat and tried to stem the flow of blood as best she could with the loose fabric of her blouse. Unable to move, she watched helplessly as Darryl and Larry struggled together on the ground. One eye on the knife still gripped in his hand. Finally, with relief, she saw it fly from his hand as they fought, and land several feet away. She glanced down at her hands, where she was still holding her bunched up blouse tightly over her wound. Blood had smothered her hands as it seeped through the fabric. Not wanting to see it, she turned her focus back to the fight.

Once the knife had left his hand, Larry became frantic. He scrambled desperately to escape, but it was no use. Darryl stopped him time and time again as he fought to reach for the knife and the power it gave him.

Darryl finally pulled him to his feet. They both stood breathing heavily from exhaustion, covered in mud and wet from the constant drizzling rain. It was over. Darryl held him by the shirt collar, his fist pulled back. Reminiscent of his fight with Mr Nelson earlier that day. But instead of holding himself back, he let his fist fly, letting out all his anger in the one sweeping motion. A punch that sent Larry hard to the ground.

'I guess you were right,' he growled, his shoulders heaving. 'Some people are just bad.'

He lifted his head, feeling victorious. Wanting to share his triumph, he looked around for Eleanor as Larry laid unconscious on the ground. She was sitting a little distance away, back near the badger sett. Her knees drawn up close. As he staggered back towards her, his own exhaustion dissipated. Her white face didn't show the joy he had expected to see from catching Larry. Instead, it showed pain. As he came closer, he saw she was clutching her side. Her knees had hidden her red covered hands and blouse. His last few steps were at a run.

'What happened?' he gabbled.

He pulled off his muddy jacket and using the clean insides; he tried to use it to stem the flow of blood.

'He – he –'

'Don't talk,' he changed his mind. Her energy was better reserved.

Looking around him, he struggled to think what to do. A million thoughts bombarded his brain at once. There was nobody else around. The nearest village was miles away, and even the archaeological site was too far for Eleanor to walk to with a river in-between. The closest thing to civilization was the farm, but even that was at least two miles across the fields.

'I'll run for help,' he said.

'If Larry wakes – he'll run—' Her breathless voice grew weaker with each word.

'Do you really think I care about that now? I'll be as quick as I can.'

'No,' Eleanor grabbed at him as he stood. 'Larry.'

'I told you—'

'No.' She shook her head. 'His phone.'

Darryl couldn't believe he hadn't thought of it. He ran back to the still unconscious Larry and rifled through his pockets. After using Larry's thumb print to unlock it, he made his way back to Eleanor. His call for an ambulance was dotted with information; his mind flitting from one thing to another. Obviously, Eleanor's wound, and the odd situation in which they could be found. But also requesting the police and DI Hutchins to attend to pick up the real killer. Oh, and there might be an issue with reaching them, as there would be two cars left in the middle of the road. And maybe a few sheep that have escaped their field because of their gate being broken.

Towards the end of the call, Larry stirred.

'Please hurry,' Darryl implored and hung up, ignoring the pleas on the other end to stay on the line.

After everything they had gone through, he couldn't risk losing Larry now. Looking around him, Darryl guessed Eleanor must have come to the same conclusion. She was struggling to remove the tie from her coat with a single hand while still maintaining pressure on her wound. With one eye on the awakening Larry, Darryl helped feed the tie through the loops, releasing it from the coat. Then he tied Larry's hands behind his back; surprised at the absence of any resistance. Lastly, he found the knife lying in the grass.

Returning to Eleanor, he sat on the ground next to her. His arm around her shoulders in a feeble attempt to warm and comfort her. Although he had a feeling her shivering may have been down to a number of reasons. Her head dropped to his shoulder, and he quickly propped it back up.

'Stay awake,' he told her.

Her face was pale and her eyes drooping. Relief consumed him at the sound of a helicopter as it appeared on the horizon. Almost simultaneously, police sirens came from the opposite direction as they surmounted the crest of a hill. The sound breaking through the drizzle.

'They're here,' he told her, hoping the news would help keep her awake. 'Come on, look. They're here.'

Though not wanting to leave her side, he tore himself away and stood, waving frantically. The quicker they were seen, the better.

Everything was going to be alright, he tried to convince

himself as he turned back to Eleanor, struggling to keep her eyes open. In a last desperate attempt, he looked down at himself and then at the state of Eleanor, both of them covered in mud and blood.

He asked, 'Do you have another one of those tissues?'

Chapter Thirty-Five

A few days later, with the hospital stay behind her, Eleanor was staring at her coat, which hung in its usual place in the hallway. Although it was a raincoat, it hadn't been made with swimming in mind, and now it hung raggedly on its hook. And then there was the bloodstain. A flowery bloom on one side. The one inch slit in the centre where the Leatherman had cut through the material. Something else Larry had ruined. She subconsciously ran her hand over the wound on her side, now healing but still sore. She'd spent too long avoiding the coat, but now, she took it off its peg and carried it through to the kitchen. The bin was the only place for it now.

When she checked the pockets before disposing of it, she found the plastic badger and folded sheets of paper ruined from the river, crumpled, and stuck together. Ink had seeped through the paper, creating shapeless blotches. She tried to unfold it, but when it ripped, she stopped. She had forgotten it had been in her pocket, but the question was, what did she do with it now? In her mind, there was only one thing to do.

Searching for Darryl, she found him sitting at the dining room table, surrounded by bags and boxes. The dining room had become the store room after they had been able to move their bed upstairs to the master bedroom. A luxury in itself, but it left the dining room free to become another place for the endless amount of unopened boxes that seemed to move round the house like a game of sliding tiles.

Darryl was lost in thought and staring at a small object in his hands. Turning it over and over in his fingers.

'Isn't that your World War I bullet?' she asked.

Darryl didn't make a sound. She wasn't sure he had even realised she had entered the room. She sat down next to him and gently placed a hand on his shoulder. He jumped at her touch.

'You OK?' she asked.

He had been uncharacteristically quiet since his friend's arrest. There was nothing she could do but give him the time he needed to process everything that had happened over the last few days.

'Larry gave me this,' he said, showing the bullet, 'on a dig we worked together.'

'I thought you were uncovering a World War II bomber. But this is—'

'We met on the bomber site,' Darryl clarified, 'but we did a couple of others too. He liked his machinery; bombers, tanks—'

'Ferraris,' continued Eleanor.

Darryl shook his head wearily. It was clear he still couldn't believe that his friend had been the culprit and not the victim.

'The trouble is,' his voice broke as he tried to speak. 'I don't know if it was his to give. Was this another of those items that he didn't record and slipped off the site? I should have seen it,' he said, his voice full of anger.

'You can't blame yourself for what he did,' Eleanor said, but she knew there was nothing she could say to change his mind. After a moment of silence, Darryl stood forcefully.

'What are you going to do?' she asked.

'I don't know. I know it's just a dumb bullet, but to me it's...'

'I know. It's more than that.'

He walked off into the kitchen and Eleanor followed. He took a plastic pot from a drawer, put the bullet inside, and sealed it.

'It can stay in here until I'm ready to think about what to do with it. Till then, it can go in the loft.' His words were defiant and hard as he pushed the box to the side of the counter, as though physically trying to push it out of his thoughts. 'What have you got there?' he said, noticing the paper in her hand. His demeanour changed. He clearly wanted to change the subject.

She hesitated to answer. She'd had second thoughts when she'd first found him, but now he needed a distraction. 'I wondered if you wanted to come to Sahara's with me.'

'Sahara's? What for?'

'To right a wrong.'

She knew Darryl's curiosity would compel him to go.

The journey itself was full of questions. Darryl persistently trying to uncover the reason for their visit. Eventually, he gave up with one last question.

'Is this something I should know about? I mean, if you're going to invite her and her brother to move in with us, I think that's something I should know.'

'No, I'm not going to ask them to move in,' she laughed. 'Don't worry, I know how much you value your solitude.'

She wouldn't say any more than that for the rest of the journey.

Standing on the doorstep, Eleanor took a deep breath and knocked, relieved to see Sahara herself answer the door.

'Hi,' she said sheepishly. 'What are you doing here?'

Eleanor took the folded papers from her pocket and held them out to her.

'What is it?' Sahara asked with suspicion, refusing to accept the unidentifiable object being handed to her.

'It's your dismissal,' Eleanor said.

'What?'

'Mr Nelson hadn't sent the paperwork in to head office,' Eleanor explained, 'and so I removed it.'

She could see the expression on Darryl's face shift as he realised this was what she had taken from Mr Nelson's file.

'She stole them,' Darryl said pointedly, an enormous grin spreading across his face.

'Ha,' Sahara blurted.

'I didn't—' Eleanor stopped herself from denying it. 'I stole them.' She turned to Darryl. 'There, are you happy now? Yes, I stole them. I have come to understand that there are times when a little light-fingeredness isn't necessarily a bad thing.'

'What do you want me to do with it?' Sahara asked.

'Whatever you like. Rip it up if you want.'

'But Mr Nelson will—'

Eleanor shook her head. 'Haven't you heard? They have arrested Mr Nelson for theft. He framed you. He used your circumstances as an excuse to blame you as soon as he needed a scapegoat.'

Sahara furrowed her brow. 'I don't understand. He was always so kind.'

'No, he was manipulative. The site is due to reopen from Monday with a new manager. I don't see why you can't have your job back. I will simply explain to the others that I was wrong and I'm sure Mo will only be too pleased to hear me admit that,' she continued under her breath.

Sahara stood quietly, thinking. 'You rip it up,' she said, finally.

'Pardon?'

'You rip it up,' Sahara repeated. 'You do it. Prove to me that you believe that I am not a thief.'

'On one condition,' Eleanor said. 'If ever you need help, you speak to us first. Do we have a deal?'

'I don't want charity,' Sahara said quickly. 'You know I—'

Eleanor gently shook her head. 'It's not charity. Just a friend helping a friend.'

Sahara took a moment to think before she smiled. 'Deal,' she said.

Eleanor held up the folded papers in front of her and tore them slowly down the middle, relishing the sound. A sound that kept Sahara her job, and finally ended the entire dreadful ordeal.

Coming next from K. McCrae

When Darryl's daughter is accused of murder, Eleanor needs to discover the truth… no matter what it may be.

Eleanor Garrett never expected a trip to the theatre could have such disastrous consequences. A sneak peek at the rehearsals where Darryl's daughter, Alex, is one of the main characters, leads to a front row seat to murder.
With every finger pointing at Alex, she sees no sign of mercy. Even the police are heading in that direction.

Books by K. McCrae

Neither Safe nor Sorry

Never Out of Mind

One Good Turn Deserves Nothing

www.ingramcontent.com/pod-product-compliance
Lightning Source LLC
Chambersburg PA
CBHW061807190726
48289CB00007B/2104